Water so Deep

Other Books by Nichole Giles

Descendant
Birthright

Water so Deep

NICHOLE GILES

For Gary, an everyday hero

One

May 5th
412 days to departure

SOMETHING WAS WRONG. Emma felt it in the dark storm raging around her. Felt it in the cold rain peppering the surface of the sea. Felt it with each jagged gasp of salt water that filtered through her gills. Trepidation twisted her insides into tight knots, leaving her muscles quivering with anxiety. Normal people don't risk swimming in a storm—but Emma Harris didn't have that luxury. The turbulent spray curled up and crashed hard against the distant shore and the wind howled, creating a churning, ripping undertow that would drown even the strongest swimmer.

Well, the fully human ones, at least.

Emma's muscles screamed, but kept her gliding, fast—faster than should be possible—as her body took what it

1

needed from the ocean. The ebb and flow, more than just waves and wind, sounded like war drums, a continuous heartbeat of a living, breathing being controlled by the moon's gravitational pull. That beat thrummed in her ears, sucked her body back, and shoved her forward, stroke after endless, exhilarating stroke, compounding her apprehension until she made it to the sharp rocks that led to the patch of sandy shore, still unsure what battle awaited her. When her head broke the surface, Emma gasped, her gills closing as her lungs filled with the sweet, fulfilling oxygen that could calm her mind in a way only saltwater could calm her body.

Hard drops of rain pelted her bare back and shoulders as she pulled herself onto the ledge and scooted across the rocks to lie on the sand, fully exposing her developing scales to the fresh water falling from the dark night sky. Her hand automatically went to her neck, where the thin slits of her gills settled below the surface of her skin.

Breath drove her into the water and breath pulled her back out. She was torn between the sustaining forces of saltwater and air—both necessary. For now. Eventually, the sea would fully claim her.

Unable to shake the dread in her chest, she dragged herself across the stony beach. The soft skin on her palms stung, scraped and cut from the rocks, and exhaustion made her limbs heavy, but she kept moving, scrubbing the salt off her legs with the aid of sand and rain, feeling rushed for no reason she could name. Drops pinged off the abalone shell hanging from her pearl necklace, creating a unique music few but Emma would ever appreciate. When the full moon peeked through the clouds, she inched backward, careful not to tear her swimsuit on the rough ground, until she reached the natural alcove where she'd hidden her clothes.

Strange to think that only a handful of hours ago, she'd spun slow circles in her prom dress with Tom, and now she was partnered with a tumultuous storm instead.

A flash of lightning rent the sky, illuminating her secret alcove long enough for her to see Merrick step from the recessed shadows near the cave wall. His sudden appearance—in addition to his complete lack of clothes—startled a scream out of her.

"What do you want?" She averted her eyes, heart racing as she forced herself not to look. Why was he here, and how long had he been watching her? She retrieved her towel, desperate to wrap up—hide herself—as she dried her now skin-soft legs, emotions swirling. Was he the reason sick fear curled in her stomach?

The merman seemed oblivious to Emma's disjointed emotional state. "Fifteen moon cycles left."

Emma squeezed her eyes shut, swallowing a knot of pain. "How could I possibly forget? I already struggle to breathe on land sometimes."

He stepped toward her. "Tangaroa has given you to me for a mate. We will join upon your permanent return."

His words sent a chill up Emma's spine. It had nothing to do with the storm raging around them, and everything to do with the one swirling inside her. She'd suddenly become betrothed without ever having visited the place she was supposed to be living within the next year. "Mate? He has *given* me to you? But you're way older than me."

"Age has little to do with the will of the Sea King." He waved a dismissive hand, walking nearer.

Everything about Merrick's world seemed foreign, unreal. Though she'd known about Atlantis for a while, understood that she would physically have no choice but to live there someday, she despised its very existence, dreaded with blind terror a future she couldn't even picture. "I don't belong in Atlantis, Merrick. Oceanside has been my home for sixteen years. My family is here, and my friends. I have a life. I don't want to leave."

She thought of Tom, and wondered if she would miss him the same way she'd miss the sunshine, driving her car, Gram, her mother, father, and Keith. Somehow, she doubted it.

A wrinkle formed between Merrick's brows. "But you must. Once your gills develop, you will need the sea water to survive. You cannot change the natural progression of life. "

Under the cover of her towel, Emma wiggled into her jeans and tank top. "Natural progression or not, I was meant to be human. Why else did the Sea King—or my parents or whoever made the freak decision—leave me ashore in the first place?"

"We cannot care for a human-ish youngling ashore, and you cannot survive the sea until your gills have fully developed." His green eyes caught hers, held, and the harsh honesty in them made Emma pause in the act of pulling a hooded sweatshirt over her head. "There is no way around it," he said. "You waste energy in empty wishing. Tangaroa's word is law."

"Not my law." Emma crammed the towel into her bag and slid her feet into flip-flops, then pushed past Merrick. "I don't want a mate. Tell the Sea King I turned you down."

Emma knew he couldn't hear her murmurs of complaint over the wind, but didn't care. She didn't plan on letting anyone—Sea King or not—force her into something she didn't want to do.

Merrick wouldn't shadow her up the steep, rocky path to where she'd left her car—too much insecurity away from the water. But she felt his eyes follow her every step of the way. That same tumbling dread gnawed at her. She picked up the pace, leaving him behind to go back to her real life. The only one she'd ever known, and the only one she really intended to live.

After the difficult swim, hiking up the slope was more work than she remembered, and Emma's steps slowed as her strength dwindled. Her muscles shook as she dug in her bag for keys.

She crested the hill, stopping when she saw the familiar figure across the road, illuminated by the beam of a streetlight. Tom leaned against her driver's-side door, still wearing the tux he'd worn when he dropped her off at home over two hours ago. The white-and-pink boutonniere hadn't even started to wilt yet.

Goose bumps prickled up and down her body. She swallowed and approached tentatively, uneasiness tightening her shoulders, skittering up her neck. "Hey, Tom."

"Have a nice swim?" He didn't smile or reach out to pull her into his arms as he had earlier. Didn't even move away so she could get in the car. Just stared, his jaw clenched in anger, eyes full of bitter loathing Emma knew was born from misunderstanding.

"The water's too rough for swimming." Her heart mimicked the thunder shaking the sky as she popped the trunk with the key fob and walked around the car to put distance between her and Tom.

He followed, stone-faced. "What happened to, 'Tom, I'm not feeling well. Take me home so I can go to bed' instead of heading to the after-prom party in Mark's hotel room?" His eyes absorbed her dripping hair and trailed to her wrinkled toes. "Obviously, you're not in bed. So where *have* you been, Emma?" Her name whipped from his mouth like he'd just tasted something bitter.

Emma cringed, fear skittering up and down her spine. How could she possibly explain that she needed the saltwater to ease the tightness in her chest, to help her breathe? She dropped her bag in the open trunk, but Tom grabbed her arm before she could close it, his fingers digging into the tender skin beneath her sleeve. "I asked you a question."

"The beach." She tried to pull away, but he only held tighter.

"In this weather? Doing what? And with who?" His lips pressed tight against his teeth, his eyes flashing.

Emma twisted, trying in vain to loosen his grasp on her arm. He pulled the towel out of her bag with his free hand and shoved it in her face while the rain continued to pelt them.

"What about this, huh? You going to tell me it's soaked from the rain?"

"I wrapped it around my shoulders to keep warm."

"What's his name?"

"Who?"

"The naked guy you were with down there."

Emma felt the blood drain from her face as the breath caught in her throat. "I didn't . . . It's not what you think."

"Like hell it isn't. Don't try to tell me you weren't naked down there too. I'm not stupid, Emma."

"I . . ." She swallowed, shaking, her brain scrambling frantically for an explanation, but all she could think of was the truth—which she couldn't give him.

"That's what I thought." He growled a stream of profanities that stung Emma's ears and brought hot tears to her eyes. His muscles bulged as he slammed the trunk and yanked her around until she was wedged between him and the car.

"I didn't—"

"Don't lie to me. Don't. Ever. Lie to me. All this time, I've given you your space, been gentle and careful because I thought you were so innocent. So pure. What a load of shit." His body trembled with rage as he pressed closer, grabbing her other arm, his breath hot in her face. "I believed you. I respected you. I loved you."

Emma's arms throbbed under Tom's grip, but she wasn't as concerned about bruises as she was about the fury in his eyes. She'd never seen that look before, and it turned her already-cool blood to ice. Her voice quivered. "I'm not lying. It's not what you think. I . . . I love you too."

The sting of his hand across her cheek left her eyes watering. *He hit me. I can't believe he hit me.* Shock rendered her speechless, immobile. He'd never hit her before.

"Shut up," he growled. "Don't you say that. Don't you ever say that to me again."

The second blow involved knuckles and sent her sprawling against the car. A starburst of pain exploded near Emma's eye when the side of her head smacked the back windshield. She pushed up onto her elbows, trying to focus, needing to get away, but her head spun, and she slipped on the wet surface. Drips of warmth rolled down the side of her face, but whether it was blood or rain, Emma couldn't tell.

"Keys," she murmured. "What happened to my keys?"

"You're not going anywhere." In the space of a single flash of lightning, Tom hauled her over his shoulder and into a small grove of citrus trees on someone's private property. She tried to scream, but his shoulder dug into her stomach, and she couldn't catch enough breath. Tom tossed her on the ground. When his heavy weight pinned her down, Emma found a well of reserved strength and fought back. She punched, kicked, bit, and finally screamed. She struggled with everything she had until the lights went on in a nearby house and someone came outside, shouting.

Emma screamed harder, crying, shuddering, and then weeping with relief when Tom sprang up and ran away as a beam of light fell across her face and the person—definitely male—shouted again. None of his words registered as anything other than loud. A blanket fell over her and someone tried to take her hand, but she refused it, curling on her side and turning her face into the rain-soaked grass, sobbing until the sound of her voice was drowned out by the wail of sirens.

I'll never trust a boy again.

Two

August 28th
323 days to departure

EMMA TOOK A CLEANSING BREATH and let it out slowly, willing her nerves to calm, her hands to still, before she emerged from the car. Eyes glued to the familiar building, she stowed her keys and hooked her bag over her shoulder. "Here goes."

"It's okay, Emma. It's just school."

"Yep. And Everest is just a mountain." She glanced at her younger brother, Keith, wondering again if it was a mistake for her parents to enroll him in regular high school. The district classified him as "special needs," and Emma agreed with that label. He was special, and for whatever reason, he thought he needed to attend school with her.

What if people were mean to him because he was different? What if bullies picked on him? What if he came away traumatized for life? Hoping he was still this excited about school at the end of the day, she nudged him with her bag. "Let's go, you grown-up high schooler."

Keith's grin split his face, lighting his eyes with excitement and pressing a wrinkle into his prominent forehead. The look melted Emma's heart. If they were mean to him, she'd destroy them. Destroy them completely.

"You'll find me at lunch, right?" He started toward the building, twisting the bottom of his T-shirt into a ball. The first nervous gesture he'd shown since they'd left the house.

"Yep. And we can eat outside on the grass if you want."

"Okay, 'cause I know I'm going to be hungry. It's my first day of high school, and Gran says teenage boys are always hungry."

Smiling at his eagerness, Emma saw Keith to his first class, where a petite woman with dark, spiked hair introduced herself. "Hello, Keith," she said. "I'm Mrs. Long, the aide. I'm here to help you learn everything you need to know about high school."

"Hi, Mrs. Long." Obviously embarrassed, Keith pulled the collar of his shirt over his face, hiding his pink-tinted cheeks.

"Is this your sister?" Mrs. Long asked, trying to force him to engage. "Are you going to introduce us?"

Hesitant to leave until she was sure Keith would be okay, Emma said, "Why don't you be a gentleman and introduce me to your teacher?" Nothing. She kept her voice light, despite the nerves buzzing along her skin. "Keith, I'm going to be late to class. You don't want me to get in trouble, do you?"

"No." He shook his head, still hiding.

"Remember what we talked about?" she asked, tugging on the wrinkled bottom of his shirt and trying not to curse her parents. "How it's polite to look at people when you talk to them?"

He nodded.

"How if you're going to high school, you have to have manners and pay attention to what your teacher says?"

This time, he let the shirt down enough that his eyes peeked over the top. "Yes."

"And do you still want to go to high school, or have you changed your mind? Because if you'd rather go home, I can take you." And she would, even if it meant missing her entire first-period class.

He let go of his shirt and smoothed it over his torso, biting his lip. "No, I'm big. I want to stay."

Pride filled the empty spaces in her chest. Keith was so much stronger than she would ever be. "Then hurry and introduce me before I'm late."

Scuffing his shoe on the ground, he muttered, "This is my sister, Emma."

"Nice to meet you, Emma," the teacher responded with a firm handshake.

Once Mrs. Long had assured Emma that Keith would be fine—at least a hundred times—Emma left him in his classroom and went to find hers. Worry for Keith tied her stomach into knots, but it also kept her mind off her own insecurity—always a good thing.

She was going to be late. If this was an indication of what

she could expect every day, they'd need to leave for school earlier. She shook back her waist-length auburn hair and straightened her abalone-and-pearl necklace, then made her way down the familiar hall to her locker, purposefully avoiding looking above anyone's knees.

Unfortunately, there was no way to close her ears. As she rounded the corner into the senior hallway, it was impossible not to hear the whispers, the comments, the jeering remarks about the "girl who ruined Tom." He'd been a school hero, a basketball all-star who led his team to the playoffs. And Emma was the girl who got him sent to jail before the championship game. Emma was the reason three different colleges retracted scholarship offers. Emma was the reason the Oceanside Pirates were now infamous for their bad-boy athletes, rather than famous for the skill with which they played.

Ignoring the chatter, she unloaded notebooks, pencils, and a magnetic photo frame with a picture of her family, taking an extra few seconds to gather her courage.

The locker next to hers slammed, and Emma's gaze riveted on the eyes of the person on the other side of the door. They were steel gray, enormous, and framed by thick lashes. The boy smiled and flipped back his dark, long-ish hair. "That your family? You look nothing like them."

"I'm adopted," she blurted, wincing at her automatic response.

That made him pause. "Lucky family. I'm James."

Emma bit back a nasty reply and forced a weak smile. Not every guy was like Tom. She didn't have to trust this guy—or any guy, for that matter—but she could talk to one every so often. Especially one who went out of his way to be nice. "Emma."

James leaned against his locker, studying a map of the school. He crossed one ankle over the other—looking both confident and casual in his distressed jeans—and waved the slip of paper. "This place is a maze. I hope you know where you're going, 'cause I'm pretty well clueless."

Emma nodded, glancing at her schedule and taking slow, even breaths. In. Out. In. Out. "English. Barnes. Room 302."

"Must be fate. Me too." James straightened to his full height—which had to be somewhere near six feet—his grin revealing a sexy dimple in his left cheek. "Do you mind if I shadow you to class? I really don't want to be late because I'm directionally challenged." He held up a notebook. "Maybe by the end of the year, I'll know my way around."

His infectious smile eased Emma's apprehension, loosening the knot between her shoulders. Across the hall, two girls glared at Emma, then bent their heads, whispering. Although it wouldn't hurt her feelings if new-guy-James never heard the rumors, she should caution him anyway. Tom's friends made sure everyone heard eventually. "I should warn you. Being seen with me could be bad for you."

"Ah." James's smile fell. "Your boyfriend's going to hurt me, huh? Don't worry." He flexed his bicep. "I can take him."

A short, quick giggle burst past her lips in a way that felt both foreign and freeing. "No. No boyfriend." Anymore. Thank goodness. They started down the hall together, her long hair brushing against her back in a comforting rhythm as she tried to decide how best to explain without *explaining*.

"All the better." His face brightened considerably. "Why would I be concerned? Are you, like, a serial killer in your spare time?"

She offered an apologetic smile. "The way people talk, you'd think it was something like that."

James glanced at her from the corner of his eye. "First day. New school. Senior year. I'm going to reserve judgment and walk you to class."

"I thought I was walking *you* to class. You know, because you don't know the way."

"You are, and I don't. But no one else needs to know that."

"I guess not." Emma fiddled with the corner of her binder, her mind scrambling for something more to say before the silence could envelop them in a cocoon of awkward. "What's it like, starting a new school senior year?"

"Not as bad as it sounds." He tipped his head in her direction. "Kind of feels like I'm reinventing myself. I get a second chance to prove who I am and what I'm capable of doing. Don't get me wrong—in a lot of ways, it sucks rocks. I mean, seriously, I have no idea where I'm going or who I'm about to meet. There's no one here who knows me. No one who gives a damn. But," he glanced meaningfully at her, "so far, I'm enjoying the view."

Emma's stomach tightened with a mixture of anxiety and pleasure. "With lines like that, you'll fit in fine at Oceanside High."

They reached the classroom, where James paused with his hand on the doorknob, frowning. "That doesn't sound like a compliment."

Emma's mouth formed an O, and she blinked, realizing how snide her words had come out. "Sorry. I didn't mean it like that. I don't even know you. And I really do hope you find your place here."

James let go of the doorknob and folded his arms across his chest, staring at Emma with a strange glint in his eye. "No apology necessary."

Behind Emma, someone cleared his throat, and James opened the door to let him through. Emma didn't move to follow, and James let it swing closed again while the uncomfortable silence roared. "Wanna know what I think?"

She arched a brow, pushing aside the awkwardness caused by her rusty manners.

He plowed on. "You know your way around, but you don't have your schedule memorized. You're obligated to be here, but expect no pleasure from it, and since you cautioned me up front about a non-existent jealous guy, I'm guessing something socially major went down with you fairly recently."

Emma's lips quirked, her eyes narrowing with amusement. "Wow. That's . . . rather astute of you."

"Astute. Never been called *that* before." Grinning, James opened the door, and Emma followed him inside.

"That was a compliment."

He raised an eyebrow, again revealing his impish dimple. "I know."

That stupid dimple did strange things to Emma's insides, so she forced herself to look away and claimed an empty seat—luckily, across the room from James—ready to focus on getting through the day. But when someone shot a spit wad at her

desk, she thought of James's plan to reinvent himself, and allowed the corners of her lips to turn up as she brushed the soggy paper onto the floor. Second chance? Yeah. She wouldn't mind one of those herself.

LATER, SHE FOUND KEITH standing with Mrs. Long in front of his classroom, fists clenched around his paper lunch sack in a sign of anxiety, but his smile was wide. "Emma. It's time to eat."

Emma nodded, waving at the teacher. "Yep. Careful not to squish your sandwich."

"It's peanut butter and jelly."

"I know. Your favorite." After everything that happened at the end of last year, she'd made a rule against entering the cafeteria, especially on the first day. Instead, she led Keith outside to a shady patch of grass and laid out her meal: yogurt, fruit cup, water bottle, a container of tuna. She'd always preferred seafood to anything else, but now that she knew what she was becoming and where she was supposed to be going, her distaste for bread made more sense.

"This is a good spot," Keith said, scraping his shoe along a patch of dirt. "I like eating outside. I'm glad you didn't leave me by myself today."

Emma reached over and squeezed his arm. "How could I desert my best pal?"

He stared at his sandwich. "Maybe you want to sit with your other friends—cool people. Seniors."

What friends? Emma ripped the paper off the top of her straw and blew the wrapper at Keith's nose. "You're the coolest person I know, even if you aren't a senior. I'd rather eat with you than anyone else. Besides, I promised, right? We have a date for every Monday. And whenever else you need me."

Keith sighed. "Yeah, but . . ."

"Have I ever lied to you? Have I ever said I'd do something and then not done it? Have I ever left you alone when we had plans?"

"No."

"Exactly."

"Sorry." He gulped down half a Milk Chug and wiped his mouth with his wrist. "You having a good day?"

Without a fork, Emma picked the tuna out bite by careful bite. "It's okay. Kind of weird. What about you? What do you think of high school so far?"

Keith shoved half his sandwich in his mouth, struggling to chew and then swallow as he scanned the rest of the courtyard. "It's really loud. People are annoying."

"Get used to it." Knowing he needed to focus on something positive, she added, "Mrs. Long seems nice. What do you think of her?"

His answering shrug was accompanied by bright red ears.

He has his first crush! A laugh bubbled up. "Pretty, isn't she?"

Another shrug.

"Okay, Romeo," she said, patting his knee affectionately. "I won't make you talk about it as long as you remember you're not allowed to date teachers. Even the pretty ones."

"Duh." Keith offered her a squished piece of his mangled sandwich. "Wanna bite?"

Emma shook her head, going along with his abrupt change of subject. "No, thanks. Would you like some tuna?"

"I don't like fish." Keith stuck his tongue out, pretending to gag.

"And I don't like bread," Emma countered, opening her fruit cup. "But we both like apples. Want one?"

"Yes, thanks." Keith took the whole cup, leaving Emma with the single apple slice she'd offered him. She laughed, marveling that anyone could think her brother was anything less than genius.

"Who's that over there, staring at you?"

Her head snapped up and anxiety coiled in her stomach. Just outside the cafeteria door, Tom's friend, Mark, waggled his fingers, his grin just sharp enough to cut down what was left of her appetite. "Let's get going."

"I'm not done with my lunch."

Emma shoved her garbage in her paper bag and crumpled it. "Bring it with you. Time to go."

Keith glared at her. "I don't want to. I want to stay here."

As she stood, she angled her gaze down at Keith to avoid looking at Mark again. "Okay, well, stay here and finish your lunch, then. Can you find your way back to class?"

"Yes. I'm in high school, you know."

"All right." But she sent more than one worried glance over her shoulder as she walked away. *If they hurt him, I'll hurt them.*

JAMES WATCHED EMMA and the boy laugh on the other side of the courtyard. When she smiled like that, unguarded and in the moment, her whole face lit up. He wasn't positive, but he thought the kid might have been in the picture she'd displayed in her locker. A brother, maybe? Clearly, he meant something to the hottie who occupied the locker next to his.

She leaned against the tree, closing her eyes. A ray of sunshine peeked through the leaves, dancing in the strands of her fiery hair and along the smooth forehead that was almost the same color as the pearls in her necklace. Something stirred inside him. Something more than the desire he was used to feeling when it came to girls. Something dangerous and forbidden. Fascination? Curiosity? He wasn't sure. There was something different about her, something he couldn't quite put his finger on. He gulped the last of his pop and crunched the can, tossing it at a nearby recycle bin as he stood from his perch on the low brick wall. He headed inside to the gym, nearly plowing over someone on the way.

"Watch it." The guy stood about as tall as James, had the shoulders of a bull, and a look in his eyes that said he was every bit as dangerous.

"Sorry, man. Didn't mean it, I swear."

The kid glowered at James, but then turned and walked away. James sighed, relieved. It wouldn't serve him well to damage his knuckles on his first day.

He wasn't the first in the gym, but it was obvious he was

the only newbie. A number of guys were dribbling, sweating, calling to each other like they'd played together their whole lives. Some probably had. James shook his head, fighting back nerves. To make it on an already established team was like trying to force through a concrete barrier, and came with plenty of risks.

But they were risks James was going to have to take. He had no other choice if he wanted any semblance of a real future.

Wrapping himself in confidence he didn't necessarily feel, he strode past the court and knocked on the office door.

"Yeah, come in."

James twisted the knob and entered.

The fifty-something coach raised a dark eyebrow, his fingers hovering over a computer keyboard. "Can I help you?"

"You the basketball coach?" At the man's nod, James offered a hand to shake. "Name's James Phelps. I'm a senior, new to the school. Thought I'd introduce myself before tryouts, since you're going to want me for point guard."

"Nice to meet you." The coach gripped James's offered hand with a frown. "Hate to flatten your fizz, but we already have most of our first-string line-up. You can try out, but even if you make the team, you probably won't be starting. And unless you've got superhuman skills, I can almost guarantee it won't be as point guard."

James rocked back on his heels, crossing his arms over his chest. "I can work with 'probably' and 'almost.'"

Unimpressed, the coach turned back to his computer. "Pretty sure of yourself."

"I know my strengths. See you at tryouts next month." James pulled the door closed on his way out, grinning. He didn't have anything close to superhuman skills. But determination was good enough, and he had bucketloads of that.

STILL WORRIED ABOUT KEITH, Emma rummaged in her locker, then slammed it, planning to double-check that her brother had made it back to class okay.

"Emma."

She whirled at the familiar feminine voice and was promptly caught up in a pair of bony arms.

"Heather!" Emma grinned, relieved at her friend's greeting even after all this time.

"Where have you been all summer, and why didn't you come find me this morning? I've looked all over for you." The dark-haired beauty let her arms drop, her gaze sweeping the length of her friend as if to appraise Emma's condition.

Emma tucked her hair behind her ear, untangling it from her silver hoops. "I've been around. Just needed some time, you know? And I looked for you this morning, but got distracted helping a new kid find his class."

Heather flipped her waterfall of dark locks behind her back and led Emma down the hall. "Ooh, is he cute? What's his name?" She paused to bat her baby blues at a guy Emma didn't recognize. So many unfamiliar faces this year.

But too many familiar ones.

"James Phelps, and I didn't notice." *Except for the dimple. And the gray eyes. And the heart-melting smile.* When the wings of anxiety started to unfurl, she blinked the thoughts away.

Heather raised a suggestive eyebrow and lowered her voice. "Judging by the look on your face, you noticed a lot."

Emma shook her head in denial. "Uh, no. I'm not going there. I have officially learned my lesson. No boyfriends for me. Ever again."

Heather stopped walking and tipped her head sideways, looking down on Emma from their six-inch height difference. "That's possibly the lamest thing I've ever heard you say. Of course you'll have a boyfriend again someday. It's only a matter of time."

Time is exactly the problem. "I'm not joking, Heather. I don't want to put myself in that situation again. Besides, I don't need a boyfriend to be happy."

The warning bell rang, but Heather didn't move. "I get what you're saying, but this is our last year of high school, and I refuse to let you withdraw into yourself and become a loser-loner who never talks to boys because you're afraid they might ask you out."

"I won't. And I don't have a problem talking to boys." Emma leaned against a locker and let her head tip back with a soft bang. "I talked to one this morning. I just don't want to fall in love, or be alone with any of them. They only complicate life, anyway." She sighed, searching her friend's face for a hint of understanding.

Heather seemed to struggle with a response, and ended

up changing the subject. "Are you coming back to cheer? We could really use you."

Emma shook her head emphatically. "No." She started walking again, and Heather followed, finally breaking the silence as they arrived at Emma's classroom. "Well, cheer or not, I refuse to let you hermit. We're going to hang out. Shop. See some movies. And you, Miss Emma, will promise to attend at least one school function—specifically, a dance."

Even the word "dance" gave Emma flashes of cold sweat. "No dances. I—"

Heather stopped Emma's words with a finger on her lips. "Wrong answer." She leaned in and lowered her voice like she was sharing a secret. "Are you really going to let that scrambled-egg-brain steal what's left of your high school experience?"

She hadn't thought of it like that. Silently cursing Heather, Emma agreed. "Okay. You're right."

Heather grinned, staring up at the ceiling. "Mark this day on the record books and watch the news for signs of frost, people, because I believe that's a first."

"What's a first?" Emma wondered. "That you're right?"

Heather swatted Emma with her notebook. "That Emma Harris *admits* I'm right. It's about time, too."

Emma opened the door, but paused before going in to class. "Don't get used to it. I don't intend to make a habit of it."

"I'm coming over tonight. Shoes, chica. I miss your taste, not to mention your shopping stamina."

Grinning, Emma left Heather in the hall and entered her

classroom, trying to decode her emotions. She couldn't decipher them all, but there was one she recognized, and it was something she never thought she'd feel again within the walls of this building. Happiness.

Three

"HEY, I KNOW YOU." James dropped his notebook on the lab table next to Emma and secured the empty seat.

She glanced up from her smartphone, remembering their earlier conversation, and tried not to be amused. "You're stalking me now?" She returned James's arch look. "And even if you thought you knew me—like, say we'd been friends for several years—how can you tell if you really know a person, what they're like deep, deep down?" She certainly hadn't known Tom, even after eight months.

James tipped his chair back against the table behind them, tilting his head and narrowing his eyes. "I guess sometimes it's a judgment call."

Unable to meet his steady gaze, she turned her head to stare out the nearby window. "Even then, you just can't know." *Some of us have terrible judgment.*

"Exactly." His voice gentled. "Which is why you should try spending quality time with the person in question—outside of school—in order to get to know them better."

"Or." She turned her head, pasting on a smile she couldn't feel. *Please don't bring out the dimple.* "You could try the more unconventional approach of getting to know that person *inside* a public setting, like school, so you can feel comfortable before going somewhere alone with them. Safer that way."

James let the legs of his chair clank to the floor and propped his elbow on the desk, resting his chin on his fist. "Skittish, are ya?"

"Cautious."

"Burned?"

"Ashes."

"So, if I were to ask you out for this weekend . . ."

"I'd say no." She returned her attention to her phone.

"Because I'm not your type?"

She scrolled through her messages, unable to focus as memories tried to claw to the surface, leaving her skin sticky with anxiety. "Because no one's my type anymore," she murmured. "I don't date."

"So noted." He stared at her, calculating. "I'll keep trying."

She opened the textbook that had been on the table before she arrived and busied herself scanning the contents to evade further discussion. Avoiding Merrick was hard enough. Having a second male-figure pursue her was the last thing she needed. "Good luck with that."

AFTER THE LAST BELL, Emma gathered her things and headed outside, anxious to pick up Keith and see how the rest of his day had gone. As she merged into the special-needs hall, a paper airplane sailed toward her nose and would have hit her had she not blocked it with her hand. Across the way, two girls scowled at Emma, muttering. In the nearly empty hall, their quiet voices carried.

"They should keep her in the special classroom with the rest of *those* kids."

"Can't believe they didn't expel her."

"Such a liar."

She had a vague memory of the girls—maybe from prom?—but nothing solid. Not that she wanted to know them. Clearly, they were some of Tom's girls.

Ignoring them, she kept going.

Keith wasn't in his classroom. According to Mrs. Long, he thought Emma was taking too much time and insisted he needed to go "save" his sister from "that boy who hits." After skillfully evading Mrs. Long's questions, Emma found Keith waiting at her car in the parking lot and sighed in relief, beyond ready to leave.

"So. How was your first day?" She unlocked the doors and stowed her bag in the trunk.

"I love high school." He climbed in the passenger seat and fiddled with the radio while Emma lowered the convertible top.

The familiar tightness in her chest, the constricting of her lungs, and prickling of her skin forced her to adjust her afternoon plans. "I'm going to run to the beach."

Keith looked up, frowning. "I don't like swimming. Gran says you shouldn't go there."

Her hand was gentle on his shoulder. "We really need to get you over this fear of the ocean. It's practically a crime to live so close and never go."

"It's dangerous. I don't know how to swim, and there are scary things in the water." Keith rolled down his window and let the wind slap his face. "You shouldn't go to the beach by yourself. Something bad might happen."

He had *no* idea.

Emma turned up the volume on the stereo, pushing aside the hurt that curled in her stomach. By the time he found out what she was, she would be leaving—if not already gone. The idea made her melancholy. Her baby brother was the most important person in her life, and the thought that he might someday have reason to despise her hurt much worse than any damage Tom could have inflicted.

She cruised onto their street and pulled into the driveway. There was no need to go inside—she kept a swimsuit and towel in her trunk. Always.

"I'm going now so I can be back in time for dinner. Will you be okay by yourself for a while?"

Keith paused with the door open. "Mrs. Hall is going to help me with my homework."

"Okay." She glanced at their elderly neighbor's house, wondering how the woman always had flowers blooming in her yard regardless of season. "I'll be back in a couple of hours. Be good for Mrs. Hall."

Emma stretched to close the passenger door, watched her brother skip across the street, then aimed her car for the Pacific coast. When she stopped at a traffic light, a motorcycle pulled up beside her. The driver turned his head, staring through his visor.

"Bye, Emma!" he called, revving the throttle. "See you tomorrow."

She blinked when Motor Boy pushed back his visor. James.

"Nice bike." A new flame of attraction fluttered in her stomach, joining the unidentifiable something that had started when she'd first seen his dimple.

James winked, dropped his visor, and took off the second the light turned green, leaving a line of black smoke behind him. Emma coughed, gagged, coughed again, and didn't accelerate until James was far into the distance. The car behind her honked and she waved in apology, hurrying toward the side road that led to her beach.

BY THE TIME SHE HIKED down the steep embankment and around the tide pools to her cove, the pressure in her chest squeezed so tight, black spots floated in her vision. Not a good sign. It had only been five days since her last swim—usually she was good for seven.

Emma hung her bag on a rock that jutted out of the cave wall and stripped off her clothes, breathing deep, squeezing her hands into fists to avoid the panic creeping up on her. Panicking stole precious air from her half-converted lungs, and she was already on the verge of passing out.

If she did pass out, she couldn't get to the water, and if she couldn't get to the water, this terrible pressure wouldn't ease, and if the pressure didn't ease, she would soon stop breathing altogether. It would be hours before anyone missed her and came looking, and by that time, she'd be shriveled like a washed-up fish, and probably just as dead.

By the time she'd put on her suit, her vision blurred and she had to step carefully, trailing her hand along the wall of the shallow cave so she wouldn't trip and hurt herself before she got to the water. Finally at the edge, she sucked in a last breath of air and dove, relieved as slits opened up to gills in the side of her neck and water filtered through them, finally allowing her lungs to expand. Scales prickled up her legs, and she tightened the strings on her swimsuit bottoms to be sure she didn't lose them. The bottom half of her suit would become unnecessary once her fin fully developed, but for now, she relished the freedom of being able to use both legs like any human swimmer would. Well, if that human swimmer had scales and webbed feet.

Once she was in the water, her vision cleared exponentially, offering a unique view of stunning corals and bright sea life Emma doubted any human would ever see the way she could—even the scuba-diving ones. A giant yellow rockfish chased a school of red-and-silver sardines, his sharp spine brushing Emma's shoulder on his way past. She jerked, and a family of white crabs clinging to the side of a multi-colored coral formation scuttled in every direction. Deeper still, a young silver stingray flapped and burrowed in the sand.

Though the world beneath the surface possessed a soft, incomparable beauty, Emma's anger covered everything in a film of resentment. Why? Why had this happened to her? Why couldn't she just stay human and keep living her life like everyone else she knew? Go to college and have a future?

She'd spent her childhood dreaming of a wedding, of a house with a picket fence and red-headed children with freckles. Things she now knew she would never have because eventually, her seawater-oxygen ratios would flip-flop, and she'd no longer be able to live on land. She'd have to leave the parents who raised her and the brother she'd grown up with, the family she loved—a future she struggled to accept every day.

The knowledge hovered at the edges of her thoughts constantly, carving away at her desire to reinsert herself into the high school social scene that had once been such a big deal to her. There were already enough people for whom she would always ache. Adding more would only make her departure more difficult.

There was no experience she could imagine that would be more painful than leaving her family behind—even after what Tom had done. Emma had no idea what was happening to her until Merrick explained just after she turned sixteen. She hated him for that. For knowing things she didn't. For insisting she couldn't stay with her family and be human. For acting smug every time she was forced back here to swim out of necessity. For reminding her over and over again that huge chunks of her life had been decided before she was even hatched.

Hatched. The very word irritated her.

According to Merrick, her sea parents deserted her as an infant, left her on her grandmother's doorstep to be raised as a human child rather than the changeling she really was. Gran remained the only person in her life who knew the truth.

In the distance, a dark form materialized as if thoughts alone were enough to summon him. Not in the mood to talk, Emma veered to the right, hoping to avoid the inevitable confrontation. Merrick followed her movement, coming closer with every fin stroke. Another right sent her back toward shore, by now over a mile away. She skirted the natural rock arch that rose a hundred feet above the surface—marking the passage that would lead to Atlantis, her future home—and behind a large wall of coral. Merrick could no longer see her, but creatures she didn't recognize blinked as she passed, reminding Emma exactly how impossible it was to hide.

I don't want this!

But even as she thought it, her body took strength from the salt water she so hated. Physically, it would be easy to walk away from her life ashore and start over in Atlantis. But emotionally, the price was high—there would be nothing easy about any part of what was coming.

With a sigh that sent a stream of bubbles trailing behind her, Emma put on a burst of speed that brought her back to the cove she considered her own. She swam the length of the inlet once, twice, then returned at a leisurely pace. After taking time to ensure she'd been in the water long enough to keep her going for several days, she hoisted herself out on scaly, but nimble, feet and stole into the privacy of the cave, scratching her itchy hips and legs.

"You cannot avoid your fate."

Emma jumped, swallowing a curse, and turned her back on Merrick, who had apparently been waiting in her cave. Why did he always come out of nowhere? "I can try."

"Why will you not swim with me?"

If she believed him capable of feeling, she would think he sounded hurt. "I prefer to swim alone." As her towel soaked the drops of salt water from her legs, the itching eased, and her white skin smoothed. Once she'd finished drying her body, Emma squeezed the water from her hair and wrapped the towel around her head, then turned back to Merrick, leveling her gaze on his face to avoid seeing the parts of him she preferred not to see. "What do you want?"

"You have ten moon cycles left."

Her neck stiffened. She hardly needed the reminder. "I think it's eleven, actually."

"We will be tied soon after your arrival." He ran his fingers along her shoulder, over her birthmark, until he touched her necklace.

Her hands stilled in the process of unfolding her jeans. She stepped away and yanked the pants on over her swimsuit, then pulled on her tank top and slid her feet into her sandals. If he didn't represent everything she hated about her future, she might at least try to appreciate his friendship or the way his boyish white-blonde hair belied the manly muscles that bulged along his shoulders. But right now, that was too much to consider. "You're too old for me, Merrick."

"You will be happier if you accept your fate." Heat radiated off him as he moved in behind her, his breath hot on the back of her neck as he forced her into the corner. "Accept me."

She whirled around, hands clenched into fists, and shoved against his chest. "Go away, Merrick. Leave me alone.

I hate you. I hate you all for giving me a family and then taking it away."

"Emmalina. I am your family now. In time, you will learn to love the sea. Your ties to land will no longer be a burden—you will forget."

"I'll never forget. Ever."

Merrick stepped back, but not far enough. Emma shoved him again. "Out of my way." She snatched her bag, keys, and cell phone and stomped out of the cave, knowing he wouldn't follow.

"I can help you," he called.

"I don't want your help, Merrick," she said. "I want a miracle."

October 7th
283 days to departure

THE TARDY BELL BUZZED as James took the stairs two at a time. Stupid bike. After all the work he'd done on it this summer, all the money he poured into rebuilding the engine, it had the nerve to pick now to up and die on him. Like he could afford to be tardy today, of all days. He wrenched the door open, but a screech in the parking lot had him turning his head to watch a red convertible pull into one of the last available stalls.

James let the door fall closed and leaned against the building. This could be interesting. Emma's brother jumped out of the car, shot across the parking lot, and bolted past James into the school. Emma put the top up, then slung a bag over her shoulder and sauntered toward him, looking like her mind was light-years away.

He waited until she got to the bottom of the stairs. "You're late."

She jerked her head up, the sunglasses sliding down her nose and revealing puffy, bloodshot eyes, like she was either exhausted or hung over. Probably the first. She wasn't the drunk type—at least, not from what he could tell. He was usually a good judge of which girls were what type, but Emma continued to throw him off balance. She met him at the top of the landing. "So are you."

He opened the door and ushered her in. "Long night?"

"Couldn't sleep. Took a P.M. and over-slept my alarm." Her voice was hoarse, low. Sexy. "What's your excuse?"

Something tugged in his chest, twisting and spiraling and heating his blood. He liked her tired voice, and attraction was a sensation he both recognized and enjoyed. "Bike wouldn't start. Had to hoof it two miles."

"Maybe we'll be doing detention together."

"For one tardy?" He couldn't afford to be shackled in detention. Not today. "They can't do that."

Emma dropped the sunglasses into her bag and opened her locker, the corners of her mouth twitching. "Hot date after school?"

"Basketball tryouts. Being late hurts my chances. Then, if I end up running laps until ten, I'll have to miss work, and my boss will be mad at me too. And if I piss him off, he might not be so flexible with my basketball schedule. It's like an endless chain of angry-James-making events." If they even let him on the team. Although, Coach Adams had seen him in open court and hadn't kicked him loose yet. James really hoped he wasn't wrong about the coach's level of interest. He'd know soon.

"Poor baby," Emma teased. "That's quite a predicament."

"Heartbreaking, really." He snagged his English book and slammed his locker, following her down the hall and falling into a rhythm that felt as natural to him as breathing. "If I started to cry, would you kiss me better?" She turned, walking backward as her smile grew into the unguarded expression he'd only ever seen her wear for her brother.

"Real men don't cry. Well, unless they're about to go to jail."

"What? You don't think long-distance phone comer-cials affect guys too?" Enchanted, he lunged forward to catch up with her, close enough that if he reached out, he could swing her into his arms and plant one on her right there in the hall. The move had worked with plenty of girls in the past, and usually they melted like chocolate in his hands. He considered trying it for a nanosecond, but decided he'd probably end up with a black eye from this particular girl, and kept pace with her instead. She paused, seeming to contemplate something, then turned and walked forward again. As she moved, her loose-fitting blouse slid to reveal part of her shoulder and a mark that resembled a fish.

James clutched his chest as the tightness moved into his throat. *Birthmark or tattoo? Girls like her don't get tattoos. Do they? Too detailed for a birthmark, though. Holy hell, which is it?*

"Don't stress," she said, waving a hand, oblivious to the direction of his thoughts. "You don't get detention until you have three tardies. Barnes won't be happy, though."

"Does that mean he'll ream us out?" They were almost to class, and James felt the need to know what was coming. He was still in the adjustment phase and preferred not to complicate his student-teacher relationships any more than necessary. Last thing he needed was to gain a reputation for the wrong things.

"No. I'll protect you." Emma flicked her hair over her shoulder and sent him a playful smile. "Watch and learn."

James frowned and opened the door. Emma headed for the two empty spots on the back row. Mr. Barnes paused mid-lecture to say, "Miss Harris. Mr. Phelps. Glad you could join us."

Murmurs traveled around the room, accompanied by strange expressions and furtive glances. For a second, Emma's face flashed stony cold. James ignored the odd looks and took the last empty seat.

"Mr. Phelps," Mr. Barnes said, singling him out. "Would you care to explain to the class why we've been so rudely interrupted?"

James cleared his throat and opened his mouth to answer, but Emma spoke first. "It's my fault, Mr. Barnes." James watched her eyes go wide and innocent. Her lashes fluttered as her lips moved into a pout. In the time since he'd opened the door and sat down, she'd transformed, looked suddenly needy and helpless. *What the hell?*

Emma continued, "I had trouble with my car on the way to school, and James stopped to help. Without him, I might still be stuck on the side of the road instead of here in my favorite class."

Barnes shook his head, seemingly at a loss for words as Emma's helpless act drew him in. He cleared his throat and finally said, "Okay. Well. I'm glad you both made it. We're on page 57 . . ." The rest of the teacher's words were lost to James when Emma winked and flipped through her book to follow along.

How did she do that? Why? She rarely gave him more than a passing glance, and suddenly—because they both showed up late to school—they're now best buds? He opened his notebook, but instead of taking notes, he doodled her tattoo / birthmark, dying to know which it was. Everything in him itched to fit her into one of his categories. Once he put a girl in one box or another, he knew what to expect—how to avoid getting in over his head or in too deep or whatever other hazard might present itself—but each time he saw her, she teetered along the lines of one type or another, or several. Something told him he should leave this particular girl alone, forget about fitting her in a box, but there was a crazy pulling in his chest, a compulsion of sorts, that compelled him to at least try.

By LUNCH, THE COMPULSION hadn't calmed. From what he'd seen, Emma ate lunch with her brother on Mondays, but the rest of the week, the kid ate in the cafeteria with other students from his special-needs class. In the weeks since school had started, he hadn't once seen Emma—or the brunette she sometimes hung out with—in the cafeteria, so James figured they left campus.

Within minutes of the lunch bell, he'd ditched the fling-worthy girls he often ate with and was outside leaning on the hood of Emma's car, waiting. Before long, she strode out alone, mumbling something under her breath. She walked around James and got in, but left her door open. "If you don't want to get run over, you'll need to move."

He didn't. "The usual practice would be to back out by putting the car in reverse, in which case, I would more likely be dumped on the ground. That is, unless you plan on driving onto the sidewalk and over the grass."

She slid on her sunglasses and started the car. "Depends on how I'm feeling. One of these days, I could snap. Drive right into the school."

"You wouldn't do that."

"How do you know?"

He straightened, catching her door before it closed, and leaned in. "Well, for one thing, it would be a crime to hurt this pretty car." She moved just enough that the vent blew strands of her hair into his face, bringing with it a soft, clean scent that reminded him of fresh air and flowers. He swallowed. "Besides, you wouldn't hurt me. What would you do the next time you have pretend car trouble?"

"Take care of it myself, as usual. And it probably wouldn't be car trouble. Maybe a female issue or something lame like that." Over the top of her glasses, her eyes glinted with mischief. "What do you want?"

"A ride."

She raised a questioning brow. "To where?"

James shrugged. "Wherever you're going. You saved my bacon this morning. I'm buying you lunch."

She relaxed into her seat. "Thanks for the thought, but that's not necessary. You were there, I was there—it worked out for us both."

"Of course it's necessary. Because of you, not only do I *not* have detention, but Barnes didn't even mark me tardy. That's huge."

Her lips twitched as she tilted her head. "He didn't mark me tardy, either."

"I know. You deserve to be rewarded. Let me at least buy you a drink. What's your favorite soda pop?" When she didn't respond, he said, "Look, I'd be happy with just a ride." For now.

She pinched the bridge of her delicate nose. Distracted? Stressed? Tired? Something. Whatever it was, her guard was lowered, however temporarily. "Fine. Whatever. But for the record, I'm still not going out with you."

He leaned closer, close enough so their breath mingled, until mere inches of air separated them and he could practically taste the honey of her lips. Inches—small ones. Her slight gasp and the anticipation in her eyes gave him a smidgen of satisfaction, but the taste of fear caused him to back off. "A fact which continues to remain a mystery. But I haven't given up."

Emma hesitated, like she wanted to do something and couldn't, or wanted to say something and wouldn't. She met his stare, mute confusion freezing her face until he closed the door and jogged around to the passenger side.

"Where's your friend?" he asked as he settled in beside her.

She maneuvered the car out of the parking lot and onto the busy road. "Tutoring. Heather's really good with English, so every Wednesday, she volunteers to tutor the kids who aren't."

Absently, he let his thumb tap to the beat of the low music. "She gives up her whole lunch period for it?"

"Yeah. It's not so bad. I did it for three years and really enjoyed it."

"You don't do it anymore?"

"Not this year."

There were about a hundred more questions brought to mind by her response, but from the tightness of her jaw, James judged that they'd crossed into a subject Emma didn't want to discuss, so he changed it. "Tell you what. You drive to wherever you want to eat, and since we're using your car, I'll buy lunch. As payback. We'll call it even."

She shook her head. "Too much like a date."

"But you're paying for gas, so that's a fair trade."

"No deal. Would've paid for it anyway. Besides, we don't need cash at this place."

James frowned as they turned into a residential neighborhood. "Where are we going?"

"My house." She shrugged. "I eat at home most days. Fast food is disgusting."

He hadn't planned on going home with her. Not that he was complaining, but the intent had been to buy her lunch, not to have her feed him. "So . . . what were you planning to eat?"

"Whatever looks good." She took her sunglasses off and

tossed them on the dash, and he caught a glimpse of her pale green irises, set off by the fiery hair that cascaded down her neck, across a thin white scar, and over one shoulder. "What sounds good to you?"

Being so close to her, about to see the inside of her house, he could think of several things, but decided for now it was best to stick with the subject of food. "I'm not picky. Maybe a sandwich."

"I can do that."

They slowed in front of a picturesque two-story with flowers lining the front walk and a variety of mature trees dotting the vast lawn. Emma turned into the driveway and hit a button for the garage. She was so out of his league, it was ridiculous. "Nice house."

Emma didn't respond. She parked carefully and turned off the ignition. James waited for her to open her door, but she sat there, both hands on the wheel, staring at the windshield long enough for him to feel uncomfortable.

Finally, he cleared his throat. "Problem?"

"I think I'm changing my mind. We should go somewhere else to eat."

James looked at the door to the house, then back at Emma. "That's fine. My offer to buy stands." She still didn't move, and she was clenching the wheel hard. "What's wrong?"

She shook her head and started the car again. Her mouth moved, but it took several tries before she found her voice. "I just remembered we don't really have all that many groceries. No bread. I'm sorry. Do you mind if we drive through somewhere?"

Something wasn't right with her, but James didn't know what it could be. He hoped he hadn't somehow caused her distress. "Sure. Yeah. Don't be sorry."

At the end of the street, they stopped at the sign. Though there were no cars waiting, she didn't proceed. "Where do you want to go?"

"Wherever you think is the least disgusting."

"There's a deli on the next block." She said it under her breath and seemed to relax as she started driving again, like she was talking herself into something. Or out of it. "I can get tuna or a salad."

"That works for me. I'll eat about anything." He stared at her profile and realized she was grinding her teeth, taking deep breaths. "You okay?"

She cleared her throat and loosened her fingers from the wheel one by one. "Yeah. Why?"

"You seem upset." He wanted to reach out and touch her, calm her, assure her that she didn't have to be afraid, but his gut told him that would be a bad idea.

She looked over, smiled, big. Too big. Not a real smile. "Sorry. I'm suddenly really hungry."

When they pulled into the parking lot, the drive-through line was seven cars long, the inside not much better. Emma's pale face had him concerned that maybe she had a health issue. She was so thin, it wouldn't be shocking. He checked his watch and figured they had time. Not that it would matter if they didn't—at this point, he was determined to see her eat. "Why don't we go inside? You can save us a table and I'll grab the food." She hesitated, so he added, "We'll eat fast."

"Okay," she said finally, and parked in a recently vacated stall. "I might even let you pay. Just this once."

James couldn't help but grin. "Deal."

SHE'D LIVED THROUGH a lot of embarrassing moments in her life, but while she saved a table and waited for James to bring their food, Emma decided the little panic attack she'd experienced in the garage at her house was near the top of the list. Seriously. Who did that? What did it say about her that she could so thoughtlessly show him where she lived, come so close to letting him—someone she hardly even knew—in the house with her while no one else was home, after everything she'd already been through? What had she been thinking?

And worse, how naïve was it that she *wanted* to trust him?

Problem was, she'd wanted to trust Tom, too. She'd wanted to love him, even though they'd never connected with that deep emotional bond she knew people in love should feel. She'd wanted to know what it felt like, even if she couldn't stay, couldn't have that fairy-tale ending she'd hoped for as a little girl.

She sighed, leaning her chin on her hand to stare out the window.

"That's the kind of loaded sigh that begs me to ask. Do you want to talk about it?" James set a berry-topped salad in front of Emma and took the seat in front of her. He tucked ravenously into his burger before she even had the chance to respond.

She picked up her fork, pushing the berries around on the lettuce. "Thanks, but no."

He swallowed and gulped his shake. "Why do I make you nervous?"

"Nosey much?" She speared a bite of the salad, twirling her fork in a practiced stall tactic. "What makes you think I'm nervous?"

If raised eyebrows were any indication, he believed no explanation was needed.

"I'm not nervous," she insisted, knowing he could see through her lie. "I just realized we need groceries and changed my mind. People do it all the time."

He set his burger down, eyes searching hers as if they were a gateway through which he could discover her every secret. Finally, after a long, tense moment, the edges of his mouth curved up and he held out his milkshake. "Want some? It's chocolate."

AFTER SCHOOL, EMMA HADN'T even made it outside the building when Heather caught up, eyes bright with curiosity. "Rumor has it you've already ruined the new guy. Obviously, I need the real details stat."

Emma groaned, further regretting her earlier indiscretion. "What did you hear?"

Heather waved off Emma's concerns and dragged her through the door. "Just that the two of you were seen leaving together, making for your house. You can imagine the rest.

No big. Something more fascinating will be happening tomorrow, and this will be old gossip. So hurry and spill before I have to get to practice."

"I saved him from a tardy, and he bought me lunch to repay the favor. That's it."

"Oh. My. That's huge!" Heather wrapped her arms around Emma as if she'd just shared some kind of noteworthy news. "You haven't even talked to a guy since Tom. I'm so proud. You must really like this guy."

Until Heather said it, the idea hadn't occurred to Emma. It was true that she wasn't big on dating lately, and she was admittedly rusty in the social sphere, but maybe there was a part of her that did like James. Just a little. And maybe, maybe, that part would grow enough to allow them to actually be friends. She pulled out of Heather's embrace. "He . . . seems okay."

Heather raised an eyebrow. "'Okay'? There are a number of guys at this school I'd label 'okay.' To have caught your attention and weaseled his way into your car, this guy has to be exceptional. Beyond exceptional."

Emma felt herself smile. "I doubt it. But maybe I'll give him a chance to prove me wrong. Maybe."

By THE TIME JAMES got to the locker room for tryouts, he'd replayed the hour he spent with Emma probably a hundred times, trying to make sense of her. One minute, she was sassy and flirty, took him home with her like she might actually let him get to know her, however reluctantly. Then the next minute, she was as pale and shaky as a wounded animal, wouldn't talk much, but let him buy her lunch, even though five minutes earlier, she'd adamantly refused.

There was no question that she was different from other girls—that much he knew—but she was also five times harder to figure out. He wasn't sure he should make the effort to try, especially now that he'd seen this new side of her—the innocent, wounded one from this morning. Something told him she could be the biggest risk of his life—though he had no idea why he felt that way.

He changed into his shorts and jersey and bounded onto the court, basketball in hand, ready to play hard. Being the new guy meant he'd have to prove himself, which started with making friends. The rest of the players had gathered on the bleachers. James plunked onto the bench next to a tall, big-shouldered guy he'd seen a few times in open court, but hadn't really cared to meet before now. "Hey, man."

The guy acknowledged James with a head bob. "Hey."

"You on the team already?" James scooted over to make room for Cameron—whom he *had* bothered to meet, and even practiced with on occasion.

"Yep. Three years."

"I hear you almost took state a couple of years ago." Having done this before, James knew the right buttons to push, and he was prepared to use them to his best advantage. "Must mean the team's pretty good."

Shoulder Guy grinned. "We are. This year, there won't be no 'almost,' either. We're after the title. Last year to play, you know?"

"Yep." James did know. It was his last year too, along with his last chance to try for a scholarship. He offered his fist. "James."

"Lyle." They bumped knuckles. "You any good?"

Now wasn't the time to brag about his past accomplishments. If this guy hadn't paid attention in open court, James would unleash his ball-handling skills when they got started. Fortunately, James *had* paid attention. He knew exactly how to beat Lyle on the court. "I'm decent."

"Who's this?" A rough hand landed on James's shoulder,

and he turned to stare down the person attached to the hand. The guy was at least six foot five, with a dent in his chin and ice-blue eyes.

"Mark, James—James, Mark." Lyle made the short-version introduction. "James plans to try out for our team."

Mark's eyebrows winged up as he glanced around the court. "Getting kind of a late start, aren't ya?"

James shook his head. So this was the infamous Mark who had led the team last year after their star player disappeared. Rumor had it Mark was a real piece of work. To James's knowledge, Mark hadn't bothered to show up in open court even once. Only the most over-confident players were stupid enough to believe they didn't need to condition. *Play it cool, man. Don't let him get to you already.* "Been playing forever. Gotta keep going, even after the move."

Mark's teeth ground hard on his gum. "New guy. Explains some."

Frowning, James turned fully, intending to ask what Mark meant by that, but Coach blew the whistle to start tryouts. It would have to wait.

Two hours later, breathing heavily and jersey drenched with sweat, James thought the grin plastered on Coach's face reminded him of a kid who'd found the prize in a cereal box. A good sign. He helped clean up the equipment and followed the rest of the players into the locker room. Coach stopped him at the door. "Well played, Phelps."

"Thanks."

Coach tucked his clipboard under his arm. "Shower up and head over to my office. Let's have a chat."

"Sure thing," James said as Coach strode away.

"Looks like you're in, bro." Lyle slapped James's butt when he walked past. "Where'd you learn to play like that?"

"Everywhere." James opened his locker and peeled off his shirt, then unlaced his shoes.

"Your life of practicing might pay off for all of us," Mark piped in, "long as you don't let the ice queen get under your skin."

The hairs on the back of James's neck prickled as he wrapped a towel around his waist and faced Mark. "Ice queen?"

"I saw you get into her car at lunch, so I'm going to warn you, because we're friends." Mark put his arm around James as Lyle closed in on the other side, his eyes narrowed. "We *are* friends, aren't we?"

Only in the sense that I just whooped your ass and now you're seeing trophies we haven't won yet. James stared, but didn't respond.

"Emma Harris is bad news, man." Mark released him with a little shove. "She may have a pretty face, but underneath that fantastic exterior hides a shark who bites hard. Trust me. If you ever want to play college ball, stay far away from that one."

As Mark strode off, James wondered if the guy's words had anything to do with why Emma had warned him off the day they met. He must be missing something, but couldn't figure out what. Not wanting to keep the coach waiting, he grabbed a bar of soap and stuck his head under a steady stream of water, trying to wash his questions down the drain.

"*THE GOOD NEWS* is that I definitely want you on the team." Coach didn't waste any time getting right to the point. "But I want to address some concerns so we can come to an agreement before either of us makes a commitment, okay?"

James squared his shoulders and sat, relieved to have made it this far, and figuring he was about to be lectured on all the stuff coaches are required to demand of players. But Coach surprised him. "Clearly, you've played before, so I don't need to tell you to keep your grades above a C average, no skipping class, and keep the tardies to a minimum."

"No, I already know all that." James shifted in his chair, wondering what the man really wanted.

"Right. That's good. You have a head start on fifty percent of the team, then. So here's the thing. I looked up your file—gotta know who's playing for me—and I noticed you have work release last period instead of a class."

"Yeah." James cleared his throat, not sure how he felt that the coach had checked up on him. What else did the man know?

"I'm concerned," Coach continued, "because I don't want your job conflicting with practice times, or vice versa. I get the impression that the job is necessary."

Tension snaked up James's spine, and he clenched his teeth to keep from cursing. "I'll work it out," he said. "My job schedule will be flexible because my boss likes basketball."

Coach nodded like this was good news. "All right, then. What about varsity team fees? We've got jerseys, travel costs, equipment rentals . . . it adds up to somewhere around twelve hundred per player, before off-campus meals. Are you able to handle that?"

James's throat felt hot, sticky, and it took him a minute to find words. So much for getting his bike fixed anytime soon.

Coach continued. "If not, I want your skills bad enough to try to set up some kind of financial assistance. Maybe a fund-raiser."

Yeah, that won't make it obvious or anything. "No, thank you. I can take care of the fees." James hated being forced to admit that he and his father didn't have much money. He hated that his paycheck paid some of their bills and left little else. More importantly, he hated having to discuss it with someone who was—essentially—a complete stranger, even if he was the basketball coach.

Coach let out a relieved breath and leaned back in his chair. "Well. You let me know if that changes. We'll work something out."

"Yes, sir." James stood and started for the door.

"James, there's just one other thing."

He turned his head to meet the coach's eyes. "Yes?"

"In the past, some of our players have had issues with the law. Just so you're aware, I have a zero-tolerance policy. You get arrested and charged—for anything—and you're out. No exceptions. No excuses.

"I expect my players to keep control of personal-type situations. I understand that kids your age have drama, especially when it comes to girls, but I'm encouraging you to keep your private life, well, private. Got it?"

"Yeah. I got it." James forced himself to close the door with a soft click. He'd played on lots of teams over a lot of time and had never—in his whole life—felt like making the team was a burden instead of a joy. Until now.

He understood the thing about being arrested. From what he'd heard, the Oceanside Pirates varsity team was infamous for past players' criminal records. He personally had nothing to worry about there. Not so much as a traffic ticket to his name. But since when did coaches warn players about girls?

The whole conversation left a bad taste in his mouth. If he didn't need a scholarship so desperately, he'd consider walking away, saying no to the controlling coach with the insane players. But he couldn't. Wouldn't. Not only did he love playing more than anything else in the world, but basketball might be his only shot at college. And college, he knew, was the best way for him not to end up like his dad. As much as he loved his dad, he had zero desire to become a middle-aged single man whose misery went hand in hand with his obesity. James detoured through the mostly empty locker room, snagged his gym bag, and took a swing at a punching bag as he passed.

The impact of his fist on the leather relieved some of his stress, so he hit it again, and then again. Apparently, playing hard wasn't nearly enough today. When his knuckles were bruised and his biceps ached with exertion, he let up on the bag and strode out, wondering what it would take to get his bike running again, and how he'd come up with the money to pay the ridiculously expensive basketball fees.

Seven

October 23th
267 days to departure

Emma closed her textbook and stood to stretch, eyeing her bed and moaning wistfully. No time for a nap. Not today.

Will I still be able to sleep when I live in Atlantis?

She had so many questions—and yet no will to ask them. Maybe it was better if she didn't know until she got there. Sighing, she tossed a clean swimsuit and towel in her beach bag and grabbed her keys. Whether or not she wanted to swim, she had to be able to breathe during school tomorrow. *Time to replenish.*

She detoured by Keith's room to say good-bye, but paused when she heard an unfamiliar voice.

"I really like your room. What's this?"

Emma peeked in without knocking. The stout, barrel-chested kid had strawberry hair and a scar on his forehead, and he held up the autographed basketball Keith most treasured among all his possessions.

"It's my ball." Keith reached out like he wanted it back, but his friend turned away.

"Can I borrow it?" the kid asked. "I just want to show it to some people."

Keith shook his head, a wrinkle forming between his eyebrows.

Emma opened the door all the way. "Hi."

"Hi, Emma." Keith relaxed his face and let out a breath.

She nodded at the boy holding the basketball. "Hey, that's not a toy. It's valuable. Signed by the Lakers. Can you please put it back?"

Keith's friend shrugged as he replaced it. "I was just looking."

His defensive tone put her on edge, and a devious spark in his eyes made her hesitant to trust him. "You guys should come downstairs to the kitchen. I'll help you find a snack."

Keith bounded down, leaving his friend to glare at Emma. But glare or not, she wasn't about to leave him alone in Keith's room unsupervised. Finally, the boy followed Keith, and Emma pulled the bedroom door closed, hoping she was wrong about the kid, but knowing she wasn't.

Once the boys were settled in front of the Xbox in the family room, Emma poked her head into her father's office to warn him. "Can you keep an eye on the boys? I don't have a good feeling about Keith's new friend. He seemed way too interested in some of Keith's more valuable possessions."

When her father's only response was a distracted, "Mmkay. I'll do my best," she doubted her words got through. Still, she wrapped her arms around him from behind and kissed the top of his head. "Love you, Daddy," she said.

"I love you too, sweet pea." He patted her arm while it was still around his neck. "Wherever you're going, stay safe."

On her way out, she sent a text to her mother, not trusting that her father would remember their conversation. Cindy responded that she would only be at the hairstylist for another half hour and assured Emma she would return home soon, but even so, Emma wished she could stay and keep an eye on the boys herself.

Trying to let it go, Emma dropped the convertible top and sped toward her beach, willing the sisterly worry stone in her stomach to melt away.

THE LIGHT BREEZE PICKED UP the hair off Emma's shoulders, weaving strands around until they tangled together in knots and then blew out again. The familiar scent of fishy-brine mixed with smoke from a bonfire farther down, twirling and swirling and drawing away many of the seagulls that usually circled near her cove. Standing on the rocky ledge, Emma dipped her toes in the cool salt water, testing. Gradually, the itch climbed up her foot, tingling in her leg until she could feel the burn, make out the shape of the scales that would rise to protect her skin underwater.

Rather than diving in, as she usually did, she kept control

and took a step back to shake the excess water from her foot, staring out at the natural rock arch, the marker to the entrance of Atlantis.

What if this could be good enough? What if she could get away with just touching the water occasionally, as she had through her tween years? That would be nice.

But even as she thought it, she knew those days were long past.

Resentment rolled over her, threatening to crush her with the weight of things she couldn't change. Tilting her head back, she closed her eyes and allowed the sun to warm her skin, soaking up radiance from being outside, in the air, living on land. She would do whatever it took to stay.

When she opened her eyes again, Merrick was there, at the base of the arch, beckoning for her to jump in the water and swim with him.

Emma shook her head and stowed her things in the cave. *Why is he always here? If I have to swim to clear my gills, can't I do it by myself? In peace?*

By the time she reemerged, Merrick had slipped underwater, his dark form moving in a zigzag pattern toward her, fast. Faster than anything she'd ever seen. He stopped twenty feet away, still in the deep water, but close enough. Close enough that if Emma wasn't careful, vigilant, he could grab her and take her down with him before she even remembered how to breathe in his world. She didn't think he would do that at this point, but eventually, he'd probably have to, since she had no intention of going voluntarily. She'd rather live alone than be forced to marry someone she didn't love. And if it wouldn't kill her, she'd give up swimming altogether to stay on land. Depending on the circumstances, she wondered if death would be a better fate.

"That's close enough," she told him.

"Come in the water," he said. "It is so dry up there, so harsh."

"I will. After you leave."

"Why do you not embrace your heritage? Your place in the sea?" He swam closer, making Emma take a wary step back.

"My *heritage* is on land. My place is here, with my parents and my home."

"What of me? Would you leave me without a mate?"

"I don't even know you."

His brows knit together and lines formed in his cheeks. "I am Merrick, your betrothed. *I* am important. Tangaroa has chosen me for you. What more is there to know?"

Emma swallowed a lump in her throat, knowing she'd never be able to make him truly understand. "Everything. There is everything to know. I don't want to live in your world. To be honest, I wish it didn't exist."

His look of hurt astonishment cut Emma in a way she didn't realize he could. "I do not understand your anger. Continuing to fight against the change will destroy you."

"You're wrong." Struggling to keep her balance through eyes blurred with unshed tears, Emma tripped over the edge of the volcanic rock and scraped her ankle. Warm blood drizzled down her heel, but she glared at Merrick. "Being forced to live in Atlantis—away from everything I know and everyone I love—that is what will ultimately destroy me. I know you think I'm selfish, but I'm about to lose everything that matters to me. I don't think you'll ever understand." Her ankle throbbed. She bent to wipe away the blood, swallowing a heavy lump in her throat. "Merrick, I would do anything, *anything* to change this part of myself."

Merrick stared at Emma, clearly perplexed. "You are right. I do not understand. Our home bursts with thriving beauty. If only you will come there, you will see how the ocean gives us life."

A tear escaped and slid down her cheek. "So does the air. The sand. The sun on my skin. I have parents and a brother who love me. I need them. I don't know how to leave them. How to exist without them."

"You have family in Atlantis. We will help you." He inched closer. "It will not take long for you to forget those you must leave behind in order to come home."

She dug her toes into a patch of sand, knowing she couldn't argue her misery away. "You keep telling me I have family there, but I've never seen them, Merrick. Never met them. Why aren't they here? Why did they send you and not come themselves? They deserted me when I was a baby. They still haven't come for me. Doesn't exactly make me want to be with them for the rest of my life. I belong here. Everything I am is here." Emma stared at orange and pink rays that stretched across the horizon and turned the water a stunning, sparkling gold. "Please go. I need to swim alone. Please."

Merrick said nothing, but nodded one last time and dove under. He didn't understand love, not the kind she felt for her family, the kind she would fight for, die for, and Emma couldn't comprehend that at all.

She waited until she was absolutely sure Merrick was truly gone, until she was sure her ankle had stopped bleeding, and then dove into the crystal blue, swimming with a ferocious speed she hoped would numb the ache and help her accept the blow fate had dealt her. As she passed schools of fish, a grouchy stingray, a rainbow of coral, she fought sobs building in her throat. There were things she'd miss if she could leave the sea and never return, but they would be small sacrifices. Fairy-tale endings follow battles well fought, and Emma would gladly draw her sword if she could find the right giant to cut down.

Living a double life would never allow her the peace she craved. An hour under was all she really needed, and once she'd cleared her gills, Emma had no desire left to swim, no matter how alive it made her feel. Every minute she spent here was that much of a loss from her real life.

When she was finished, she pulled herself ashore, shaking her legs dry. The breeze, cooler now as the sun disappeared below the horizon, caressed her skin, raising goose bumps and making her shiver as she picked her way around tide pools—busy with sea life—and slippery, but sharp, volcanic rock to the secluded alcove.

By the time she got to her car, the breeze turned into a strong wind, blowing her hair in a wild mess, tangling the fine strands into ropes that slapped her face and stung her eyes. She dug an elastic out of her purse and bound the mass at the nape of her neck.

Sometimes she liked to drive down the coast road to decompress after swimming, to compose herself before going home to face her family and pretend that everything was normal and fine. But not today.

Today she needed her family close, so she slid on her sunglasses and headed home, trying to decide what would make a quick and easy dinner, since it was her turn to cook.

Near the high school, she passed a tall, muscular figure with long-ish hair. She slowed, glancing in the rearview to confirm that it really was him before she stopped along the curb. "Hey, James."

His lips turned up, but his eyes didn't sparkle the way she knew they could. "Hey, there. Going somewhere fun?"

"Yes, home. Long day. You?"

"I'm going home too." He draped his arm over the edge of the windshield where the convertible top would be if it were up and let his hand dangle in the air, exposing slightly bloody, purpling knuckles. "Longest ever."

The frustration in his voice gave her the urge to take him home and bandage his hand, feed him dinner. He looked so tired. But she knew she couldn't do that. Wouldn't. Never again. She shook her head, wondering why the sight of his bloody knuckles didn't scare her. "Jump in. I'll give you a lift."

He sighed in relief and opened the passenger door. "You're an angel."

"What happened to your hand?"

James lifted both and turned them over like he was just now noticing something was amiss. Emma let out a tiny sound of sympathy. "Both hands. Were you in a fight?"

"If I were, would you kick me out of your car?"

"Depends on who you hit." She flipped on the blinker and merged into traffic. When he didn't say anything, she probed further, needing to be sure. "So . . . who was it?"

"Everyone who has ever made me mad rolled up in a punching bag filled with sand." He stared at nothing, frowning at some kind of inner turmoil. "I stayed after practice to work out, clear my head."

That he wouldn't look at her dried Emma's throat with an anxious kind of pain. He'd heard the rumors by now, she was sure. Mark and Lyle had done a great job of making people believe that what Tom did was somehow her fault. That she lied, led him on, blah, blah, blah. Didn't matter that it was their skewed version and totally untrue. In James's eyes, she'd changed. Become something he didn't like, and might even come to hate. Maybe he was too kind to treat her the way they did, but his view of her was forever stained. Swallowing her regret, she asked, "Did it work?"

James flexed his fingers and rolled his shoulders in a smooth movement that rippled the muscles in his arms. He didn't answer for several seconds, which, in her experience, was not a good sign.

"I don't know where you live, so you'll have to give me directions," she said.

That seemed to snap him out of his thoughts. "Sorry. Turn right at the stop sign up there."

She did as he said, hating the tension she could feel pulsing from him, at once desperate to be rid of him.

"The blue house, fourth on the right."

Afraid to look into his eyes and really see how much things had changed between them, she stopped next to the curb and stared at the house, knowing she couldn't undo the damage, and surprised by how badly she wanted to.

His wasn't the shabbiest house in the neighborhood, but from the appearance of the painted wood siding, she guessed it was only a step up from a mobile home. The yard was more dirt than grass, though what little grass she could see was well trimmed and deep green. A lone tree stretched tall enough that its protective branches touched the tiles on the roof. The crumbling driveway was empty, and in the carport, peeking over the clutter, were the handlebars of the sleek black motorcycle she'd seen James drive to school.

They sat silently, Emma waiting for him to get out, and James not acting like he was going to do it anytime soon. Finally, she couldn't take it anymore. "Guess I'll see you tomorrow."

"Can I ask you something?"

"Depends." She stared at her thumbs.

"Will you look at me first?"

"No."

He sighed and reached out a hand, but let it drop onto his knee without touching her. "Why do people keep warning me to stay away from you? They say you're dangerous. Call you an ice queen. But I can't see it. You've never been anything but nice to me. Makes me wonder what you did that caused them to say those things."

Her defensive wall shot up, her heart hammering with hurt while anger smoldered in her chest. It always came back to prom night. "Nothing. *I* didn't do anything."

He shook his head against her angry glare and squeezed the strap of his backpack until his hand curled into a fist. "There has to be something. People don't say things like that without a reason."

The plastic film she'd wrapped around that part of her life started to split, and a torrent of emotions rushed through. However much she liked James, she wouldn't unwrap her pain, her humiliation. Not now, after all her efforts to store it away and focus on the present. Her voice cracked when she said, "Apparently, you know all about it, so why even bother asking? Has it even occurred to you that it's none of your business? Or theirs. And maybe, just maybe, I don't like talking about the past."

"I want you to tell me they're wrong. They're lying. That you didn't do whatever they think you did."

More memories. More ache. The slit ripped further. "What if it's true? Whatever they told you and probably a whole lot more."

"No one has told me anything. I just want to know what you did."

"Nothing." She turned her head to hide her inner turmoil. "I told you the first time we met. *I* warned you. I'm like poison to your reputation. It's your own fault you didn't listen."

He didn't respond—probably didn't know how. Eventually, James opened the door. "Thanks for the ride."

"Sure." As soon as he stepped back, Emma put the car in gear and drove off, wiping away a few hot tears. Regret formed a tight knot in her stomach, but she'd deal with it. She was getting good at dealing with regret. The tires squealed as she turned the corner out of James's neighborhood and away from his friendship.

Once again, Emma knew better than to look back.

Eight

October 29th
261 days to departure

EMMA *PRESSED HARD* on the gas, then hit the brake just as hard as she pulled into the school parking lot. She'd tried not to let it bother her, but for whatever reason, the confrontation with James had fixated in her mind, replaying over and over like a bad movie she couldn't forget no matter how hard she tried. After six nights of very little sleep, Emma was so grumpy she could barely stand herself, let alone anyone else she might encounter. She knew her anger was out of control, but couldn't manage to rein it in.

She refused to allow James to make her second-guess what happened, blame herself for what Tom did to her. Not that she'd been completely innocent. She *had* lied to Tom— though really, there was no other choice—and he'd hurt her for it. He was paying his price—first with six months in the county jail, followed by probation and a protective order—and she continued paying hers.

Still, James had no business asking her to explain. Their relationship might border on friendship, but that was all. She didn't owe him anything—especially not details. It made her feel better to slam her car door, so she stormed into school and threw open her locker, then rocketed it closed again. And because that felt so good, she did it one more time, just because she could.

"You know, beating up school property isn't going to change anything." Heather caught Emma's hand before she could abuse the locker a third time. "But it might get you suspended, if you try hard enough."

Emma scowled at her friend. "So?"

Heather tried to scowl back, but it looked more like a squished-up smile. "So, you've never been the get-suspended type. What's up? Haven't heard from you in days."

"Stupid boys. Stupid prom. Stupid . . ." *Change.* She trailed off, wanting to tell Heather what was happening to her, and knowing she couldn't. Instead, she finished with, "Stupid boys."

"You said that one already." Heather grabbed Emma's sleeve and pulled her into the girls' bathroom. "What's going on?"

Emma shook her head. "You know how the rumors never used to bother me? Well, now they do. I'm bothered. I'm annoyed. I'm flat-out steamed."

Heather raised a speculative eyebrow. "Is this about the guy from the next locker over? James?"

"No. Well, not entirely. I just . . . Why do Tom's cronies have to sabotage everything? I'm not even allowed to have friends."

Looking hurt, Heather stepped back. "If that's true, what am I? Some of us know the truth, Emma. If Hot New Kid has half a brain, he'll figure it out too. And if he doesn't, I don't care how gorgeous he is, he will never be good enough for you. Got it?"

Emma blew out a breath and leaned her forehead on her friend's shoulder. "You're right. I know you're right. But it still makes me angry."

Heather patted Emma's back. "I know. Tell you what. We'll start an angry girls club, and every Tuesday, we'll all stomp around the school, beating up lockers and pushing boys into puddles. Then the principal will suspend us all, and we'll spend the week at the beach eating clams. Sound good?"

Emma nodded against Heather's shoulder. "Yeah, it does. But why Tuesdays?"

"To keep the tradition real. You started on a Tuesday, so it's official."

Emma straightened, grateful for Heather's support.

Heather continued, grinning. "Besides, no one wants to be suspended on a weekend. The sports teams wouldn't have any cheerleaders, and what if there was a dance? Weekdays are much safer. Plus, the beaches are less crowded."

"Good point." Emma allowed herself to smile as they left the bathroom and wound through the crowded halls. Sometimes it just took a good friend to put everything back into perspective. She caught Heather's purse strap before they separated. "What would you think if I decided to start working out with the cheer squad again?"

"I'd say it's about time." Heather's eyes lit up. "No one can top the pyramid the way you did."

Emma shook her head. "I'm not coming back to cheer. I don't want to deal with Tom's friends at the games. But I miss practice. And you girls. Maybe I can help train the new recruits?" She could use a good distraction.

"Be in the locker room at practice time and we'll figure it out. Coach Gina misses you. We all do."

Funny. Until Heather said it, Emma hadn't realized anyone missed her. But now that she thought about it, she realized she missed herself. Maybe it was time to do something about that.

"HEY, JAMES." LAURA—at least, he thought that was her name—leaned against the cafeteria table, her skirt inching up her thigh in what he was sure she considered an invitation. This one fit in the "trouble" category. "Wanna get together after school? I'd love to go for a ride on your bike sometime."

James finished chewing his pizza, using the time to come up with an escape plan, except nothing came to him. "Uh, yeah. That would be good, except my bike is having issues right now. And after school I have . . . basketball conditioning. Maybe some other time?"

"That's what you said last week." She stuck her lip out in an exaggerated pout, and James had to consciously stop himself from rolling his eyes. "I'm starting to worry that you don't like me."

The collar of his crew-neck T-shirt suddenly felt tight. "It's not that, I promise," he said, standing with his tray. Unfortunately, Laura stood too, blocking him from any kind of graceful retreat. Why couldn't he enjoy his senior year in peace? He glanced around the room, desperation mounting. "I'm just super busy this week. And next week. Maybe you should hit me up next month?"

With a totally fake, ridiculously contrived laugh, she walked her fingers up his chest. "One of these days, maybe I'll show up at your house." He took her wrist, letting go when she got the hint and stopped touching him. He was almost prepared to tell her that he just wasn't into girls who wore skirts *that* short, whose favorite perfumes were covered over by the cigarette smoke that always clung to their skin, and who had a reputation for giving it up to anyone who asked. But before he could say the words that would forever stain his player reputation, salvation arrived.

Emma's brother walked in with some kids from his special-needs class. They got in line with everyone else, giggling like kindergarteners. Lyle, sitting at a nearby table, shouted, "Looks like it's happy hour in the cafeteria." Several people laughed.

Needing the escape, and worried that Lyle or someone else would say something really mean, James made a split-second decision. "I have to go," he told Laura. "I'm meeting a friend."

She stood her ground, her eyes narrowing into angry slits. "What friend?"

James nudged Laura aside and caught Keith just as he set his tray at an empty table, looking around as if waiting for someone to sit by him. "Hey, there. Keith, right?"

The boy nodded, his eyes widening with anxiety.

James offered Keith his uneaten cookie. "I'm James. One of Emma's friends." Maybe he didn't quite qualify as a friend, but Keith didn't need to know that. The boy was old enough to make his own friends.

"Hi, James," Keith said, biting into the cookie.

"Mind if I sit here?"

"Guess." Keith nodded, allowing James a breath of relief. "Why?"

James nodded at the table he'd left, where Laura glared at them, eyebrows raised. "See that girl over there? She likes me, but I don't like her, and she won't leave me alone. I sort of told her I had plans to sit with another friend, because I don't want to hurt her feelings. Can I eat here with you?" *Please, please, please.*

"You want to eat with me? You want to be my friend?"

James patted Keith on the shoulder as they were joined by two other kids from Keith's class. "If that's okay. That is, if you don't mind having a loser like me join all you cool kids."

Keith snickered. "Sure, I guess."

They chatted for several minutes, during which James discovered that Keith had a serious crush on one of his teachers. "Aren't you the little Romeo," James said, eyebrows raised. "You know she's off limits, right?"

"Emma says Mrs. Long is too old for me, but I still like her." Keith folded his arms on the table and buried his face in them. "She's just so pretty."

James could relate. "Some prizes are meant to stay out of our reach," he murmured, thinking of Emma. The conversation continued, moving on to beautiful movie stars, and James found himself so entertained by Keith and his friends, he spent the rest of his lunch hour visiting with them long after he'd finished his pizza. The next time he looked up, Laura was gone. "Keith, I think you've officially earned your wingman status."

"Wings? I get wings?" Keith asked.

"No, you're a wingman. That means you help me out when I need to escape from girls."

Keith grinned around a mouthful of chips. "I like being your wingman."

James stood, patting his new friend on the back and taking his tray for him. "I like having you for a wingman. Let's do it again next week, yeah? Maybe Thursday?"

"Sure." Keith's eyes lit up, and James swore the whole cafeteria got brighter.

"Okay," James said. And strangely, he looked forward to it.

THE MUSIC SWELLED, and pride sparkled in Emma's eyes as the girls struck their ending pose on cue and with aplomb. Their performance had been far from perfect, but since Emma had started working with them, the freshman girls had improved dramatically enough that she believed they could do well in a competition. Especially if Coach Gina allowed

Emma to continue to choreograph the moves. "Great job, girls," she told them. "Let's end on a high note and call it a day."

Whooping with jubilation, the girls gathered their belongings off the grass and started for the locker room. Emma jogged to catch up with Heather, who was already on her way to her car.

"How'd it go?" Heather asked, slowing her pace through the lot. "They pick up on that last bit okay?"

Emma nodded, turning away from her own car and toward Heather's. "I'm so proud of them. They've worked hard to come this far."

Heather grinned. "They aren't the only ones." She waved off Emma's questioning glance. "Where's Keith tonight?"

"That kid Jonathan's house." Her senses heightened at the thought of Keith's friend. "Spends a lot of time over there these days. They seem to be hitting it off well."

"Does it worry you?"

"A little," she admitted. "But he seems like a nice kid, and I have no reason not to trust him." Except the devious vibe she'd caught the day she met him.

Heather tossed her bag in the back, then leaned against the closed door. "I'm glad your trust issues don't extend to Keith's friends. Now we just need to get you to the point where you'll talk to some guys *our* age."

"I tried that already. I'm done." Scowling, Emma flicked a glance toward the other side of the lot where James usually parked his sometimes-running motorcycle. Other than that brief hour in biology during which they only spoke when necessary, most days Emma managed to avoid James. Somehow, in silent mutual consent, they'd worked out a locker schedule that kept them from having to face each other. Days had passed with no communication between them, and then weeks. Every so often, she saw someone walking home from school and slowed down, but it was never James. Probably best that way.

"I heard he's seeing Elana Jay on the swim team," Heather murmured. "You should move on."

"From what?" Emma tore her eyes from the bike. "There wasn't even a relationship to end. Besides, rumor has it he's also seeing a soccer player named Windy. I have no desire to be part of a harem."

"I'm glad for that." Heather's answering giggle lightened the tension. "But give the guy a break. You know how the rumor mill works."

Emma nodded. She did know. All too well, unfortunately. And that was exactly the problem. Luckily, James Phelps and his love life were none of her business. She didn't care if the rumors were true or not. She was over it either way.

Seeming to sense that Emma had been pushed to the limit on the subject of boys, Heather asked, "Are your parents still planning that trip to Greece?"

"Yes. My dad is dying to do some research, and he's determined to go this year. They leave mid-February."

Heather grinned. "Pa-artay!"

Emma shook her head. "Um, no. No parties for me, thanks. But I am looking forward to the quiet."

"My mom wanted me to make sure you know you can

call her if you need anything. In fact, if your parents are working late again, why don't you come over for dinner tonight?" Heather opened the driver's side door and climbed in. "I think we're having meatloaf."

"Wish I could," Emma said, her mind scrambling for an excuse she hadn't used yet. "But I have to study for a test."

Heather's forehead crinkled with suspicion. "You said that yesterday."

"It's math, and I suck at math." As much as Emma ached to tell someone about the changes she was experiencing, she couldn't bring herself to share the problem with her friend. And every four or five days, she begrudgingly took a solo trip to the beach, hoping Merrick wouldn't be waiting to swim with her.

Sometimes she got lucky. She hoped tonight would be one of those times.

"You sure you don't want me to help?" Heather tossed her keys in the air, catching them in her palm over and over again. "Seems like you spend a lot of time studying lately, and not enough time playing."

"Just trying to graduate," Emma hedged, feeling that familiar tightness in her chest.

"Please tell me you're not planning to study the entire time your parents are in Greece," Heather said. "Then I'll really worry about you."

"No need to worry," Emma said, hugging her friend. "But don't expect a party, either. Keith would totally rat me out."

"At which point, grades would be the least of your problems," Heather agreed.

An engine revved, and Emma whipped her head around, strangely disappointed when it wasn't James on his sexy motorcycle.

"Speaking of grades, I should get going," she murmured.

They said their good-byes, and Emma jogged to her car, wishing more than ever that she could tell Heather everything.

She was certain that by the time she was done swimming, her last conversation with James would slip farther into the back of her mind until she no longer caught herself watching for him in the halls or parking lot or on the street. At some point, she'd stop worrying about what he'd heard and what he thought.

Unfortunately, whenever she saw a motorcycle zipping around town, she couldn't resist craning her neck and squinting. It was a habit she feared she might never break.

ONE DREARY AFTERNOON in late November, Emma left class to retrieve an assignment she'd left in her car. Distracted and in a hurry, she rounded the corner and ran headlong into James's back as he was making out with his latest flame. "Sorry," she muttered, averting her eyes.

"It's fine." Drawing in a breath, he unwrapped himself from the tall blonde whose hands and arms seemed to be everywhere, and faced Emma. "Are you okay?"

Eyes round and startled, Emma nodded, unable to find her voice, confused about why seeing him like this made her chest burn. She turned around and picked up her pace, needing to get far, far away.

"Hey," James said. "Wait. Where are you going?"

Emma walked faster and faster until walking became running and she'd made it to her car. She wasn't jealous. Not of James or the blonde. But she was envious because she knew she would never again be half of a couple, one of two people who were so in to each other that they would risk sneaking away during class to make out in the hall.

Her breath hitched, and she took a moment to sit and compose herself, then returned to class via the long way, hoping to avoid a repeat performance between James and his latest of many girlfriends.

Nine

December 14th
215 days to departure

EMMA CLOSED HER LAPTOP and moved aside her textbooks and papers as the doorbell chimed for the third time. "I'm coming!" By the time she got down the stairs, she'd worked up a speech on doorbell etiquette for whoever was on the other side. The entire lecture fled her mind when she answered for the uniformed police officer who'd brought her brother home—in handcuffs.

"What's going on?"

"Are your parents home?" the officer asked.

"They're at work. But I can call them." Though her hands shook with worry, she put on her most grown-up face and ushered the police officer and her brother into the living room.

"That would be a good idea," the officer said, reaching

behind Keith to remove the cuffs. "It's important that I talk to them."

As the door closed, Keith broke into sobs. Through his distress, the only words she could understand were, "I'm sorry, Emma," over and over again. Heartsick, she wrapped her arms around him, soothing as best she could, trying to convince him everything would be okay—even though she had no idea whether or not her words were a lie.

Officer Patterson—according to his name badge—stood back, letting Emma take care of her brother until he'd calmed, a fact for which she was grateful.

Not wanting to upset Keith again, she stepped into the kitchen to call her mother. When Emma returned to the living room, she brought three bottles of water and offered one each to Keith and Officer Patterson.

After she assured Keith that their mother was on the way, she asked, "What happened?"

"It's because Jonathan wanted to play the shopping game. I don't like the shopping game because it makes people mad sometimes, but it's Jonathan's favorite so I said I would play and then Jonathan ran away and I got in trouble."

Perplexed, Emma wrapped her hand around one of Keith's. "What's the shopping game?"

Blowing out a breath that pretty much meant, "Duh," he said, "It's when one friend decides a special thing we have to shop for, then the other one has to find it and put it in his pocket, then run away as fast as he can before the other friend can catch him."

Emma's stomach plummeted to her toes. "When you play the shopping game, do you run out of the store?"

Again, the breath, accompanied by rolling eyes and hand gestures. "Of course we do. That's the only way we can touch home base and win the game."

"Where's home base?"

"Jonathan's car. It has to be the car so we never forget where to run."

Quivering with anger, Emma turned her eyes to Officer Patterson. "Shoplifting?"

The man nodded, frowning. "I suspected someone else had put him up to it, but your brother wouldn't talk. At all. He seemed paralyzed by fear, so I brought him here rather than having your parents meet me at the mall. I'd hoped he'd be comfortable enough to give a statement."

Her sharp intake of breath was involuntary. Though he seemed kind-hearted, Officer Patterson's words worried Emma. "My mother won't want him to make a statement without her present—she's an attorney."

Patterson's sympathetic smile took the edge off her discomfort. "That's perfectly fine. I wouldn't want it any other way—especially since your brother is a minor."

Keith sniffled. "Am I going to jail?"

Patterson was spared having to answer by the sound of the garage door opening, followed by heels click-clacking across the kitchen tile. "Mommy, hurry," Keith yelled. "I'm arrested and maybe I have to go to jail."

Cindy Harris strode into the room, bringing with her a draft of cool winter air scented with oranges and powdery-soft perfume. She bypassed Keith and faced off with Officer Patterson. "Sir, would you please explain why you've brought my disabled son home in handcuffs?"

The officer stood, clearly used to livid-mother confrontations. "Yes, ma'am. I'm happy to tell you what was caught on the security cameras at Macy's. But you might prefer to hear his version, since your daughter managed to get him talking better than I could. In fact, I'd love to hear more myself, if you don't mind."

Cindy scowled at Emma. "You know better than to give a statement without me."

Emma squeezed Keith's hand. "We didn't. We were just talking, and he told me what happened. It's not his fault, Mom—it's that boy Jonathan."

Cindy shot the officer a look, and he gave her an encouraging nod.

By the time their father, Russ, came in, Keith had given details, not only about that day's adventure, but others.

Mortified, Cindy and Russ assured Officer Patterson this would not happen again and that Keith would receive just punishment—meaning, among other things, no more Jonathan. They were all happy to discover that Keith would not be spending the night in jail, though he would have to pay a fine.

At the end of the night, Emma returned to her room, infuriated about how easily her brother had been used, and sick with worry about what would happen when she was no longer around to look out for him. The day's events culminated in a ball of stress that left her struggling to breathe, even though it had only been two days since her last swim.

Since she usually swam after school while her parents

were working, Emma hadn't needed to sneak out since the night Tom caught her. Now, because of the using, abusing, sick-joke-of-a-human Jonathan, she had no choice. She sent a text to Gran and gathered her things. As she unlatched the window and climbed out, she vowed to pay closer attention to Keith's friends from now on.

Ten

January 27th
171 days to departure

JAMES *DIDN'T GET WHAT* the big deal was. They were locked down, trapped in biology—his least favorite class, and by far the looniest teacher in the whole school—just because some idiot-crazy-moron shot someone blocks away. It wasn't like the suspect was going to hide inside the school or anything. But James hoped the cops would find the guy fast so they could all go home.

He seriously wished Emma was in class today. They hadn't interacted much since their last confrontation, but the whole thing still bothered him. He'd been unnecessarily harsh, he knew. But so had she. They hadn't even gone on a real date, but he'd liked her more than seemed wise, and it scared him. Felt like he'd needed an excuse to stay away, so she gave him one and he took it. But whenever he saw her, that familiar pull dragged him under all over again, leaving his stomach tied into billions of tiny knots only Emma could untie.

She was different from other girls. More fragile. More frightening. More everything. And he still needed to find out if that mark on her shoulder was a tattoo. Not knowing might make him crazy.

Ironically, though Emma wasn't in class when the school went into lockdown, her brother was. He'd come in on an assignment from his teacher and ended up stuck there, without his sister to help keep him calm. So James had taken the job upon himself—though he really had no clue how Emma would handle the situation. Fortunately, Keith was unpredictably composed. And as James had already discovered, the kid was entertaining as hell.

"How long do you think we'll be stuck here?" Keith asked.

"I don't know." James stared at the covered window, wishing he could see the storm rolling in from the west. "Probably till they catch the guy or get sick of keeping us here."

"Do you think they'll at least let us eat lunch?"

"Doubt it." James dug in his pocket for a pack of gum and offered Keith a piece. "Probably won't even let us to go to the bathroom for a while."

Keith folded his gum wrapper into a tiny square. "What happens if I need to go? Really, really go?"

"Guess you'll be forced to hold it." James leaned back in his chair, pointing the toe of his shoe at a row of glass beakers. "Unless you were hoping to borrow one of those."

"Yuck. I don't think that's allowed. The police might arrest me again." Keith whacked James's foot so his chair clattered back on all four legs. "Besides, peeing in a bottle— that's disgusting."

"Just an idea." Surprised by the talk of criminal activity, James asked, "When were you arrested?"

Keith turned his head, deliberately ignoring the question, and stared at the window. The whirling blades of a helicopter cast moving shadows of ghostly images around the edges of the blinds and rattled the windows with the force of manmade wind. James shook his head in annoyance, vowing then and there that if he were ever going to commit a crime, he'd at least have the courtesy to do it early in the morning so all the school kids would be locked down at home.

Keith leaned his elbows on the table, dropping his head in his hands. "I want to go home. I need my sister and my mom and dad. What if the bad guy comes here?"

James put a comforting hand on the younger boy's back, feeling protective. "He won't. Not unless he's dead-ass stupid. If he's got any brains at all, he's on his way to Mexico by now. If it were me, I'd rent a cheap little boat and float my way to freedom before the cops even knew I'd done anything wrong."

Keith looked up, a hint of concern in his eyes. "But you're not a bad-guy-murderer. Are you?"

"Hell no." James ruffled Keith's hair. "I'm just saying that's what I would do if I were the brain wizard who started this mess. 'Course, shooting a person in broad daylight and in front of witnesses—not exactly a brilliant thing to do. Smart is definitely not his strength." Keith's face paled, so James patted his shoulder, mentally kicking himself for telling Keith details the students probably weren't supposed to know—but which were posted all over social networking sites, and kept his smartphone chiming with nonstop notifications. "But even someone that stupid has a basic gut instinct to run. He's long gone by now. This whole lockdown business is just a precaution. It's built into the district rules, that's all."

Keith sighed in relief. James glanced at the window again, mesmerized by the shadows and the occasional flash of red and blue that told him the police were parked out there. He wondered what Emma was doing—where she'd gone. He wished he'd known she was going to skip class. Today would have been a perfect day to follow her example.

AFTER A BRIEF CONVERSATION with one of the officers, Emma turned around and headed home, no longer worried about making it back to school in time for the biology quiz. The classes were in lockdown; there would be no tests of any kind today. She glanced in the rearview mirror, hoping Keith was all right, and wondering how she'd know when to pick him up. He was probably freaking out about now.

She parked in the garage and flipped open her cell phone as she walked in through the kitchen, stopping to grab a mango from the fridge.

"Hi, Gran. I need you to excuse me from school."

"Why?" Gran's voice sounded raspy. Maybe she'd been sleeping?

Sighing, Emma cradled the phone between her shoulder and ear and searched for a paring knife. "I couldn't breathe this morning. It's only been three days, and I felt like I was suffocating. So I dropped Keith off at school and went to swim."

"Are you planning to go to any classes today? I don't like you skipping the entire day just for an hour swim."

Emma dug around in a drawer and barely avoided slicing her finger on a butcher knife. "I tried, but the school's locked down. Cops won't let anyone in or out. Nothing too serious, just a precaution to protect us from some lunatic in the area."

"What about your brother?"

Having found the knife she wanted, Emma paused, staring at the sharp blade. "He's there, but I can't get him. I mean, I *will* get him, but I can't until they unblock the roads and stuff."

A muffled sound on the other end made Emma wonder if Gran had dropped the phone until she said, "I hope those teachers are well trained. Can't even imagine how he's reacting to the situation."

"Me either," Emma murmured.

"Tell you what," Gran conceded. "I'll excuse you, but I expect to see you on Saturday. We have some things to discuss, you and me. If it's only been three days, your change is progressing faster than we thought. No more putting off writing those letters. Also, as soon as you have Keith in your car and safe, I want to know."

Emma set her mango on the cutting board, then the knife, before she could follow the impulse to stab the blade into the wood. "Fine. And I'll be there Saturday. But then you're going to tell my parents that you lied to them and their daughter isn't actually human. Tell them I'm going to disappear soon. No more putting that off, either. I can't keep lying to them. It's not fair. They deserve to know what's going on."

"Baby doll, you just need to let me handle this situation my way." The pitch of Gran's voice rose, giving way to apparent nerves. "I raised your mother. I know she won't react well to this. Neither, I suspect, will your father."

"I know, Gran, but it's time. Way past time. I only have six months left."

Gran's mumbled response was inaudible to Emma, but rather than continuing to argue, Emma let it go. "I'm going to take a nap," she said. "We can talk about this on Saturday. Love you, Gran."

"I love you too, honey." More mumbling as the line went dead.

Emma slid the phone across the counter and turned back to the cutting board, going to work on the mango. She managed to peel off the skin and cut more than half the fruit before slicing her finger. Swearing, she dropped the knife and ran her hand under the faucet, gritting her teeth as she watched the bluish-purple blood wash down the drain. The cut wasn't deep—nothing some antibiotic cream and a Band-Aid couldn't handle—but the color alarmed Emma all the same.

Dumping the mango in the trash, uneaten, Emma bandaged the cut and went to her room to lie down. Some days, even sleep couldn't help her forget. But now seemed like a good time to try.

"*THIS SUCKS.*" *JAMES STORMED* to his locker, leaving Keith to scramble behind him.

"At least we don't have homework." Keith caught up and leaned against the metal doors. "I like no homework days."

"Yeah, me too." James left the books in his locker and grabbed his leather jacket, instinctively reaching for his motorcycle keys before he remembered his bike still wasn't running. He sighed. For the past few months, all his free time had been spent working his tail off for his uncle's company. There were girls in his life—lots of them—but none who mattered enough for him to cut back his schedule. None on which he cared to waste precious time or money. None he kept around for more than a few weeks before dumping them. He'd paid his team fees, and would soon have enough to fix the bike. He hoped. That was what mattered most in his world. "I should've been to basketball practice at two forty-five."

Keith followed him outside. "The gym was locked down too, remember? Didn't they cancel practice?"

James flipped his dark hair out of his eyes and forced his frown to level. "You're missing the point. We've got an important game next week, and the team has to be ready. *I* have to be ready. A basketball scholarship might be my only chance for college."

"Oh. I want to go to college too, someday." Keith hugged his stack of textbooks to his chest as James slid down the stair rail and started along the sidewalk. "I'll practice with you. So you can be ready. No homework today. Got some free time now. I'll practice with you today."

A trickle of guilt had James jogging back. With Emma gone, he wondered how Keith was getting home. He wasn't sure if being alone was something Keith could handle. "Hey, I wonder where your sister is."

Keith's eyes grew wide with distress as he looked around. "I don't know. Her car's gone."

"Wherever she is, I bet she's worried about you." Leaning against the stair rail, James wished for the five-hundred-and-sixty-seventh time that he could afford to hire a mechanic to fix his bike instead of trying to figure it out himself. "How will you get home?"

Keith shrugged. "I sometimes walk home when Emma is sick or when she has to do cheerleader things." He stared at the ground, distress evident in his posture. "I hope they put that bad guy in jail."

Grudgingly, James climbed the concrete stairs to where Keith stood at the top. "Why don't we walk together?" It was about a mile out of his way, but the exercise would do him good—especially if a conversation with Emma was the final payoff. He figured it was about time they cleared things up. "I'd offer you a ride, but . . ." James cleared his throat.

"Your motorcycle's broken. I know. I see you walk a lot."

"Mm-hm." James flipped his hair again, narrowing his eyes. "What else do you see?"

"You look at my sister sometimes. I think you like her."

This kid was more than smart—he was observant. "Nothing gets by you, does it?"

"Emma says I'm a genius." Keith hooked a thumb in his pocket, looking smug.

James sent him a warning glance. "Well, Mr. Genius, you just keep your mouth shut about the me-staring-at-your-sister-thing, and I may let you live. Let's call it our little secret, okay?" They cut across the black top and headed east up the hill.

"You'll let me live anyway. You're too nice to hurt me."

Something about the trust in Keith's voice bothered James. "How do you know? I mean, I *wouldn't* hurt you, but you should be careful who you trust. Some people will try to take advantage of you if you're not careful."

Keith stared at the ground. "Okay."

James paused, worried he'd offended the kid. In a gentle voice, he murmured, "Is that why you got arrested? Did someone trick you?"

Keith shook his head, pressing his lips together.

"You can tell me if you want. I won't be mad or judge you or anything. But I would like to have a chat with whoever it was." When Keith's eyes filled, James decided it was time to change the subject. He started walking again, urging Keith to do the same. "So tell me more about Emma. I haven't talked to her in a while."

Eleven

JAMES STOOD BEHIND KEITH on the stoop, eyeing the door and trying not to be nervous. *What am I doing here? She hates me.*

Keith tried the knob, but found it locked, so he rang the bell. James shuffled his feet. *What's taking so long?* After what seemed like forever, footsteps pounded down the stairs on the other side of the door. "Guess she's here."

Keith slid one arm out of his backpack strap. "Only one other place she would go."

James's hope plummeted. Of course. Her boyfriend's house. Girls who looked like her never stayed single for long. The door opened before Keith could answer, and James's pulse skipped. He'd never seen her flaunt her beauty, which made her way more attractive to him than flamboyant girls—

like Nettie, his current flame—who wore their skirts too short and their tops too low. Emma rarely wore much makeup, and other than an occasional clip, didn't appear to go to extreme efforts in the hair department either—not that she needed to. The wavy red curtain flowed down her back however it fell, accentuating her smooth, fair skin and complimenting her unusual pearl-and-shell necklace. A light sprinkle of freckles dotted her nose and cheeks, a result of time spent riding around with her convertible top down. She stared at him with luminous green eyes, and though she appeared sleepily confused, her lips curved into a polite smile.

While James searched for his voice, Keith said, "Me and James got stuck in your biology class for hours and hours. They locked us in the school and you weren't there and I thought maybe the bad guy got you and then James brought me home. Where were you, Emma?"

Emma squeezed Keith's shoulders. "I had to come home for something, and then the police wouldn't let me back in. I've been worried about you." She eyed him up and down. "Looks like you survived."

"Yeah. Did you go to the beach?"

The beach? That thought hadn't even occurred to James.

"Uh . . ." She twisted a lock of her hair. "For a little bit." She backed away from the door, gesturing for them to follow her down the hall and into the bright kitchen, where she flipped on a small, flat-screen TV. It was tuned to the evening news. James followed Keith, taking in everything he could about Emma's home. Earthy browns, reds, and greens, cushy leather, multi-stained hardwoods, natural travertine. Family pictures adorned the walls next to tasteful art he was pretty sure were original paintings—or really expensive replicas—and on the table, fresh flowers. Keith dropped his backpack on the floor and perched on a high-backed leather barstool pushed against a long granite counter.

Emma uncovered a plate of cookies and set it in front of them, then pulled a pitcher of juice out of the refrigerator and poured burgundy liquid into three glasses. "So . . . you guys. Been hanging out a lot lately?"

James tapped Keith's shoulder with the side of his fist. "Well, you know, your brother is a pretty cool guy."

She frowned, seeming irritated by his answer.

Keith accepted a glass from Emma and snatched a cookie. "We're going to play basketball together sometime, huh, James?"

Emma handed James a glass, eyes narrowed.

"Thanks." James held up his glass, studying the contents. "What is it?"

"Pomegranate-grape juice. Try it. It's good."

James gulped, barely tasting the tart mixture as he met Emma's eyes over the rim of his glass. "Something wrong?"

She looked away. "What are you doing here?"

He'd known the question was coming, had even formulated an answer along the way. Unfortunately, that answer—along with every other rational thought—disappeared the minute she'd opened the door. "I . . . uh . . ."

"He brought me home, Emma," Keith interjected. "Because we're friends, like I used to be friends with Jonathan, but now I'm friends with James. Only he's nicer."

She set her glass on the counter so hard, James wondered if it cracked. "Like Jonathan? And do you and James play games like the ones you played with Jonathan?"

Keith grinned. "We're going to play basketball because James is practically a pro. And maybe he'll teach me how to drive a motorcycle when he gets his fixed. But first he has to get money."

James cringed at the offhanded remark. Yeah, they'd talked about his bike, but he had no intention of letting anyone other than himself drive it. And the money thing—he hadn't meant to tell the kid that. It just slipped out.

The look Emma shot him mirrored sheer and utter hatred, something James couldn't even comprehend coming from her. "What?" he asked.

"Thanks for bringing my brother home, but I think it's time for you to go."

Bewildered, he didn't move. "What? Why?"

Emma's hands curled into fists. "I'm not very tolerant of people who use my brother just because he doesn't understand. Also, my mother's an attorney who has no problem sending high-school-age boys to prison. Our parents aren't very tolerant either."

His eyebrows pulled together while he attempted to make sense of anything she'd just said.

"No!" Keith yelled. "Mom won't send James to prison. He isn't the bad guy—the other guy is the bad guy and James is my friend. He sometimes eats lunch with me and I like him and I won't let you send him away." He jumped off his chair and seized the front of Emma's silk blouse. The action nudged

James out of his shocked stupor. He took hold of Keith's hands and pried them away before he could actually hurt Emma. "Come on, man. You don't grab girls like that. It's not cool."

"You can't send my friend to jail, Emma. I promise I'll be good and never get arrested again." Keith's voice shook, his eyes wide and worried as he clutched her wrists and held on.

"Okay." She managed to keep her voice calm, soothing. "We won't send James to jail. But it *is* time for him to go home. Say good-bye." Emma pulled Keith's fingers off her and led him to the stairs. "Why don't you go to your room and read for a while?"

Keith's eyes glazed over, but he nodded and stomped up, turning at the top of the landing. "Good-bye, James."

Not understanding what had just happened, James said, "Bye, Keith. See you soon."

Emma sighed, bending over to pick up the backpack. "Sorry. I'm not usually so rude to our guests. I guess I'm overprotective lately."

"What was that all about?"

"Jonathan." Emma smiled ruefully. "Taught my brother how to shoplift for him—pretended it was a game—then ran away when the cops busted them. Left Keith alone to take the fall."

"Right." James didn't know what to do with his hands, so he picked up their glasses and walked over to put them in the sink. "And you think I'm using him too? That's . . . well . . . great. I'm flattered you think so highly of me."

Her eyes flashed. "What else am I supposed to think? You haven't said a word to me in months, and out of the blue, you show up on my doorstep with my little brother. *That's* not suspicious or anything."

James leaned against the counter, not sure where else to go, since every available exit was on the other side of Emma. "Excuse me? Okay, Miss High and Mighty. Let's talk about who hasn't said a word to whom. *You* haven't given *me* the time of day in months. In fact, you even refused to acknowledge my presence when you plowed me over in the hall that time."

She took a step toward him. "Me? You're the one who heard a stupid, screwed-up rumor—which, by the way, is absolutely untrue—and ran away like your shoes were on fire."

James narrowed his eyes against the venom in hers. The setting sun glowed in the window behind her, turning her hair to flames. He'd never been more attracted to a girl than he was to Emma in that moment. "That is *so* not what happened. The minute you found out I'd been talking to some of my teammates, you shut down like you were disgusted. Wouldn't even look at me. You kicked me out of your car like you wished you'd never met me."

"I did not kick you out of my car!" Her voice rose with fury. She stepped closer, arms tensed and hands folded into fists. "You wanted me to explain things that are none of your business rather than taking the time to get to know me and find out the truth for yourself. The minute I didn't give you what you wanted, you bailed."

She was within arm's length now, and it took every ounce

of restraint James possessed to avoid reaching out and pulling her to him. He wondered if she'd taste as hot as she looked right now. But this was not the time, not with her. He had to work hard to keep his voice steady. "You may not have said the words 'Get out,'" but the implication was clear as a neon sign. What did you want me to do, physically grab you and force you to help me sort out the confusion in my head? I'm not that guy, Emma. When a girl needs me to leave, I leave, whether she asks out loud or not."

She sighed like a balloon that had been poked with a pin, long and slow. "That moment is now. You should go. Between bringing Keith home and having a mercy conversation with me, you've officially fulfilled your charity quota for the day."

"My charity quota?" James moved to step around her, pausing when his chest grazed her shoulder and he felt a tremor ripple up her arm. "Why do you hate me, exactly?" he murmured. "Just so I'm clear."

Emma swallowed, inching away. "Look. I know what you're about. Big, tough, motorcycle loner latching onto a disabled kid, hoping you can trick him into doing things for you—possibly illegal things. While you're at it, maybe you'll get me on the back of your bike—as soon as you dump your current flavor of the month." She gulped in a breath. "I'm telling you now. Don't waste your time."

James stared, speechless for the second time since she'd opened the door. Where had all that come from? Apparently, when she said she'd been burned to ashes, she wasn't joking.

She stepped away from him, her eyes bright and hot, and

instinctively, James followed. "What the hell are you even talking about? I know we haven't seen a lot of each other, but I hoped you knew me better than those bullshit accusations."

"I'm talking about Keith—and your agenda."

Temper, hot and ripe, boiled up in James. How could she think him capable of such awful things? Shoving his fisted hands in his jacket pockets, he stomped out of the kitchen, Emma not far behind. "You don't know anything about me, least of all my so-called-agenda. I happen to genuinely like Keith. And I didn't want him walking home alone."

He wrenched the door open. "All this time, I've thought you were different from the shallow snobberazzi. Thanks for proving me wrong before I really started to like you." As he pulled the door closed behind him, he shot one last look over his shoulder and caught Emma's expression of shock.

He would never, in his whole life, understand women.

EMMA SLAMMED HER BEDROOM DOOR and flopped on the bed, unable to decide who she was more angry at—herself or James.

Who did he think he was? And why did it seem like every time she turned around, James Phelps was there, staring at her with those mysterious eyes? If he wasn't the epitome of every badboy she'd ever gotten mixed up with—and then some—she'd be intrigued, maybe even interested. But guys like him were tough to figure out, and Emma preferred to have everything figured out.

Begrudgingly, she thought back to the day they'd had lunch in the deli down the street. He'd been sweet and accommodating, so concerned about the insane panic attack she'd suffered in the driveway of her house. But he'd never asked why, or what was going on, or nosed into business that wasn't his. It was like he knew exactly where her personal boundaries were, and how to put her at ease.

Most likely, he'd been that way with Keith this afternoon too.

She'd always been defensive of her brother, but after Jonathan, well, maybe she was more on edge, more defensive than usual. Maybe she'd taken things a tad too far.

Her phone chimed with a text from Heather and she stared at it, knowing she had the number to call and apologize to James, but dreading the conversation. He probably wouldn't answer anyway. When he left, he'd been pretty steamed.

Steamed was the one emotion Emma couldn't—wouldn't—deal with from a boy. The conversation would go better if she let it rest for a day or two, gave them both a chance to cool off.

Keith knocked on her door, then let himself in. "Hey."

She sat up and patted the spot next to her. "Hey. Sorry I wasn't there to pick you up. I fell asleep. I thought someone would call me. Were you scared?"

Fiddling with a string on one of his long sleeves, he shrugged. "Kind of." He sat next to her and leaned his head on her shoulder, and she draped her arm around him.

"Sounds like you did okay, though."

"James took care of me. He even walked with me all the way from school. If his motorcycle was fixed, he said I could ride on the back."

She didn't know why she would be surprised about

James's protective side, but she was. "He walked you here? How's he getting home?"

"Walking. Because of his motorcycle being broken."

But he lives at least a mile in the opposite direction. "Why would he go so far out of his way?"

"Because what if the bad guy came after me? What if he followed me home and killed me before he ran away to Mexico? James didn't want me to get killed, so he walked me home to be safe."

"I'm glad James protected you, but I don't want you to think something like that would ever happen."

Keith twisted the string around and around his finger, his voice trembling. "You weren't there. They had police cars and helicopters and we couldn't even go to the bathroom. They didn't let us eat lunch, and I was starving, so James gave me gum. We were worried about you, too. Because you were supposed to be there."

I should have been there. "Well, I'm fine, and you're fine, and James is fine too. So the day turned out okay, right?"

"Except I'm starving." Keith stood. "I'm going to get a snack to make my tummy stop growling."

"Good plan." Before he could close the door behind him, Emma said, "Keith, I know James is your friend. He's my friend too. But you should always be extra careful about what you do for people. You never know who is going to turn out to be like Jonathan. Don't ever let James—or anyone else—trick you into doing something bad again. You tell him no, okay?"

"Why would he want me to do bad things? James is a nice person. He even wants to go to college so he can learn how to fix machines and play basketball for a scholarship."

College? Scholarship? "Wow. Good for him. I hope he gets it." She opened her laptop and scrolled through the documents to find her partially completed English paper.

Keith stood in her open doorway. "Emma?"

She looked up. "Yeah?"

"I don't want to stay at Mrs. Hall's house when Mom and Dad go to Europe. She's mean and her food doesn't taste good. Can I stay here with you? When you're not home, I'll go to Mrs. Hall's house like I usually do, but when you're here, I want to be here too. I promise I won't cause trouble."

Closing her computer again, Emma stood and met her brother's eyes. "You never cause trouble. I thought you *wanted* to stay with Mrs. Hall. You always have fun over there."

Staring at the ground, Keith shook his head. "I do, sometimes. But ten days is a really long time, and I want to stay home with you and with all my stuff. In my own house."

"Okay." She squeezed her brother's hands. "I'll talk to Mom and Dad, tell them I need you here. That I don't want to be alone. I didn't realize you'd been thinking this way or I would have brought it up weeks ago."

"So I don't have to go?"

She shook her head. "Nope. We'll have to work together, take care of each other. We have to become a team, okay?"

He nodded, eager. "I'm always on your team."

Emma smiled, her heart swelling with love. "I know you are, buddy. We make a great one."

Now happy, Keith bounced down the stairs. Emma closed the door with a soft click and dove onto her bed, burying her head in a mountain of pillows, and ignoring the chime of a second text.

There were so many good things about her life on land. How could she ever let them go and say good-bye? She needed to talk to someone. Someone who was allowed to know the whole truth. This was not something she could tell Heather. For all that she loved her best friend, Emma knew exactly how far their friendship would stretch, and it was not into supernatural territory. Gran knew, and she was great for venting, but not so much a problem solver when it came to Emma's plight. Yes, Gran stood to lose a granddaughter, but the rest of her life would go on as normal once Emma was tied to Atlantis. On the other hand, Emma stood to lose everything she'd ever loved. The only way for her to keep it was to reverse the process of her change.

And much as it pained her, Emma knew all too well that DNA isn't something that can be changed. There was no reverse button to auto-fix her life.

Thirteen

JAMES THREW HIS JACKET down on the counter and stuck his face under the faucet for a long drink of water. What just happened? He'd walked two miles out of his way to make sure Keith got home safely, and now Emma thought he was using her brother for . . . well, who knew what.

That she'd turned out to be just like the rest of them made the back of his throat burn with anger. How could he have been so wrong? Even now, knowing what she was really like, the way she really thought, something about her still pulled him. She was like an itch he couldn't reach, and he'd never had this problem before. Ever. He didn't like it. At all.

He tossed the jacket on his unmade bed and kicked some dirty clothes around on the floor in the dark bedroom until he uncovered his basketball shorts. He needed to think. To vent. To play.

The makeshift court in his driveway was pitted and rocky, and no matter how often he swept the crumbling concrete, it was inevitable that he'd end up chasing the ball into the neighbor's bushes at least once. He'd saved up for a month to buy the used hoop and backboard and screwed it directly into the carport overhang, knowing no one cared one way or another if he put holes in the seventy-year-old structure.

His forehead and back were covered in dust and sweat, and he'd sunk at least a hundred shots by the time the old Chevy pulled into the drive. "Dad!" James hollered. "Can't you park on the street? I need court time today."

"Too far to walk." Richard Phelps slammed the door with a sigh, limping away from the car. "Besides, it's getting too dark to see the basket." It took him a while to navigate the fifty feet to the house, his belly hanging several inches below his belt and his back bent with the extra weight. "What's for dinner?"

James caught the ball on the rebound, working around both the car and his father. Story of his life. "Your turn, remember? I'm supposed to be at practice."

Richard scowled. "But you aren't, are you? What'd you do, skip?"

He shot again.

"I'm talking to you, boy. What are you doing home?"

Dancing around the car, James jumped high for a lay-up. "Coach cancelled practice after the lockdown. Got stuck in biology all day."

"Been home a while?"

"Not long. Had some stuff to take care of on my way."

James shook his head, pivoting next to the rear bumper to shoot a three-pointer.

"And getting food on the table wasn't one of those things?"

James caught the ball, ruthlessly shoving down the budding guilt as he met his father's eyes. A year ago, he would have just done it, but Rachelle, the social worker, had warned him about taking on too many of his father's responsibilities or problems. No one could prevent Richard from going off his depression meds if he chose, but James refused to make it an easy choice. "I told you. It's your turn to cook." The old man grunted, climbing the two steps to the door. James leaped up and opened the screen for him. Some habits were hard to break. "I have to practice every day. College isn't going to pay for itself—I have to get a scholarship, remember?"

Richard huffed his way to the one and only recliner in the tiny living room. "Still got to eat. What we gonna do for food now? Been working all day. I'm too tired to stand in the kitchen."

"If my bike was working, I could run out for burgers or tacos, but . . ."

"Don't know why you can't just drive my car," Richard grumbled. "Nothing wrong with a vehicle that gets you where you're going."

James peeled off his shirt on his way down the hall, irritated by his father's lack of motivation even when it came to food. This was an argument they had four or five times a week, but it never got them anywhere. "Told you a million times, I can't drive it with the seat stuck so far back from the wheel. When you get that fixed, we'll talk." He grabbed a towel and headed for the bathroom, determined not to get sucked into being his father's slave. Most kids he knew weren't expected to take care of their parents so early in life. James had been doing it since his mom left two years ago. "Let me know when you figure it out. I'm taking a shower."

"How much did you say that bike would cost to fix?" Richard hollered.

James stripped off his shorts and turned the water on pure hot, then opened the door a crack, standing there in his underwear. "Probably about six hundred. Won't know for sure until I get it looked at."

"Too much." Richard grunted, already flipping through the channels with his universal remote. "Still don't know what we're gonna eat."

The bathroom door clicked shut. James leaned against it, resisting the urge to bang his head on the wall. According to Rachelle, his father's depression was only going to get worse with time. Eventually, he'd stop going to work, stop getting out of the chair, and start needing round-the-clock care for the most basic things. James loved his father and would do anything to help him, but he knew the social worker was right. If James let him, his father would steal both their lives.

And however much he loved his father, James was determined to live a very different kind of existence. One that included stability and happiness, regular meals and bills he could actually pay. He wanted a career—didn't even care doing what—that would allow him vacations and sick time and maybe give him a chance to see the world.

James knew Richard's condition was medical, and that his father's aspiration to live in a five-year-old recliner could be overcome. He had never been more relieved than he was the day Richard's boss had sent Rachelle over to help them. But he felt guilty because the majority of the relief came when Rachelle gave James permission to live his own life.

The problem was that Richard was in no condition to support or encourage James in any way. That's why he played like his life depended on it. He had to get a basketball scholarship—it was his only way out.

Fourteen

February 11ᵗʰ
156 days to departure

"ARE YOU SURE THE TWO of you will be okay?" Emma's mother barely glanced at her, focusing instead on fitting the last of her clothing into a large suitcase. "It was bad enough when you were going to stay here alone, but looking after your brother on top of everything—that's a lot of responsibility."

You have no idea what kind of responsibility I'm about to be stuck with.

Letting go of Keith's hand, Emma gently folded one final blouse and handed it to Cindy. "We'll be fine, Mom."

Cindy stopped packing to look—really look—at her children. "I should stay. You need me here." She picked up her cell phone and pressed a button. "Your father will understand."

Emma took the phone and ended the hastily made call.

"No, he won't. He needs you. Dad won't stop long enough to eat or sleep if you aren't there to make him. Besides, you've been looking forward to this trip for over a year. "

"True." Cindy perched next to Emma on the edge of the bed, playing absently with her daughter's necklace. Her fingers stilled, and she frowned at the faint white lines on Emma's neck. She rubbed her thumb over the top of one of Emma's gills. "What—"

Emma shot forward, faking a cough and forcing her mother to move her hand. "Just a scar."

"We should be taking you with us," Cindy said, replacing her frown with a smile. "You'd love the Greek islands."

The idea of a vacation halfway around the world was tempting, but unrealistic for Emma this close to the end of her time. And selfish as it was, she needed her brother nearby while their parents were gone. "Stop with the guilt. We'll be fine, and you and Dad will have a wonderful time."

Cindy took Emma's chin in her hand with a sigh. "When did you become such an adult? How can you be so calm about everything when I know you're more stressed than you've ever been? So much has happened lately. And it's senior year. You're getting ready for college, real life, and you're just so practical. It's scary how fast time is passing."

She has no idea. "Keith and I will be fine. And we'll call if we need something, okay?"

"Yeah, Mom. Emma will take care of me, and I'll take care of her." Keith pulled Cindy's arm around him and nuzzled her neck. With her free arm, Cindy pulled Emma in as well, the three of them hugging until Emma's throat felt swollen and sticky with grief.

"I'll miss you so much," Keith sobbed. "And Dad, too."

As if he'd been summoned, the front door slammed, and their father's footsteps hurried up the stairs. "Cindy? Are you about ready? The shuttle will be here any minute." He blew into the room like a tornado, spinning with life and energy and excitement. "Oh, good. You're all here." After wiping Emma's tears and murmuring encouragements to Keith, he rattled off a list of instructions while he tossed last-minute additions into his suitcase. Once the zipped and labeled luggage had been hauled to the front door, Russ engulfed each of his kids in one last bear hug. "Take care of each other, Team Harris. I love you both. And don't forget to check in with us every once in a while. We'll answer no matter what time it is, as long as we have a signal."

"Call us every day," Cindy clarified. "I mean it. I want to hear from you as often as possible to know how things are going."

"Mom, that will cost a fortune." Emma wiped one more tear, wondering, hoping, praying she wouldn't change too much in the next ten days.

"I don't care, Emma. Every day." She grabbed Emma's hand and squeezed. "Promise me."

Emma nodded. "I promise."

The shuttle pulled into the driveway, and before the driver could even honk, Russ strode out with two suitcases. Cindy wrapped her arms around Emma, cocooning her in warmth she could only find being held by her mother. "I am the luckiest woman in the world to have been given you as my daughter." Cindy sniffed. "If you need anything, or if something happens, you call me. I don't care how stupid it sounds. If necessary, I'll be home on the first available flight."

"What about me, Mom?" Keith whined. "What if *I* need you?"

"I'll fly home if you need me too." Cindy hugged her son. "Don't give your sister too much trouble, okay? And you stay away from Jonathan. He's bad news."

Keith shrugged out of her arms, pouting. "I know. You keep telling me."

"Don't worry, Mom. I'll watch out for him."

Cindy handed Emma an envelope with several hundred dollars in cash. "For groceries and other necessities. Let me know if something comes up and you need more. I'll transfer some into your debit account." She wound her arm around Emma's waist and squeezed. "Mrs. Hall will check in on you, and says you're both welcome at her house anytime."

Emma folded the envelope and crammed it into her pocket. "I can handle things. We don't need Connie to take care of us."

"She's just checking in and spending time with Keith, like she does when I'm here. Even I need help sometimes."

"Okay."

"Will she make us cookies?" Keith asked. Despite his claims of dislike from days ago, he had long been a fan of their neighbor's baking abilities.

Cindy kissed her son's cheek. "Maybe if you ask her nicely."

Emma watched through the doorway as the shuttle driver loaded her parents' bags and closed the hatch. Russ jogged

back to the open front door, and excitement lit Cindy's eyes. They dimmed again when she looked at her children. "Are you sure—?"

"Yes, Mom. I promise." Emma hugged her mother and gave her a gentle shove toward the porch, ignoring the ache of knowing her time was limited. "Be safe, have fun, and I love you."

"Me too." Keith added. "I love you too."

Cindy wiped a tear from the corner of her eye as she climbed into the van. "We'll call you when we get there. And if you need anything—anything at all—you ask Mrs. Hall. She might even be willing to bring dinner, if you want."

"We'll be fine. And I promise, neither of us will starve. Have a great trip." The lump in Emma's throat was uncomfortable, but she couldn't seem to swallow it. She and Keith waved from the curb until the van was out of sight, then she led her brother back into the house. "Just you and me, Keith."

"Yep." Forlorn, Keith started up the stairs toward his room. Emma dug into the pantry for a recipe book, feeling both exhilarated and lonely. As she flipped through the pages, she dialed Heather's number, determined to make plans. Best to stay busy tonight.

Fifteen

February 14th
153 days to departure

"FOUL!" COACH BLEW THE WHISTLE and James doubled over, holding his gut where his own teammate had just sucker-punched him. "What was that about?"

James stayed quiet, fuming. He couldn't afford to lose it now—not with their game schedule going full swing. Every instinct begged him to jump Lyle and pummel his face until it caved, but James held back, knowing the action would earn him suspension from the team. Especially since Lyle's dad and the coach had been rather chummy lately. "Nothing," he wheezed. "It wasn't about anything."

Coach Adams raised his eyebrows and rested a hand on his hip. "Didn't look like nothing. Lyle?"

Lyle's smug grin heightened James's urge, but he suppressed it for his own good. "Just playing the game, Coach. You know how it goes."

"James?" Coach asked. "You wanna sit the bench for a few?"

James shook his head, straightening his spine and let his arm drop to his side. "Nope. I want to play."

The whistle blew, and James jogged into the key to take his foul shots. The first one hit the rim and swirled around the edge before falling in. The second wasn't so lucky. Too much power behind the throw, and it bounced off the backboard and dropped to the right of the hoop. He'd been missing his shots far too often lately, and it frustrated him.

He'd like to believe he was distracted by dodging girls who, for some reason, expected him to send flowers or candy or other expensive crap. Seriously, today had to be the biggest joke of a non-holiday anyone ever concocted. But he knew that wasn't really the problem. No, this was much bigger than stupid Valentine's Day. The real problem had red hair, green eyes, and stood about five three, even when she stretched tall to yell at him.

Tonight. He'd go talk to her tonight, and one way or another, he'd either get past that gigantic "keep out" wall she'd put up or clear her from his mind for good. Figuring out why Emma hated him had just become priority one on James's list of things to do. Ever since the day of the lockdown, she'd been cool as the ice queen Mark and Lyle said she was. Like she couldn't stand looking at him, let alone being in the same classroom.

He'd tried to do something nice, and he couldn't figure out how it had backfired so beautifully. Story of his life. Might as well get one of those cardboard crowns they hand out at fast-food places and write "loser" on it in big fat letters so everyone in town would know. So they would see him coming.

James Phelps, king of Backfire City. They had no idea how much *more* he could handle. How much more he could be.

Lyle had the ball. James covered him, stole it in a moment of weakness, and sent it sailing across the court for a swish worth three points as the final whistle blew. Practice was over.

"Think you're hot, do you?" Lyle shoved James from behind, sidestepping around to get right in his face. "Play better than me just because Coach has you starting?"

"You said it, not me." James pushed past Lyle and headed for the locker room.

"Lucky shot. I dare you to try it again."

James shook his head. "Tomorrow. I'm hitting the showers."

Mark blocked the way. "You really should. Maybe a shower could wash away the stink that follows you around on the court."

"Yep, I stink so bad, I took your starting position." James seethed. "Outta my way, Larson."

"What's the matter? Got somewhere better to be?"

"Yep. I do." He glanced at the clock on the wall, hoping Emma hadn't left yet. She probably had plans. How could she not?

Lyle spoke from behind. "If he doesn't hurry home and make dinner, his dad might start eating the furniture."

James's self-control nearly snapped. Lyle could know

nothing about his father without having read James's school file. His arm cocked back, fist at the ready, his other hand gripping the front of Lyle's jersey. *No one insults my dad.*

"Problem, guys?" Though Coach Adams' voice sounded mild, it held an undercurrent of warning.

James let go, his chest heaving with pressure. "No. No problem at all." He pushed past Mark and headed for the showers, ignoring the smirks and guffaws behind him as he reminded himself that it didn't matter what they knew or if they liked him. Basketball was still his only means of escape.

EMMA PAUSED HER MOVIE and straightened her tank top, her ponytail swishing against her shoulders as she bounded down the stairs to answer the door. The persistent knocking threatened to bring on a headache. "I'm coming!"

When she peeked through the side window and found a dangerous-looking James on her porch, she flung the door open, annoyed that his anger only made him more appealing. "What do you want?"

"To talk to you." James's expression softened, though Emma hadn't done anything except fold her arms and lean against the doorframe.

"About what?"

He braced his hand on the wall next to her shoulder and leaned close enough to make her squirm, but not close enough to make her panic. "Why do you hate me?"

His words pricked a hole in her defensive bubble, and she scrambled to patch it. Her tongue felt thick. "I don't."

Moving in closer, he raised an eyebrow. "Liar. It's evident in the way you look at me. Normally, I wouldn't notice, and if I did, I wouldn't care. But for some reason, coming from you, it bothers me. A lot."

She lifted her gaze to meet his for the first time in days, but couldn't force words to come. It had been months since her heart had beat so erratically. Having James loom over her sent a shiver of anticipation up her spine. Her own lack of fear surprised her.

"Why can't I get you out of my head?" He brushed a loose lock of hair behind her shoulder, then let his hand drop—careful not to touch her. "I know I scare you. But I'm not as bad as you probably think."

He had a ring of deep blue pigment surrounding his gray pupils. She hadn't noticed it before, but now it was all she could see. His presence filled up the space in the doorway, shoving aside the dark and reflecting the warmth and light that would otherwise spill out and disappear into the night. She pulled in a deep breath and pressed her hand against his chest, nudging him away. Distance. Distance would help her catch her breath and think straight.

He stepped back, careful, cautious. But only one step. Determined.

Care and caution, she could resist. Determination, she could not. Not when coupled with a presence as large as his. Emma opened the door wider, inviting him inside. She glanced at the clock. Keith would be home from baking with Mrs. Hall any time, so they wouldn't be alone for long.

She led James through the kitchen and into the sitting

room, where a floor-to-ceiling window overlooked the pool. With the help of the rising moon, wavy lines of blue reflected through the glass and onto the walls, giving the illusion of being underwater. If only she could breathe as she needed here. Too bad her parents' chlorinated pool didn't do the trick. She snuggled into her favorite recliner and pulled her knees up to her chest, leaning her chin on them, and gestured to the sofa.

He sat, draping his arm across the back, and settling his ankle on his knee in a deceptively casual pose. Emma forced her eyes away from the corded muscles that bulged under his T-shirt and along his arms. No wonder she thought he was dangerous.

Tension filled the space between them until Emma felt like the oxygen was being sucked from the room. She lifted her head. "I owe you an apology. I'm overprotective of my brother these days, and you caught the backlash from that."

One brow rose at that. "But?"

She squirmed. How did you tell a guy you didn't like being around him because he was too attractive for his own good? Or that you didn't want to be one of the many? She was done with guys anyway—maybe she should just tell him that. "But nothing. I'm sorry. That's all."

His eyes clouded with confusion, but he shrugged. "Apology accepted. I still don't understand why you hate me."

Studying his face, Emma tangled her fingers together around her knees. "I really don't. It's just . . . I have trust issues. And I don't know anything about you other than what I've seen at school. My brother isn't the only one whose character judgment has landed him in trouble."

James made a face, puffing his cheeks out. "One of your friends got you arrested for shoplifting?"

Shivering, Emma pulled a throw blanket off the back of her chair and wrapped it around her shoulders. "No. Not that kind of trouble. It was . . . um . . . worse than that. Different." She drew in a calming breath. "I'm cautious because I have to be."

"Noted." He tipped his head sideways, speculating. "Listen. I know you have no reason to believe this, but you can trust me. If not as your friend, as Keith's."

"Thanks, but we don't really need—"

"Yes, you do. Or at least, Keith does." He leaned his arms on his knees, his jaw tightening. "That day, in biology? He was on the verge of freaking out, so I talked him through it. Got to know him better. He's a good kid who tries really hard to overcome society's view of what others wish he was, as opposed to the awesome person he truly is. Walking home the other day—that wasn't the first time I've hung out with him, and it won't be the last. I talk to him a lot, Emma, and wave when I see him wandering the halls. And anytime he wants to sit with me at lunch, or anywhere else, I'm happy to have him."

Their gazes locked in a tug-of-war. "He's real. And in case you haven't noticed, there aren't a lot of 'real' people at Oceanside High."

Though she hated to admit it, James's words softened Emma, regardless of his current "player" status. It sounded like he genuinely liked Keith, and though it surprised her, she wondered if James was having a hard time fitting in too.

"Thanks for taking care of my brother." Emma sighed, staring out the window where a gust of wind bent an orange tree to one side, ruffling the tiny budding leaves. "I bet he loves sitting with all your girlfriends."

James cringed. "Uh, no. That'd be like throwing him into the shallow end of a pool. But he makes a great wingman."

"Wingman?"

"Knows how to help me escape." He waved off her confusion. "It's a guy thing."

"Escape from what, exactly?"

"The snobberazzi." James's lips turned up with a rakish smile that made Emma's heart stutter. "Maybe you'd feel better if we spent some time together—got to know each other. You know, to avoid future misunderstandings."

A slow smile erupted, and Emma allowed it to spread into a grin because she finally felt like they might be done playing games. "Isn't that what we're doing right now? Have some patience, and maybe by the time Keith comes home, we'll be best friends."

His chuckle was deep and rumbling, and held an undercurrent of something Emma couldn't place. "I've got buckets of patience. But being friends isn't exactly my goal."

She had to look away to avoid losing her train of thought. *He's good.*

"I have a question." He rolled slowly to his feet, his expression lightening into curiosity. "What are you doing home alone on a Friday night? It's Valentine's Day. Why don't you have plans? A date or something?"

Emma stood too, bringing the throw blanket with her,

trying to keep up with his change of topic and mood. "I do have plans. I'm watching a movie and eating an entire carton of peanut butter cup ice cream while I wait for my brother to come home from the neighbor's house."

"An entire carton? By yourself?" His eyes traveled the length of her thin frame, deliberately slow. "Shocking."

Emma marched into the kitchen, the blanket billowing like a cape behind her. "More shocking than my being home alone on Valentine's Day?"

He nodded. "A little bit, yeah."

It felt good having him here. Natural. Right. She decided to go with it this once and just see. "Well, here's another one, then." She opened the freezer and removed the ice cream, then produced two spoons and set them on the counter. "I stay home every Friday night because I like it. Sometimes Heather comes over, but more often than not, her Fridays are dedicated to dating. I'm okay with it, though. I'd much rather spend quality time with myself than waste time with a jerk who wants nothing more than to put his hands where they don't belong."

He accepted a spoon, but paused in the act of opening the carton. "You seriously don't date? Like, no boyfriend?"

She shook her head. "Nope."

"At all?"

"Only in the past." She set the cardboard lid he'd handed her on the counter and scooped a bite of ice cream into her mouth, spoon upside down, and closed her eyes. "Oh, yeah. That's good."

James dipped his spoon in, taking his time. "Mmm." He

closed his eyes too, and Emma noted his apparent enjoyment of her favorite flavor. Then he asked, "Why not?"

"Why not what?"

"Why are all your boyfriends in the past? No current interest?"

She swirled her spoon around the top, digging out a peanut butter cup and avoiding his eyes. "Commitment is overrated."

Their spoons clanked together as they shared more of the ice cream, having hit a lull in the conversation. Halfway through the carton, Emma looked up and found James staring at her, looking like he wanted to say something. "What?"

"Me neither," he said. "I don't have a girlfriend."

She gawked at him. "You could've fooled me. What do you call that . . . ahem . . . make-out session I witnessed that one day?"

He dug his spoon back into the carton with renewed vigor. "That wasn't what it looked like."

"Really?"

"Yeah, really."

"So what was it, then?"

James swallowed a mouthful of ice cream. "Momentary pleasure. Temporary insanity. A huge damn mistake. Take your pick."

His response startled a giggle from her, but she managed to rein in an actual laugh—out of respect. Or self-preservation. She wasn't sure which. "I'd rather have you explain how sucking face with what's-her-name doesn't constitute her being your girlfriend."

His sigh was long-suffering. "First of all, we weren't sucking face. She kissed me, okay? What was I supposed to do—reject her? And for your information, you running into me at just the right moment would've been the perfect escape if you had slowed down long enough to talk to me."

Emma tossed her spoon in the sink and walked around the counter to perch on a barstool. "Okay, fine. Whatever. So, you aren't hooked up with that blonde—even though I've seen her hanging all over you on more than one occasion. I'll bite that bait. How do you explain the rumors about you and that other girl, the soccer player . . . what was her name? Windy something or other. Sounded like you two were an item not long ago."

He slammed his spoon on the counter. "Damn gossips. That was an absolute rumor and I have no idea how it got started. Really. None." His eyes danced with merriment. "I swear. I don't even know Windy what's-her-name. Besides, if I did have a girlfriend, don't you think I'd be required to some obligatory Valentine's Day activity?"

"Whatever." She slid him a sidelong glance, grinning. "Okay, so why *don't* you have a girlfriend, then? In your twisted mind, what's wrong with committed relationships?"

"Too much effort. Between school and basketball and work—who has time? Especially senior year."

Emma opened her mouth to ask about his job and maybe his plans for college, but a loud crash interrupted her thoughts and sent her leaping off the stool. The security system wailed as she bolted into the entryway, James close on her heels. Glass glistened around a brick on the hardwood floor, but Emma scampered over the mess, barefooted, and threw open the door, peering out at the dark yard. A rustle in the lilac shrub had her shouting, "Hey!" A figure scooted between the fence and the greenery and bolted down the street.

James sailed past her and leaped over the porch railing, running after the intruder, whose face was covered with a ski mask. Hands shaking, Emma stumbled into the kitchen and grabbed her phone to dial 911. "I need help," she said, her voice wavering. "Someone just tried to break into my house."

Sixteen

JAMES CHASED THE VANDAL through the bushes, into the neighboring yard, and down the street. His basketball training kicked in and kept him running hard for several blocks until the guy turned down a narrow path into a park. All James wanted was a good look at the guy's face, but it was covered with a ski mask. The vandal wasn't much taller or more muscular than James, keeping things fairly even should it come to a fight.

Breathing steadily, he stretched his legs, pushed himself, closing the distance between them. With a diving leap, he tackled the guy. They hit the grass hard, momentarily knocking the wind out of James—who had somehow landed on the underside of the pile—and rolled over and over and down an incline, where they came to a stop inches away from a pile of dog poop. It was sheer luck that James ended up on top the second time.

His lungs screamed for air, and his hold on the bad guy loosened from the lack of oxygen. The man struggled, clawing and scratching at James's arms, kicking his legs, and nearly breaking free before James was finally able to pull in a breath.

"Let go of me!" the man screamed. "I could kill you right now."

"With what?" James panted, tightening his hold around the guy's arms and torso. "Your fingernails?"

"Grrruh. No." The man panted as he continued to struggle. He wiggled, bent, and managed to pull a knife from a hidden sheaf on his ankle.

James's heart leaped into his throat, and he let go as the masked man slashed the knife awkwardly at everything within his limited reach. The blade sliced a shallow ribbon in James's forearm as he disentangled himself, but he ignored the sting and scrambled backward up the grassy hill, panting against a different kind of adrenaline. The kind brought on by fear.

The vandal wiped his mouth with the back of his wrist, brandishing the knife at James. "Stay away from the redhead."

Though the breath had been knocked out of him seconds earlier, it now came in short, burning heaves, and James's brain scrambled, his eyesight blurring. He blinked his vision clear as the guy took off across the field, his blade glinting in the light of the half moon. James pushed himself up to standing, ignoring half a dozen bruises and aches. "What the hell was that about?"

The wail of sirens cut through his brain fog and he jogged

back to Emma's house, realizing he'd left her alone and cursing his stupidity. What if there was more than one vandal? Emma could have been in danger while James—idiot king of distraction—took off to run after the guy with the knife. He picked up speed, leaping over shrubs and waist-high fences as he cut through yards and wound around cars to get back to Emma. His heart pounded as he imagined all the terrible things that could've happened after he left her.

It never occurred to him to wonder why he now felt responsible for her. He just did.

Four police cars with flashing red-and-blue lights lined Emma's street, blocking the front of her house. His heart pounded into his throat until he saw Emma standing on the porch, right where he'd left her.

The breath he'd been holding flew out in a rush as he pushed through the growing crowd of concerned neighbors. An officer stopped him at the curb. "Sorry, you're going to have to stay back while we search the premises."

"Unless there's more than one person, he's not here," James panted, extending his arm and pointing in the direction from which he'd just come. "That way. He got away."

The officer eyed him suspiciously, seeming to take stock of James's long hair, the scar on his jaw, and the cut on his arm. "How did you get that?"

"Not by breaking her window. The guy in the ski mask tried to stab me."

"James!" Emma rushed to him, a mixture of fear and relief flickering across her face. She threw herself into his arms, making his heart race with something he hadn't felt for a long time, if ever. "I can't believe you chased him." She pulled back to look in his eyes. "Why did you do that?"

"He broke your window." If he'd hoped to catch his breath and slow his pulse, having her in his arms blew that idea to bits. He could think of a hundred different reactions to this sudden development, but reminded himself they had an audience and settled on pulling her close and leaning his cheek against her head, staring at her shoulder. A birthmark, not a tattoo. Definitely a birthmark.

"Glass is replaceable." She frowned, turning her head to inspect his cut. A line of blood ran down to his elbow, where it dripped slowly, but steadily. She made a sound of dismay and twisted around, but didn't pull away. Not out of his arms, like he expected. "Why not just call the police?"

"I don't know—instinct, I guess." He brushed a lock of hair away from her eyes, searching, checking, making sure. "Are you okay?"

Closing her eyes, she tucked her face against his chest, trembling like a motorcycle running low on oil. Clearly, she was not okay—at least emotionally—but didn't have a chance to vocalize an answer.

"Ma'am, do you know this man?"

Though he wanted nothing more than to hold her exactly where she was, James released Emma so she could address the officer. For all the vulnerability he'd felt in the embrace, Emma managed to pull herself together. "Would I be hugging him if I didn't?" She tossed her head—a haughty move James had seen her make at school. "I already told that guy–" She motioned to the open door of the house, where another cop sifted through the broken glass. "James and I were in the kitchen having ice cream, about to go upstairs and watch a movie, when the window shattered. We came to check it out, and James saw someone in the bushes and chased him."

The officer wrote some things in a palm-sized notebook, then glanced at James. "Did you get a good look at the perpetrator?"

Frustrated with himself, James shook his head. "No. He was wearing a ski mask. I tackled him in the park, but he had a knife." A drop of blood slid down his arm, and he wiped at it. "About the time he started slashing, I let him go."

"Wise choice." The officer nodded in approval, frowning at the cut. "Do you want me to have someone come look at that?"

"What, you mean like an ambulance?" James pressed his lips together to keep from smiling. "I'm fine. Nothing a Band-Aid won't cure." He extended a hand to the officer. "James Phelps. Do I need to give you a statement or something? Whatever I can do to help catch that guy, I'm willing."

"Lieutenant Peters," the officer returned. "A statement would be great. Why don't we go inside and have a seat?"

"No problem." He glanced at Emma. "I just need a minute, then I'll be in."

Peters nodded and walked away, leaving them temporarily alone.

Emma's hand slid down his uninjured arm, and her fingers tangled with his. Like she wanted him here. Like he made her feel secure, safe. He could only hope it was possible.

"Thanks," she murmured. Her soft green eyes betrayed a hint of vulnerability. Something dangerous and unstoppable flickered in James's chest, but he forced a smile, tried to shake the feeling away.

"Emma! James!" Keith hollered from the other side of a patrol car. "What's going on? Are you guys okay?"

Emma let go of James's hand with a groan. "I was hoping Mrs. Hall would keep him inside until this was over." She took a step away, then another. "I should reassure him. Do you mind giving that guy your statement now? I'd like to get rid of the police before dawn."

James watched her walk away, fighting an insane flare of jealousy for every guy she'd ever dated. The feeling was beyond ridiculous, especially considering his own history, but he felt the blaze anyway and had to grit his teeth against a tumult of emotions he couldn't name. Rather than spending the rest of the evening trying to figure out exactly what he wanted from her, he trudged into the house, careful to step over the broken glass.

Seventeen

EMMA *HID HER SHAKING HANDS* behind her and pretended—for Keith's sake—that it was no big deal. They had been victims of vandalism before, right about the time Tom went to jail. "Really," she assured Keith. "It's just a broken window."

"We can't stay home alone." Keith clutched Emma's arm, attempting to pull her toward the neighbor's house. "Mrs. Hall says we should stay at her house tonight."

Emma shook her head. As it was, Mrs. Hall was probably on the phone with their parents, insisting that they come right home. "I need to clean up the mess and finish dealing with the cops. Why don't you go ahead and stay there? When you talk to Mom, tell her everything's fine, and I'll call her in the morning."

"But it's dangerous for you to stay all alone." Keith stared at the house, and Emma's gaze followed.

"I'll be fine. James is here. Tell Mrs. Hall I might come over if it's not too late when I get everything squared away, but not to wait up."

It took some convincing, but eventually, Keith headed back to Mrs. Hall's house—where, Emma hoped, he'd report to their mother that everything was under control. His fear tolerance capacity had been met for the week, so having him stay at the neighbor's was probably best for both of them.

She found James in the den—sporting a giant bandage made of gauze and tape he'd probably found in the first aid kit in the bathroom—talking into a voice recorder held by Lieutenant Peters, the same officer who brought Keith home after the shoplifting incident.

"And then he said, 'Stay away from the redhead.'" A bead of sweat rolled down the side of James's face, and he wiped it away with the back of his hand. Guilt wrapped around Emma's throat, squeezing tight. *Bet he never expected* this *when he knocked on my door.*

When he'd finished questioning James, Lieutenant Peters turned to Emma. "Do you have anything to add? Any thoughts on who would do something like this? Someone who might be angry with you or your other family members?"

Several suspects came to mind, friends of Tom's, but she hadn't had problems with any of them in months. The very idea that Tom's friends could be targeting her again both exhausted and infuriated her. Her voice trembled. "This has happened before. I'd guess the same people are likely involved. There's a list in my file. You should probably start there."

James eyed her quizzically, but she turned her head.

"What about your brother's friend? The one who taught him to steal?"

Emma scowled, her nerves fraying like shredded fabric. "Keith didn't know he was stealing. He thought it was a game."

Lieutenant Peters guided Emma to the chair next to James and eased her into it. "I remember. And I'm not accusing your brother, Miss Harris. But we did pull Jonathan Dahl in for questioning after the shoplifting incident, and considering his state of mind, I'm wondering if we should add him to the list of suspects."

Doubt it. "Go for it. Investigate everyone I know, if you think it will help." *I hope all this stops when I'm gone.*

Peters flipped open his notebook and made some marks. "How long are your parents out of town?"

Ignoring James's sound of surprise, Emma answered, "At least another week. Longer, if my dad gets caught up in his work. They're touring Greece while my father researches the lost city of Atlantis for a science journal. He's a professor of history at the university."

Lieutenant Peters made another note, then pocketed his notebook and stood, frowning. "What are you planning to do about this broken window? It's unlikely you'll get a glass company out here to replace it until morning. Is there somewhere you and Keith can go for the night?"

"Keith's staying at the neighbor's." Emma took in the glass all over the floor, the cool breeze blowing in, and had to swallow a lump in her throat. "I don't know what to do about the window."

"I'll help her take care of it." James reached across the arms of their chairs and took her hand, palm to palm, an offer of solid support—friendship. "Do you know if your dad has any plywood lying around?"

"Probably." Her head spun as the initial adrenaline rush wore off, but she squeezed James's hand, grateful. "Thanks."

He shook his head. "Don't worry about it."

Peters leveled his gaze on James. "You planning to stick around for a while?"

James hesitated, his eyes searching hers for approval. "As long as Emma needs. I'll help her clean up, make sure she's not alone if the vandal comes back."

Something stirred, fluttered, in Emma's chest, soft, like the tentacles of a jellyfish in motion. She tried to push the feeling away, but James held tight, and the warm sensation traveled up her arm and spread through the rest of her body.

Tread carefully, Emma. Go slow. Don't dive in just because it feels good to be touched, to have someone worry about you. James moved her in foreign ways, from places no one else had managed to reach. By all accounts, he should be forbidden territory. She couldn't ask him to stay, but tonight, she didn't relish the idea of being alone, either.

Another officer poked his head in the door. "Lieutenant, we're clear out here."

"Thanks, Brown." Peters handed Emma a business card.

"Here's my number. I'm on duty until two a.m., but you can call anytime."

"Thanks." She ran her fingers over the card as Peters strode from the house, closing the door behind him. Outside, the cops got in their cars, turned off the flashing lights, and one by one, drove away.

A familiar sensation of dread poured into her, raising goose bumps on her arms and bringing the shaking back full force. Even knowing James was standing right behind her, she found herself fighting off memories she'd long suppressed.

Hands running up her side, under her blouse. A struggle. A forced kiss, void of affection. A rough voice.

"Come on, Emma. You know you want to. This is where we've been headed all year." Hands on her skin—in unwelcome places. Panic.

"No!" she screamed, fighting. Fighting. Fighting. Screaming. Crying.

A hand over her mouth, pushing the screams back down her throat.

Pain. In her eyes. In her throat. Her stomach and chest. Dirt in her hair. On her face. Covering her clothes. Pain and dirt. Dirt and pain.

Saved by the red-and-blue flashing lights.

She let out an involuntary whimper when James wrapped his arms around her from behind, his presence helping to push away the memory-induced panic.

"Shh," he whispered. "Just me."

James's voice soothed her, helped her relax enough to

turn into his embrace and let him hold her until her nerves settled and the shaking subsided. "Sorry. No need to fall apart. It's only . . . a broken window."

His arms squeezed. Not hard, not tight. Secure. Firm. Gentle. "Still scary."

She nodded into his neck, holding on to him in silence until her heart calmed enough for her to breathe normally, to pull herself together. Then she withdrew and turned to look at the piles of shattered glass. "Guess I ought to vacuum that up before one of us gets cut."

James crunched over the pieces to inspect the window frame, where large pieces of sharp glass hung precariously. "Where would I find some plywood?"

Emma forced herself to smile. "Try the woodshop—the shed-looking thing on the far side of the pool in the backyard. There's got to be something we can use out there."

Rather than going outside immediately, James stayed where he was.

She tried smiling again, but failed. "What?"

His mouth opened like he wanted to say something, but then he snapped it closed. "Are you really okay? Really?"

"Mm-hm." Emma nodded, hiding her trembling hands behind her back. "Just, you know, a little dazed."

"More than a little," he murmured. "You're completely freaked."

She turned away without responding. The lump in her throat grew as she watched James head out back in search of supplies. What was she thinking? She couldn't afford to get involved with him. Not now. Not ever.

In a closet near the door, she found a pair of gym shoes and put them on, then filled a plastic bucket with larger pieces before plugging in the vacuum to suck up the smallest shards of glass. As she finished, James carried in a slab of plywood and leaned it against the window frame. A power drill stuck out of his waistband, and something clinked in his pockets.

"I've never seen a woodshop like that before," he said. "I expected to find birdhouses and … you know, shelves and junk. Not . . ."

Emma chuckled. "What? Don't all men carve sea life sculptures in their sheds?"

"Not hardly." He measured the open space, then repeated the action on the wood, making intermittent pencil marks. "Are your parents going to be pissed at me for putting holes in the frame?"

"Holes?"

"Well, something's got to hold the plywood up. I figure screws are the best bet." He wielded the drill, pressing the button so it whirred. "I'll need your help."

"I doubt they'll be mad at all. More likely, they'll thank you." She helped him position the wood and watched as he drilled into the first corner. The sight of his flexed biceps made her insides go melty. "Thanks for doing this. For helping me. I . . . just. Thanks."

He glanced at her, his eyes like gray smoke and his lips lax, full, unsmiling. "Anytime."

She squeezed her eyes closed, remembering a months-old conversation. "Huh. This is definite irony."

He pushed the drill harder, forcing a screw into the wood. "What?"

"Remember how I saved you from detention and you thought you owed me? Looks like the tables have turned. Guess I owe you now."

"Shit . . . I mean, um, crap. Sorry." He winced sheepishly and moved to drill the next corner of the board. "I hope you don't think I somehow arranged for this to happen. I'd never do that. Contrary to your earlier opinion of me, I'm not that guy."

"Relax." She tapped the side of her fist against the plywood as he ran the drill again. "The thought hadn't even occurred to me. Although, now that you mention it, maybe it should have."

"No, it shouldn't. Forget I brought it up and finish what you were going to say before I put impossible ideas in your head."

"You have to admit, it looks bad for you." She winked, biting her lip to prevent giggling.

"I didn't set this up, I swear." He narrowed his eyes at her and tested the strength of the first two screws, then set the drill on the floor, looking a tad playful, ready to pounce. "But if you're going to keep trying to make me into a bad guy, I might just have to give you a reason to think that way."

His words should've made her uncomfortable, maybe even nervous, but they didn't. Not one bit. All her instincts told her James was nothing like Tom. His eyes challenged her to keep pushing, and Emma found she wanted to. She closed the space between them until they were just short of touching, and stood on her tiptoes so they were almost eye to eye—almost. "Okay. So, assuming I decide to believe that you being here was a total coincidence, what exactly would I owe you for your help? Exactly?"

His eyes drifted to her lips, then back up, and down again, making Emma squirm. She might have pushed too far.

"Ice cream," he said. "I want to help you finish off the Ben and Jerry's in your kitchen. One carton, two spoons, no dishes."

He didn't back off, and neither did she, even though his nearness made the breath catch in her lungs. "It's melted by now. Probably a huge mess all over the counter. But I can offer you a rain check and buy more."

"Deal," he said, finally breaking the spell and moving away. He picked up the drill and returned to securing the plywood. "Since the ice cream idea is shot, what about popcorn? Do you have any of that?"

"Popcorn? Probably the microwave kind. Why?"

The drill screeched as James forced another screw into the plywood. "You told the cops we were going upstairs to watch a movie. I assume that means you were about to invite me."

Heat flooded Emma's cheeks. She hadn't meant to voice the idea—it just slipped out during questioning. This guy had good hearing, and she made a mental note to remember that in the future. "Do you want to?" Then, as an afterthought added, "I mean, it's Friday night, and you probably have other plans. You don't have to stay. But I wouldn't hate it if you did."

He gripped the sides of the plywood and tugged—testing that it would hold, she assumed—then turned to grin at her, pretending to twirl the drill like it was a gun and he was a hot-shot cowboy. "Beautiful. I wouldn't hate it either. In fact, even if I did have plans—which I don't—I'd cancel them. I'm in, with or without the popcorn."

JAMES AWOKE ON THE FLOOR of Emma's upstairs movie room, tangled in a comforter, and fought to free his limbs. The place was dark except for a sliver of moonlight that crept through the blinds and fell across the sofa where Emma lay sleeping. The soft glow gleamed off the tiny pearls around her neck, highlighted her cheekbones, and silhouetted her nose and lips, giving her a radiance that all but stole his breath. Her folded hands, propped on the cushion next to her face, reminded him of a sculpture he'd once seen in a museum—except Emma was more beautiful, and much more real.

Needing to assure himself that he wasn't dreaming, he reached over and ran his finger down the thin, white scar on her neck. Emma stirred, then bolted upright, her hair falling around her shoulders in a tangled mass, wide eyes startled and afraid.

"Sorry," he murmured. "I didn't mean to wake you."

Shaky fingers combed through her hair. "It's okay." She blinked, turning away from the light so it highlighted her fiery hair and cast her face in shadow. "What time is it?"

James reached in his pocket and realized his cell phone

must be on the floor somewhere. "No idea. Probably pretty late."

Emma felt around the sofa cushions and found her phone, illuminating the face. She locked it again with a moan. "It's ten to four. Your parents are probably ready to murder you. I'm so sorry."

"Doubtful my dad even noticed." He climbed onto the couch next to Emma. "Will yours be mad?"

She shook her head, pulling a throw blanket over her knees and leaning against a cushion. "Only if I'm stupid enough to tell them." She turned her head, a wicked glint shining in her eyes. "And I'm not stupid."

"Do you want me to go?" James kept his volume low, despite knowing they were the only people in the house. "I mean, it's late enough that I might as well stay. If you want. I can pretty much sleep anywhere, and your floor isn't half bad." He flicked his hair out of his face. "I know you'd be fine, but I still hate to leave you here alone after everything."

She rolled her shoulders, stretching. "From what I recall, your bike still isn't running. I assume that means you walked here, and there's no way I'd ask you to walk home in the middle of the night. Especially after everything you've done to help me. I don't care how tough you are—it's dangerous. Just stay." She straightened her tank top and pulled her hair around her neck, covering the scar. "How long has it been since I told you thanks?"

"Four or five hours." He tried not to be surprised by her unexpected invitation to stay, reminding himself that the entire visit had turned into a parade of surprises.

"Well, again, thanks." She let go of her hair and lay on the arm of the couch, eyes closed, exposing the underside of her chin and the soft, white skin along her neck. If he kissed her there—in the hollow at the base of her throat, just above her necklace—what would she taste like? How would she react?

"Anytime," he murmured, more tempted than he liked. Knowing the timing would be bad for both of them—vulnerable and unguarded in this world of half-wake, half-sleep—he ignored the urge and scooted back to the floor, where he wrapped Emma's comforter around him and lay his head on Emma's pillow, where he fell asleep on Emma's floor, and dreamed . . . of Emma.

Eighteen

February 15th
152 days to departure

EMMA RUBBED THE STICKY GRIT out of her eyes and stretched, taking advantage of the quiet morning to peer at James in his unguarded state of sleep. With his eyes closed, body relaxed and sprawled across the floor, he had an innocent, boyish appearance that reminded her—surprisingly—of Keith.

Careful to step lightly around her sleeping guest, Emma crept to the bathroom. Her need to shower was more habit than vanity. On the other hand, the extra time she spent blow-drying her hair and applying makeup—that *was* vanity. And no matter what excuse she concocted, she knew it was because of James.

They were friends. Nothing more. Being friends was perfectly normal. Absolutely okay. Nothing wrong with being friends with a nice guy.

And James had proven that he was truly nice.

When she emerged, she fully expected James to be awake, maybe even getting ready to leave, but he was still fast asleep. She reached out to wake him, but at the last second, pulled back and tiptoed out of the room. She headed to the kitchen to make Keith's favorite breakfast—banana pancakes, scrambled eggs, sausage, and orange juice.

On her way downstairs, she paused to check the boarded-up window. Did the person who had done this know her parents were out of town? Would they come back again tonight when James was no longer there to keep her calm and make her feel safe? She detoured into the den to look up the phone number for a glass replacement company and accepted their first available appointment time, despite exorbitant same-day charges.

Twenty minutes later, James wandered into the kitchen, his long hair wild, eyes bloodshot. He sniffed as Emma flipped the last pancake onto a short stack and set the tray on the table next to a plate of sausage. "If that's for me, I might have to propose. Just FYI. There's something incredibly sexy about waking up to the smell of food cooking."

"Good morning. Of course it's for you." She handed him an empty plate and gestured for him to help himself.

Plate loaded, James sat next to her at the table. "Thanks for breakfast. If it tastes half as good as it smells, I'm serious about that proposal."

With a hand on his wrist, she stopped him from taking the first bite. "If you do propose, I'll have to say no. I'm just not in the market for a husband right now. Don't know how

I'd fit one into my schedule." Grinning, she let go of his wrist and watched him shovel food into his mouth.

"Damn. Are you sure you won't marry me? I'd hate to have to fling you over my shoulder and go Cro-Magnun, but I could seriously die a happy man if I woke up to this every day."

She stifled a giggle. "Sorry. No can do. But you're welcome to check back in five or ten years."

He polished off another bite and pointed his fork at her. "Done."

A sharp pain poked through her ribs when the fantasy flashed across her mind like a sappy movie, but she forced a smile and asked, "Do you always sleep like the dead?"

"Sometimes. When I'm exhausted. Sorry about that." He ran a hand through his dark hair. It was longer than she thought, curling halfway down his neck, free of his usual ponytail.

She tried a bite of sausage, cringing, and sipped her juice to cut the spiciness of the meat. "It was kind of a long night. Thanks for giving up your Friday to help me out. I don't know what I would have done if you hadn't been here."

"Believe me." He paused, fork poised in front of his mouth, dripping syrup back onto his plate. "It wasn't a sacrifice."

"I appreciate it anyway." He would never know how truly touched she was by his actions.

He scooped the last of his eggs, chewed, and swallowed. "I'd say the food is thanks enough, but then I'd regret it forever. Maybe if you go out with me?"

She swatted playfully at his knee. "That's not fair and you know it. If I were to go out with you, it would have nothing to do with you helping me or me helping you."

He draped his arm around her chair and leaned closer. "Oh? What *will* it have to do with?"

The touch of his fingers on her shoulder thrilled a tingle into her toes. She turned and found their faces inches apart, and had to clear her throat to find her voice. "Mutual respect. Enjoying one another's company. Common interests. Stuff like that."

His gaze dropped to her lips. "Respect, check. Enjoyment, check. And I'm interested in spending more time with you—don't much care where or what, as long as the when is soon. That enough for you?"

She pulled back and stood up. Had to—if he moved any closer, she wouldn't be able to breathe. "Maybe. At some point."

Thankfully, he took the hint and didn't push any further. "You gonna call someone to fix that window today?"

"Already did." She stacked his empty plate on top of hers and carried them to the sink. "They're coming at four."

"Good." He followed her with their glasses. "You'll be secure by tonight, then. Safe."

"As secure as I was before, anyway. Gives me time to run errands before they get here. Pick up some groceries and stuff." Translation: clear her gills in the ocean, visit Gran.

He rubbed his stubbly chin, glancing at the door as Emma rinsed the dishes. "You probably need to get rid of me, then. No sweat—I'll just grab my stuff and get on my way."

She blinked, paused in the act of rinsing a fork. "What's your hurry?" Her eyes found his and held, not wanting him to think she was pushing him out. She'd enjoyed having him there. In fact, she wouldn't mind having him stick around, getting to know him better. But she really needed to swim today, too. "I can drive you. You know, whenever you're ready to go. If you want."

The corners of James's eyes crinkled when he turned his smile on full wattage. "Here's a thought. What if I go home and get cleaned up, let you do your thing, then come back and hang out until I have to leave for my game?"

She'd spent the entire night with him and only now remembered that he played basketball with Tom's old friends. "Oh. I forgot about the game."

"I don't have to be there until five," he said, rubbing his chin again. "But, uh . . ." He pulled out his shirt and sniffed it. "I really need a shower."

She wrinkled her nose with a lighthearted sniff. "Yeah, I wasn't going to say anything, but now that you mention it . . ."

"Okay, enough." James tugged gently on a lock of her hair. "I get the point. Let me grab my stuff and you can drop me off."

While James gathered his belongings, she texted Heather to cancel their evening plans, and then called Keith at Mrs. Hall's house. Once she felt reassured that he was happy and occupied for the afternoon, she grabbed her keys, tossing them into the air and catching them again. It was going to be a beautiful day.

Nineteen

U SING ALL THE SPEED she could muster, Emma darted into a coral cave guarded by a patch of colorful seaweed. She had spent the first fifteen minutes of her ocean time drifting aimlessly, enjoying the sense of giddy pleasure brought on by thoughts of James. That pleasure made her careless enough to swim past the arch and directly into Merrick's line of sight. Why couldn't she be allowed to swim alone today, of all days?

Now, Emma found herself involved in a somewhat childish game of cat and mouse, with her playing the part of the mouse. Or, rather, the cornered mermaid.

Leave it to Merrick to find a way to spoil such rare happiness as she'd felt when she woke this morning. She peeked around the sea grass, trying to decide if she could get back to shore without having to talk to him, and paused, her grip tightening on the greenish blades at the sight of the shark circling nearby. An ominous chill flared along her scales and up her spine.

It wasn't huge, by shark standards, but it was a great white, with rows and rows of razor-like teeth. She didn't stand a chance against it, even if it was a baby. The shark circled again, and was soon joined by a second, which was closely followed by three more, two of which were much larger than the others. Emma shrank into the shadows, terror gripping her throat, hoping the coral and seaweed were enough to keep her hidden from the predators. Even though the sun was still high in the sky, this far down, the ocean was dark and cold, muting colors that she often found vibrant and heightening her growing fear.

Now would be a great time for Merrick to find me. Unfortunately, for the first time all day, he was nowhere in sight. Panic threatened to overwhelm her, but Emma kept still, fingers clutching clumps of seaweed, and watched as the sharks continued to circle overhead. Maybe there *were* benefits to having Merrick around.

Unfortunately, even he was no match for a pod of sharks. And on the day she was most excited to go home, she settled in to wait it out. Alone.

It felt like hours passed while she hid in the shadows of coral, heart pounding, doing her best not to make any sudden movements that might attract the predators' attention. Where was Merrick? Was he really cowardly enough to be hiding?

She didn't want to think of James, didn't want to fantasize about what it would be like to have him hold her like she meant something to him, but hiding in the cold dark water, fearful of each movement, each throb of her heart as the current pulled her hair in circles above her head—she couldn't help it.

In Merrick's ocean, when she encountered danger, when she most needed help, he—the merman who was destined to be her mate—left her for the sharks. Yet last night, when trouble had come to her home, James—who had no obligation to her whatsoever—dove to the rescue without question or hesitation.

After what had to be more than an hour, maybe two, the sharks swam out of her sightline. Emma's muscles shook with anxiety. She couldn't move. Logically, she knew she should leave, that the sharks had probably found an interest other than a skinny, tasteless mermaid, but instinct held her back, kept her silent and still in her tiny place of hiding for another twenty or thirty minutes. It wasn't until an injured swordfish lumped along, leaking a thin trail of blood behind it, that the sharks shot out of hiding and ripped apart their new prey.

Seizing the opportunity, Emma swam in the opposite direction, skimming the sand until she was certain she was out of sight—and then she aimed for shore with everything she had, determined to survive—somehow.

A GLANCE AT THE CLOCK had Emma almost cursing. Almost. Keith was probably sick of Mrs. Hall by now. Or vice versa. The glass replacement people were supposed to be at her house ten minutes ago, and James an hour before that. She put the car in gear and peeled away from the curb, zooming up the street and through a yellow light.

It was all Merrick's fault. If she'd been any bigger, or that coral formation any smaller, she'd have been a goner. Thank goodness her diverse and lovely corner of ocean had a few spectacular places to hide.

She sped across town, blowing all speed limits until she hit the brakes and turned onto her street at a more reasonable pace. A breath of relief filled her chest when she saw the glass replacement truck in the driveway, large panes of glass strapped to its side and two men already inside pulling the plywood away from the window frame.

Keith met her on the sidewalk, twirling Mrs. Hall's key ring around his finger. "Where've you been? Mrs. Hall said you shouldn't have left me at her house so long, so I went home. I've been worried sick."

Emma's gut twisted with guilt. She'd planned to take him to visit Gran today, but obviously, that was out. "Sorry. Got stuck in traffic."

His mouth formed an O, his eyebrows raised in disbelief as he followed her up the sidewalk. "You've been gone forever. Anyway, it's a good thing I was here. The glass guys were about to leave."

"Yes, good thing you were the responsible one today. I don't know about you, but I don't want to spend another night with a broken window."

"I would make you come with me to stay at Mrs. Hall's house."

She squeezed her brother's shoulder. "Well, that won't be necessary because the window will be fixed soon, thanks to you."

Emma introduced herself to the men replacing the glass, offered them bottles of water, and apologized for being late. When she checked on Keith in the kitchen, the lingering scent of sausage reminded her of her playful conversation with James that morning. "Do you know if James came by?"

"Yeah." Keith dug in his pocket and handed Emma a folded piece of paper. "He said to tell you he's sorry he missed you, and he wants you come to his basketball game tonight if you can. He said I can come too."

"He did?"

"Yeah."

Emma unfolded the paper and read the hastily scrawled note:

Don't argue. Just come. Bring Keith. We'll get food after. Please. James.

"Those glass guys said they'll take about two hours," Keith said.

Emma peered around the corner to check on the progress. One man carried the plywood out the front door, while another pulled a tool out of a sling on his hip and went to work, removing the rest of the broken pane.

"Can we go to the basketball game when they're done?" Keith pleaded.

James had mentioned the game when they arrived at his

house. "Game's at six, if you're interested." Then—almost as an afterthought—he had picked up her hand and grazed his lips across her knuckles. "It was great to spend the night with you. I hope we can do it again really soon."

She must've looked shocked because he grinned and jumped out, fleeing to the house to wave from the porch. In that moment, she'd known she'd probably end up at the game, even though she hadn't attended a sporting event since last year.

James had been there for her when she needed it, so she should support him by going to watch him play. That was what friends did. Wasn't it?

Starting a relationship with him couldn't end well. He was human, and in five months, she'd be a full-on mermaid. They couldn't end up together long-term. Yet, hadn't a relationship already developed between them? It didn't really matter how that relationship was defined, just that it existed. If she was careful, kept an acceptable distance, they might be able to be friends. Friends were good. When she disappeared, James would probably be sad—and she would definitely miss him on some level—but they'd both be able to move on and get past it. In time.

Maybe it was okay to be his friend.

But.

Things between them had changed. Hard as she tried, Emma couldn't deny that James wasn't the kind of person she'd originally thought. He was so much more. And less. The idea of just being his friend while he went back to seeing someone else made her sick to her stomach. Now Keith was urging her to go, and take him with her. Not to support her school or feel spirit for her team, but to see James play. To support him the way he'd supported her last night. *I owe him that much.*

Besides, she'd promised Heather she would go to some school functions. Maybe Heather could break away for a minute and sit with them. She wouldn't mind watching the squad perform at halftime.

"Earth to Emma." Keith waved a hand in front of her face. "Do you want to go or not?"

"Oh, all right. We probably should." She took out cheese, sandwich meat, and bread and began building Keith's dinner. "I owe him at least that much after last night."

Keith had to raise his voice over the sound of a power drill. "I told you he's nice."

Emma had to bite back a smile. After spending a day and night with him, she knew James wasn't a bad guy. He had shown her a soft, protective side Emma never imagined he possessed. It was time for her to admit that this time, she'd been wrong, and Keith was right.

A *RIVER OF SWEAT* rolled down James's back as he limped to the bench. It was almost halftime, and he hadn't seen her. Maybe it was better this way—he sucked tonight. They were behind by twenty, in large part because he couldn't keep his head together. It was no wonder, after spending the night at Emma's—even on the family room floor.

Considering their recent history, his time with her seemed hard to believe—unreal, even. The day they met, she'd become a sort-of fantasy, the essence of everything he wanted in a girl but could never really have. A mystery he would never solve. Fragile enough to fall apart in his arms, and then strong enough to straighten her spine and clean up the glass. Breakable, like one of the porcelain sea sculptures on the mantle in her house, yet sturdy enough to be fiercely protective of Keith. Untouchable as jewelry in a glass case until he'd somehow managed to see how she fit in his arms last night.

He'd gone there to get her out of his head, and she'd pitched a tent and started a raging bonfire.

Someone handed him water in a paper cup. James dumped it over his head and gulped from his bottle, listening to Coach feed them a new strategy for the second half. His eyes kept drifting to the bleachers, watching for Emma's fiery red hair, hoping those bright green eyes might be there, seeing him play.

"You got that, Phelps?"

James's attention snapped back to the coach. "Yes, sir."

"Start making some shots and landing some rebounds if you don't want to sit the bench. We don't go to state if we lose more than two games. You know what state could mean for us."

"Yeah." James wiped the sweat off his forehead with a towel. "No championship for you—no scholarship for me. I got it." When the buzzer sounded, he took his place on the court and glanced one last time at the bleachers.

And there she was at the very top, leaning against the wall between Keith and one of the cheerleaders—that Heather girl—looking exhausted, fragile, and as beautiful as ever. As his heart swelled, his frazzled nerves calmed.

She came.

He didn't care what being here meant to her, because she *was* here, which told him he had a chance. Maybe just one. But one was enough. He'd make it enough.

In the second half, James focused, got his head in the game in a way it hadn't been in the first half, and helped his team bring the score to a more manageable level. With five minutes on the clock, it was anyone's game. James got his hands on the ball and drove, dodging a guard, then jumped high for a layup. The guard rebounded, dribbled to half court, and passed the ball to El Camino's center. James caught up with the center under the basket and grabbed hold of the ball, wrestling for it. The whistle blew, and the referee called a jump ball in the Pirates' favor. The center—a tall, gangly kid barely old enough for the two long hairs on his chin—scowled at James, swearing under his breath, and vowed to get even.

James stood on his side of center court, waiting for Lyle to pass him the ball. Lyle's tongue snaked out to lick his lips. He nodded, leaving their personal antagonism off the court in an unspoken mutual understanding. This could be an important win. With a minute left, Lyle hurled the ball. James caught it, pivoted toward the basket, and made for the three-point line. Mark moved into defense, clearing the way so James could take aim. As the ball left his hands, sailing toward the basket, an elbow caught James in the stomach, doubling him over, where he caught a fist to the face. The blows knocked him flat.

A whistle rang in his ears. He pounded the floor with his fists and opened his stinging eyes. His teammate, Cameron, offered him a hand and pulled him up off the floor. "Hey, man, you okay?"

"Yeah." James wiped blood from his nose with the bottom of his jersey, swearing, and shook his head to clear it. "What was that?"

"No idea." Cameron wiped sweaty hands on his shorts. "But you get a shot."

James grinned at the scoreboard as the numbers jumped. 37-38. El Camino still led by one point. On the court, Lyle and Mark were nose to nose with the El Camino guards, exchanging heated words and open threats. The ref called a flagrant on El Camino, giving James two shots rather than just one. James grabbed Mark's jersey and pulled him back. "Let's play."

The players positioned themselves behind the foul line with thirty seconds on the clock. James dribbled the ball once, twice, three times and took aim, hoping Emma was paying attention. The ball swished through the net without touching the rim, and as the audience cheered, Cameron slapped his hand in a show of support. The ref threw the ball back to James, and he glanced into the stands as he dribbled, setting himself up for the second shot.

She was still there, hands clasped together and pressed against her chin in anxiety. He winked, vowing to make this one for her, and shot. It wasn't as clean as the first, taking a long moment to swirl around the rim, but then it fell through the net, jumping the Pirates ahead by one.

A cheer erupted in the stands as James chased the ball and Mark and Lyle blocked El Camino from taking more shots until the clock ran out.

After the buzzer, James jogged across the court to a cluster of people, ducked past a bunch of girls—including Nettie, his one-time hallway flame—and grabbed Emma around the waist, twirling her in a circle as her cheerleader friend waved and jogged toward the girls' locker room. Emma squealed in surprise, but was grinning when he set her down. "Glad you finally made it. I thought you weren't going to show."

"Sorry we were so late." She hitched her purse up higher on her shoulder. "The glass guys took longer than I expected."

James wiped a bead of sweat off his forehead. "Doesn't matter. You're here now."

"Yep, I am." She slid her hands in her back pockets, like she didn't know what else to do with them. "Good game. I'd forgotten how much I enjoy watching basketball."

"Hi, James." Keith sidled up to them, a can of pop in each of his hands. "I got you a drink, Emma. The other machine was broken, so I couldn't get any snacks."

"Thanks. A drink is great. Give me a sugar boost till I can get some food." At James's quizzical look, she added, "I haven't eaten since breakfast."

"You shoulda had a sandwich like I did," Keith scolded. "Bread is good for you like vegetables are good for me."

She shook her head as if this was an old argument. "Not even close to the same."

James glanced at the locker room doors, wondering if the coaches had started the after-game meeting yet. "Can you hang out while I shower?"

"Um . . ." Her eyes darted nervously to the same doors.

Nettie caught his eye, her face twisting into what James could only imagine was her look of death. No wonder Emma hesitated. "I'll hurry and clean up so we can go get something to eat." He pulled his jersey away from his sticky skin, hoping he didn't reek, but pretty sure he did. "I mean, if you don't mind driving."

She was still watching those doors, lip caught between her teeth, trepidation in her eyes, but then she took a deep breath and looked at him. Really looked. And smiled. "Okay, sure. That's fine. Just . . . please don't leave me out here very long."

Without thinking, he stepped close and pressed his lips to her forehead. "Be back soon."

It took everything in him to resist the urge to look back and see her expression as he started for the locker room. The kiss wasn't even in the vicinity of her lips, and shouldn't have made his nerves jump the way it did. Emma brought out a gentle side of him he'd never found before, never shown to any other girl—including his long-estranged mother.

"Hey." Heather caught his jersey before he could enter the locker room.

James glanced at Emma, relieved to see that she was focused on Keith, and still grinning. It wouldn't help to have Emma think he was picking up on her best friend. "Uh, hey?"

"I just need to say one thing," Heather murmured, her

voice low enough that James could barely hear. "You be careful with Emma." She didn't say anything more, but the way her eyes pierced him spoke volumes more than any words could.

The locker room smelled like a cave of sweaty old men just off a five-day fishing trip, but James was so used to it, his nose didn't even burn anymore. He leaned against a locker, listening to the last of the team meeting.

"One point won this game, but your performance tonight was just not enough. Not if we're going to make it to the finals." Coach paced in front of his office, his eyes catching and holding those of each person on the team, but resting longer and harder on James. "You've got to keep your heads together. Put your hearts and souls into the game. Starting next week, we're extending practice by thirty minutes a day, and adding 'voluntary' conditioning whenever the court's available on weekends. That might mean evenings. And by 'voluntary,' I mean 'mandatory.' There will be no missed practices, no exceptions. Now, go celebrate your victory and then get some rest this weekend. You're going to need it."

James took a quick shower—soaping twice to be absolutely rid of the stink before he got in the car with Emma—then pulled on clean clothes and dabbed his neck with cologne. He was running a comb through his hair with the help of a mirror stuck to the inside of his locker door when Mark and Lyle approached.

"Dude, Lyle," Mark said, all traces of teamwork and friendship gone. "Did you see the tweet? Our boy James laid a lucky kiss on the ice queen."

Lyle laughed, low and mean. "Sounds like the whole school saw."

"Careful, James," Mark warned. "Get caught in her snare, and your life will change forever."

James ground his teeth, clenching his hands into fists, and then forced himself to relax. He closed the locker, turning slowly to face the guys. "Who did you just call an ice queen?"

Lyle laughed, but his eyes were hard as granite. "She's using you, dude." He squeezed James's shoulder, hard. "Let her get close enough, she'll screw up the team."

James restrained himself, knowing Emma was waiting, and shoved past his teammates. "Emma Harris couldn't hurt a fly." He started to walk away, but then Mark was in his face, shoving him against a locker.

"I know exactly why you were so screwed up during the first half, pretty boy. We all do. But I'm telling you now, that girl is trouble with a capital T."

"Shut. Up," James said through clenched teeth. The urge to fish hook Mark in the side of the head was overwhelming.

"You wanna go messing up your life over a crazy girl with ice water for blood, you go right ahead. But wait until after State—you hear me? She'll twist your head so far into the ground that you won't be able to breathe without her help, and then drive away in that pretty car of hers without a backward glance, just like she did to Tom. Guy was an all-star center with pro potential before her. Now he's screwed forever. Because of her."

Liquid hot rage boiled up in James, but he tamped it down, determined not to be provoked into getting himself suspended from the team.

Lyle moved in next to Mark, his hot breath carrying a hint of the smell James associated with the stinky locker room. "I'll tell you now—she feels as good as she looks. I would know." His hands caressed empty air. "Still not worth it. Get over the curiosity and move on."

Mark's hands grasped James's shoulders and were the only reason James didn't lose control and wail on Lyle. What was left of James's lunch churned in his stomach, his shoulders aching from the words his brain was still trying to process.

"There's poison under that creamy skin." Lyle walked away, and Mark shoved James against the locker once more, and then followed his friend outside.

James turned and punched a locker, wincing when the metal sliced through the skin on one of his knuckles, and then he hit it again. He sank onto a bench, dropping his head in his hands and taking deep, measured breaths as he tried to make sense of what they'd said.

He already knew Emma didn't date much. She never even spent time with friends, other than Heather. She had secrets—lots of them—but that didn't mean she was using him. What did Lyle even mean by that? The thing that heated his blood was the insinuation that either of them had been intimate with her. Could that part be true? She had seemed nervous about sticking around to wait after the game.

Maybe it was irrational to be jealous about guys in her past, but he couldn't stop the overwhelming rage caused by the very thought of Emma and Lyle together.

James stayed in the quiet locker room for another few

minutes, trying to piece together the things he knew about Emma firsthand and what he'd just been told. By the time he stood up, his hands shook—though he couldn't decide if it was rage, fear, or nerves. There were a lot of things he didn't know about Emma, but also a lot of things he did—things he'd learned in a few short days. Whatever those guys said, Emma wasn't *that* girl. She couldn't be.

He smoothed his hair and took another calming breath, then grabbed his gym bag and headed for the door, not wanting to keep her waiting any longer.

Tonight, he'd celebrate with Emma and Keith. And tomorrow—if he was still bugged by this newest development—he'd investigate the accusations. One way or another, he'd find answers.

JAMES GRABBED A PIZZA (with a side salad for Emma) at a small family-run joint, happy to be within walking distance of Breakwater Way beach. Emma had been edgy at the school, and he'd watched her visibly relax as they drove nearer to the ocean, like something about the combination of sand and water brought her peace. Or maybe it was the growing distance from other people, distance from her memories. He hoped the sea air would bring him peace as well—or at least help calm the storm of confusion Lyle and Mark had started.

He met her and Keith at the car with the food, a six-pack of pop, and a stack of napkins. "Picnic, anyone?"

Emma nodded, her eyes questioning. He forced himself to smile and rested his hand at the small of her back. The immediate jolt to his system should have surprised him, but it didn't. Not at this point. Why did it hurt so much to look at her?

"Sure." Keith bounded across the street to the soft white sand. "Race ya."

They let him go, both aware that once again, something had changed between them.

"What's wrong?" Emma's bleak tone had him turning his head to meet her eyes. She blinked, her candid green eyes absorbing the chill. A flood of warmth rolled over the frost he'd felt in the locker room, thawing the fist of ice that had seized his chest and suspended him in confusion, preventing him from feeling, saving him from falling. He might not know her as well as he'd like, but right now, she deserved better than his doubts. The warmth he'd drawn from her flowed into his voice. "I think I'm crashing after our adventurous weekend."

Emma's expression softened. "It *has* been rather exciting. Guess neither of us got a lot of sleep." She grabbed his bicep for balance, her thin fingers squeezing while she kicked off her sandals, and James's heart fluttered. "I'm not sure what I would've done if you hadn't been there last night. You're a good friend."

"Friend."

Emma bent to pick up her shoes and James bent with her, setting the pizza box and pop on the sand so he could grab her hands as they both stood again, Emma's shoes forgotten. "What if I want more than friendship?"

"What if?" she breathed.

His thumbs drew circles over her knuckles as he inched her closer until his hands rested on her shoulders, careful to keep his touch soft, light, and allow her the freedom to pull back and run away at any point, if she wanted. Space he sensed she needed. But she didn't move.

"I don't know much about you. I don't know your parents, or what you were like as a kid, or even your favorite foods—yet. But I know you and I were not made to be 'just friends.'"

Her quick intake of breath didn't surprise him, but the frank honesty reflected in her emerald eyes did. "Maybe not. But what if friendship is all I can give?"

"Then I'll stick around and keep trying until you change your mind." The breath he'd been holding trickled out slowly as he bent toward her—his heart pounding a hard and heavy rock song.

"Hey!" Keith stood on a concrete picnic table down the beach. "You guys coming, or what?"

Ignoring the interruption, James didn't drop his hands until Emma pulled away. "Yeah, we're coming." She turned to stare across the endless expanse of ocean and lowered her voice to speak just to James again. "It's a bad idea for us to be more."

"Why?" he asked from behind her.

"It's just . . . We should talk. But not . . ." She picked up the food and took a step toward Keith. "Not now. Later. We'll talk later."

She walked to the table and set the pizza on it, beckoning for him to hurry up. Everything about her filled his mind until she was all he could see, all he could think about, even when he was playing ball. No girl ever had that effect on him before, and he found it both refreshing and terrifying. Whatever she had to say—whatever secrets she told—wouldn't, *couldn't* matter. Mark and Lyle were wrong. There was nothing hard or cold about her. Emma Harris was the softest, warmest person he'd ever met. And he was crazy about her.

Circled around one end of the picnic table, James and Keith devoured the pizza and Emma polished off the salad, all three watching the white-capped waves crash into the shore.

"Pizza's better than meatloaf." Keith wiped away a string of cheese stuck on his chin. "Last Saturday, we ate meatloaf. I like this Saturday better. Pizza goes good with basketball."

Emma wrinkled her nose. "Basketball pizza? Gross."

"Too chewy," James added.

"You can't cook a basketball." Keith covered his smile with a napkin. "Duh. If you put one in the oven, it would stink like a pile of fish guts and dirty socks."

James let out a bark of laughter. The more time he spent with the kid, the more he liked him.

Emma looked horrified. "How would you know what cooked basketball smells like?"

"Because I cooked one once. And then there was a fire in the oven and so I had to call the fire department and Mom was going to murder me, but then she didn't because it was an accident."

Her hands covered her mouth in horror, but her eyes danced with merriment. "When did you do that? Why don't I remember?"

He tapped his chin with a finger. "A long time ago. Months. You were at a sleepover with Heather and some other girls. Mom and Dad said I am never allowed to use the oven again."

"I wondered where that rule came from." She burst out laughing. "Thinking back, I do remember something about a weird smell that didn't go away for a long time. Why didn't anyone tell me?"

He bit off a good fourth of his slice of pizza, chewed, and swallowed. "'Cause it would make you worry more."

"You make it sound like that's all I ever do." Emma brushed off her hands, then flattened her pop can against the table and tossed it in the empty pizza box, along with her salad container. "Besides, that's my job as a big sister."

Keith smashed his can as well. "But I'm big too now, Emma. I'm growing up fast."

Emma shook her head sadly. "I know."

While James took care of the trash, Emma ambled to the wet sand and let the water lick her toes. Tendrils of hair curled around her face, twirled and tossed in the breeze. The three-quarter moon shone brightly overhead, reflecting off the water and making her hair glow like fire. A wave crested in, splashing her feet and ankles, and she laughed—a high, soft-pitched trill that sounded one-hundred-percent female.

The breath backed up in his lungs. "Keith, can you do me a favor?"

"Okay, James. Okay."

James picked up Emma's keys off the table and folded them into Keith's hand. "Go hang out in the car. I need to talk to Emma. Privately."

Keith opened his fist and stared at the keys. "I'm not supposed to touch Emma's car without permission."

James's eyes had returned to the vision on the beach, and his heart thudded with intent. "You have my permission. I'll give you five bucks for five minutes."

"I want a ride on your motorcycle."

"Fine. Whatever. Just stay there until we come back, okay?"

Emma faced the horizon, staring far into the distance as James approached. His footsteps caused little splashes and ripples in the otherwise peaceful ebb and flow of water swirling near her feet. She turned, and her smile faded; the pulse at the base of her throat jumped. He slid his fingers into the hair at her neck, pulling more pieces out of the clip, and stroked her jaw with his thumbs.

"Emma," he murmured. "Please don't say no."

Her eyes widened, and her full lips parted, but she didn't say the word that would have stopped him. He touched his lips to hers, soft. She melted into him, molded her lips to his so they fit together like pieces of a puzzle. His world tilted, spun on its axis, and he drew her closer for balance. Her hands slid up his chest, wrapped around his neck, and James lost himself in a kiss that was far more than he ever imagined. *More. More. More.*

About the time breathing became difficult and he contemplated moving their relationship to the next level right there on the sand, he pulled away. It took more strength than it should have to break apart and nuzzle his face in her neck. How was it possible to feel your heartbeat in your toes with your feet submerged in cold water?

Finally, Emma broke the silence. "Wasn't expecting that."

Still clutching her against his chest, James groaned. "Honestly, neither was I."

"About that conversation."

James loosened his grip so he could rest his forehead against hers. "Can it wait? I mean, I want to talk, and we will. Soon. But let's not ruin this perfect moment with imperfect words."

"Yes. It can wait. It should wait." Her shoulders relaxed, and a relieved smile found her lips. "You're right. Now's not the time for a deep discussion."

She nestled against his chest, arms clasped around his waist. A swell pushed against their calves, then reversed and sucked back out again. Emma giggled. "If we don't move, the tide might catch us up and drag us under."

"I don't mind getting pulled in, as long as you're with me." James said, holding her arms to keep them both steady. "We'll drown together."

Something flickered in her eyes, but she blinked and it was gone. "True enough. Together is always better than alone." She backed out of the water and unrolled the cuffs in her jeans, then stood, looking around, as if remembering something she'd lost. "Where's Keith?"

"I sent him to wait in the car."

"Oh, no." Emma's eyes grew wide, her expression urgent. "Does he have the keys?"

"Yeah," James said, hesitant. "I thought he might want to listen to the stereo."

She turned, swore, and pulled James with her. They splashed to where they'd left their shoes, then Emma let go of

James's hand and bolted up the slope of sand to the parking lot.

"What?" James yelled after her. "What's the matter?"

"The last time Keith got a hold of my keys and sat alone in my car, he tried to drive it." A gust of wind swallowed the rest of her words, but what he heard was enough. Emma reached the edge of the sand just as an engine revved hard. James lengthened his stride to catch up. Keith wrecking Emma's car wouldn't be a good way to end the night.

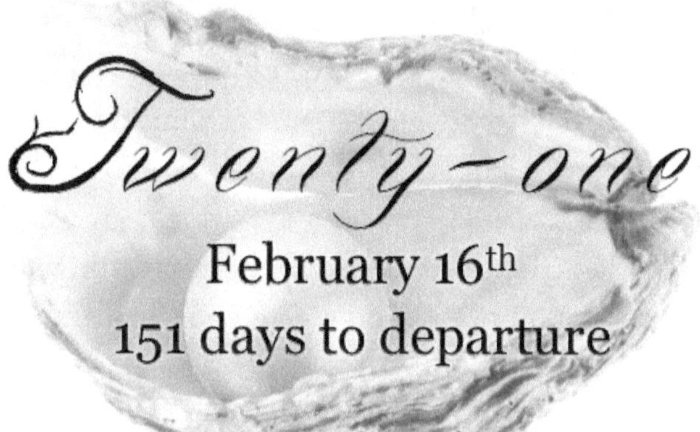

Twenty-one

February 16th
151 days to departure

SUNDAY MORNING, EMMA WOKE early and helped Keith iron his shirt so he could attend church with Mrs. Hall. He'd been a visitor in the elderly woman's congregation every Sunday for close to two years, not necessarily because he was religious, but more—Emma thought—because he enjoyed escorting the plucky widow to her most favorite location to collect gossip. Plus, according to Mrs. Hall, the congregants adored him.

Emma loved that he went because it left her free to visit Gran without having to worry about what her brother overheard in their conversation. And with everything that had happened lately, Emma needed Gran's listening ear more than ever.

"Stay out of Mrs. Hall's driver's seat," Emma warned, straightening Keith's tie. "I mean it."

"I wasn't going to drive your car," he mumbled. "I just wanted to see what would happen if I pulled the lever."

"Thank goodness for the emergency brake, or both you and my car might have ended up in the ocean."

"It's not a boat, Emma. Boats don't have wheels."

"Exactly the problem." She tried not to dwell on the rush of fear she'd felt, or how Keith had almost ruined the giddy sensation that had overtaken her on the beach with James. Luckily, they had ended the night on a high note, with James sneaking in one last, quick kiss when Keith wasn't looking.

Her phone buzzed, and Emma glanced at the text from Heather, wondering if her friend could now read minds.

Dying here. Need details, stat.

She watched Keith cross the yard, look both ways, twice, and then continue across the street, before replying:

There was kissing. I like him. A lot.

She grabbed her keys and buckled into her car, grinning when the reply came:

YES! I knew it.
Next stop: date-land
Congratulations
You're in a relationship.

Relationship. That word—that one word—snapped Emma back to reality.

How had she let this happen?

Though the clouds were dark and heavy, she put the top down for the drive. Even a distant flash of lightning didn't change her mind. Getting wet was the least of her worries, and she hoped the ocean air would help clear her head. The powerful harmony of Secondhand Serenade poured out of her stereo as she cruised up the coast, remembering the sweet warmth of James's arms around her. She'd never been kissed like that before, by Tom or anyone else. Like she was fragile and precious, like she was both air and water, like a line of electricity zipped from him into her, where it lit up her insides, lighthouse-style. She licked her lips, hoping to find a leftover taste of him, but got her coconut lip gloss instead. Maybe later she'd invite him over.

Yes, good idea, Emma. Spend more time with him. Fall in love if you want. Then take him to the cove and introduce him to Merrick. That'll turn out well.

Her shoulders tensed when she thought about how fast her time was ticking away, second by second, whirling into a black hole until life as she knew it was over.

At the assisted living facility, she parked near the entrance and breezed through the lobby and down the hall to her grandmother's room. She knocked lightly, hoping Gran was awake. Here was the one person who knew the whole truth about Emma's heritage and where she was headed, and the only person with whom Emma could talk about it.

"Gran?" She twisted the knob and pushed the door open.

"He escaped." Gran, reclined in a cushy chair on the other side of the room, turned down the volume on her TV.

"Took him twenty years, but he tunneled through the wall—outsmarted them all."

"Always does." Emma stifled a giggle as she perched on a chair next to Gran's recliner. The movie replayed at least once a month. Gran had probably seen it a hundred times, yet continued to be surprised by the outcome. "How are you feeling today?"

"I'm all right." Gran tucked a hair into her loose salt-and-pepper bun and lowered the foot rest on her chair with a great deal of huffing and grunting. "Don't move as easily as I used to. Feel like every part of me creaks." Indeed, the recliner groaned as if to prove the point, while Gran's chocolate eyes appraised Emma with a shrewd once-over. "You seem happier than usual."

Emma had to bite her lip to keep from grinning like a fool. What was wrong with her? "Someone threw a brick through our window Friday night."

Gran tapped the edge of the armrest with yellowed fingernails, shaking her head. "Always a reason to smile."

Emma caught the sarcasm in the tone and pressed her lips together. "It is when you're in the kitchen arguing with a boy you thought you hated, and he comes to the rescue like a . . . a . . ."

"Movie hero?" Gran supplied.

"Yes." Emma nodded. "Exactly." She told Gran about Friday night, including how James slept over, then skipped to the following evening and the picnic on the beach. "He kissed me, Gran. I tried not to like him. For the past several months, I've dug out every possible reason why I should hate him, but I just can't. I don't."

"Honey, you shouldn't do this to yourself. It'll only make your future harder."

"I know, Gran. But he makes me feel . . ." *Special. Happy. Alive.*

Gran leaned forward to squeeze Emma's knee with a misshapen hand. "You're not human. And as much as I've searched for a way—any way—to halt the transition you're experiencing, there's nothing we can do."

Emma's breath hitched. Wasn't this what she'd been telling herself all along? But hearing the words from Gran's mouth made reality so much more stark, more hopeless. Emma's eyes prickled, her voice cracked. "I hate them. All of them. They left me, Gran. Abandoned me—an infant—to be raised by the very society they pretend to detest. And except for Merrick, none of them has ever come to see me, to meet me. But you—and Mom and Dad—Keith. You would never desert me. You would never have expected someone else to take care of me, would you?"

Gran stood, feet shuffling across the cool tiles so she could sit next to her granddaughter and pull Emma's head to her shoulder, stroke her hair. "No, darling. We wouldn't have left you. I've loved you from the moment I opened my door and found you on my porch, and I'll continue to love you forever and always."

Emma allowed a hot tear to blaze down her cheek. "I'm changing fast now. Have to swim for at least two hours every couple of days. We should tell Mom and Dad. I don't want them to think I ran away on purpose, that I'd choose to leave them."

Gran's foot twitched in a spasm. "I'll explain when it happens. If you tell them now, they'll do everything they can to stop time—and we both know time can't be stopped. Save them the torment of knowing they're about to lose you and can do nothing about it."

"If they knew . . ."

"No. They wouldn't have gone to Greece. Nothing could have taken them from you so close to your change. You know as well as I do that they probably wouldn't allow you out of their sight—and I know you need your freedom. Especially juggling this James boy with your Merrick."

Emma's head snapped up, glaring out the window. "He's not *my* Merrick. Do you know what he did to me yesterday, Gran? He chased me into shark territory and left me trapped in a coral formation for three hours. Three. I had stuff to do, and he found it highly entertaining to watch me cower from five very large predators with extremely sharp teeth. Just because I'll be forced to live in Atlantis doesn't mean I have to marry that imbecile. I refuse."

"Sharks?" Gran's face paled. "He chased you toward sharks? How could he put you in danger like that?"

A sob worked out of her throat. "Because he doesn't care if I die. Not really. Probably hopes I will so he doesn't have to deal with the mermaid who wishes she was a human girl."

"It can't be that."

"Really, Gran? Then why?" Emma curled a lock of fiery hair around her fingers until it pulled painfully. "Every time I swim, he follows me, chases me around, tries to escort me wherever I go. And I'm pretty sure it's not always his choice. He makes me feel like an object instead of a person."

Gran patted Emma's knee. "Oh, my darling, just when I thought you might be gaining a better understanding of men. Remember in kindergarten when that boy pushed you down every day at recess? Your parents were so angry. Your father marched to the principal's office demanding that the boy be punished. Remember?"

"How could I forget?" Emma smiled, despite the tears on her cheek. "Poor kid must have been terrified. I was."

Gran shook her head. "All he really wanted was for you to notice him."

"Okay, Gran, but we were five. Merrick's a full-grown merman, at least five years older than me. Way past the kindergarten stage."

"Maybe not." She covered a yawn and reached a box of tissues off a nearby shelf. "We can't put a timeline on a civilization we don't understand."

Emma accepted the entire box, removing several to dry her cheeks and blow her nose. "Why me, Gran? Why couldn't I just be human?"

Gran sighed, wiping a smudge off Emma's cheek with her thumb. "I've been asking God that question for seventeen years."

"So what do I do?"

Gran stood and waddled to her recliner. "Tolerate Merrick—and if he ever chases you into danger again, punch his lights out." She sat, groaning, and pulled a blanket over her lap. "And I'm so sorry, darling, but you have to let this new boy go. For his sake, and yours. Last thing you need is another broken heart to leave behind."

"And if I don't? If I can't?"

Gran tilted her head against the cushion. "Then warn him that you'll hurt him, and make the most of whatever time you can steal. But be prepared. Something like this will make your leaving so much harder."

EMMA KNEW SHE OUGHT to hurry home, but as she started her car, she realized that the tears she'd shed in Gran's room were only the beginning. Unreleased sobs gathered in her chest, making it difficult for her to drive, so she stopped at the first beach she found and ran to the edge of the sand, screaming angry profanities and hurling rocks at the water.

"I hate . . . I hate . . . I hate you. I hate them. I hate the ocean. I hate my skin that turns to scales and my gills that keep me coming back here again and again and again. I don't want this! Do you hear me? I don't. Want. This."

Throat raw, hands stinging from the sharp edges of the rocks, Emma fell on her knees in the sand and sobbed out the hopelessness that had become her life. A long time later, she trudged back to her car, feeling lighter, if still conflicted.

The drive home brought her to some decisions. Gran was right. She couldn't tell her parents. Not until the very last second. She would spare them the heartache she'd been living with for the last two years. In the meantime, she'd do her best to teach Keith how not to let people take advantage of him.

And she'd let go of James.

He was a good guy. A nice guy. And he didn't deserve to

have his heart broken over her when she had the ability to prevent it.

When she arrived home, she called for Keith, but he didn't answer. Mrs. Hall must have taken him to lunch. Exhausted from crying and unable to consider doing anything productive, she crawled fully clothed into bed and buried herself under a mountain of blankets.

THREE HOURS LATER, her complaining stomach forced her out of bed. She stumbled to the kitchen, determined to ice her sticky, puffy eyes before they got any worse. If they looked as bad as they felt, people would think she'd been beaten. Again.

"Keith?" she called. "Are you here?"

No answer. She ran into each of the rooms in the house, shouting his name. When she didn't find him, fear snaked up her spine and had her pulling out her phone. "Mrs. Hall? Is Keith still with you?"

The voice on the other end came across confused. "No, dear. I took him home right after services. Needed a Sunday nap. Did you check his room?"

"Yes, I did." She spun around, her eyes darting every which way. "How long ago did you leave him here?"

"Oh, honey, hours ago."

Emma stopped cold. "Hours?" Mrs. Hall said something on the other end of the line, but Emma clicked "end" without hearing. *Where would he go?* Sliding on her flip-flops, she grabbed her keys and opened the garage, wondering where to even start. She drove up and down streets, around the school, double- and triple-checked a nearby dog-walking park where Keith liked to watch owners and animals play. After over an hour, she headed home, deciding it was time to call her parents and maybe the police. When she saw the figure sitting on the front porch, twin bombs of relief and anger exploded in her.

Without bothering to close the garage, she slammed the car door and stalked to her brother. "Where have you been? I've been searching for you all over town. I was just about to call the police."

He wouldn't look her in the eyes, which meant he was trying to hide something. "I went for a walk."

"For four hours? Where did you go—San Diego?"

"No, I went to visit my new friend Max, and we played video games at the pizza place where you and me went with James."

She closed her eyes and lifted her face to the sky, gritting her teeth. When she thought she was composed enough not to yell, she opened her eyes and used the calmest voice she could muster. "Keith, you're supposed to tell me when you're going somewhere, and you're not allowed to go places with friends until I've met them, remember?"

Keith stood and stomped his foot, folding his arms across

his chest, equally frustrated. "You weren't here, and I didn't know where *you* were, so I couldn't tell you. And you have met Max. He said he talks to you all the time."

"Max who?"

"I'm not telling you anymore." Keith pivoted on his heel. "I'm going inside."

"Keith." Emma kept her voice firm. "The next time you decide to go somewhere and can't find me for whatever reason, you leave me a note. Or better yet, call my cell phone and leave a message."

He humphed, but didn't answer.

"Leave me a message, Keith. And when Mom and Dad get home from Greece, we'll talk to them about getting you a cell phone so I can track you down when you disappear."

Still scowling like a drama queen—or king, as it happened—he stomped up to his room and slammed the door, then opened it and slammed it a second time to make his point. Emma considered doing something similar. Instead, she opened the fridge and rooted around, trying to decide what to do about dinner.

Half an hour later, a couple of chicken breasts sizzled on the George Foreman grill, steam poured from the rice cooker, and a fork in a tender broccoli stalk proved Emma had cooked it to perfection. She situated two place settings on the table and was just about to call Keith to come eat when her phone rang.

"If you haven't found that boy by now, I'm calling the police."

"Hi, Mrs. Hall. I did find him. Sorry I forgot to let you know."

"That's all right, dear. Would you mind asking him if he knows what I did with my diamond-and-ruby cuff bracelet? Seems like I had it last Sunday, and this week I can't find it for the life of me."

Emma hurried up the stairs and walked through Keith's open door. "Hey, do you know what Mrs. Hall did with her red-and-white bracelet?"

He'd strewn half a Rubbermaid of Legos across his bedroom floor and continued fitting them together, ignoring Emma. She sighed. "Mrs. Hall needs to know." Nothing. "Fine. It's time to eat."

She put the phone to her ear again. "I'm sorry, Mrs. Hall. He's mad at me right now, but I'll try asking him again after dinner."

"Appreciate it," she said. "It's driving me crazy that I can't find it. Jack gave it to me for our twenty-fifth wedding anniversary. Real diamonds and rubies. Not a cheap piece of jewelry, you understand? I won't be able to sleep until I figure it out."

"I don't blame you." Emma clicked "end" and crept into the hall to watch her brother. His behavior today was beyond unusual. She was certain he was hiding something, but she was equally certain he'd guard his secret until he was good and ready to share it—or until he was discovered. Whichever came first. She watched him try to fit a bent block onto a straight one, growing more and more frustrated until he threw the entire handful against the wall, then picked up another handful and threw it, too.

Keith stood, pointing his finger at the scattered Legos. "I hate playing Legos. They're baby toys, and I'm not a baby anymore, and I'm throwing them in the garbage tomorrow." Before he could march down the stairs, Emma scampered ahead, reaching the kitchen only seconds before him.

"Ready to eat?"

"I'm hungry," he growled.

"I know." She imitated his tone, which made his frown deepen, so she frowned back. Eventually, he gave up the grump and got down to the business of eating. Relieved, Emma followed suit, and before long he'd forgotten he was angry and started talking. Not about where he'd been, or Max, or Mrs. Hall's bracelet, but at least he was talking. Emma figured that was a start.

She dreamed of James, and woke up Monday morning questioning her decision to let him go. But no matter how she justified it, she couldn't see a relationship with him coming to any kind of happy end.

The problem was that the minute she sought him out, he'd look at her with those startling gray eyes and she'd forget why they couldn't be together. She figured the best way to set him free was to do it quick and hard, like pulling off a Band-Aid. Which meant she couldn't talk to him in person.

Knowing it was cowardly, she sent a text while he was at basketball conditioning that morning.

I can't do this. I'm sorry.

And then, she resolved to avoid him, the same way she did Merrick.

Unfortunately, that was not as easy a feat as she'd hoped. She spent most of Monday and Tuesday slinking through the halls like a ninja spy, slithering around corners and hiding behind random people, using her car as a locker so she wouldn't have to risk running into him. And for the first time ever, Emma skipped class for something other than swimming, which meant lying to Gram about why she needed to be excused. Had to. James now shared her table in biology, and was only a row away in English. On Wednesday, she got smart and stayed after school, where she cornered the biology instructor and asked to be reassigned lab partners.

"Has James done something to necessitate this change?" Mr. Jensen asked.

Emma shook her head. She refused to get him in trouble. "No. It's my fault. I find it difficult to concentrate while sitting next to him, and I worry that my grade will suffer for it." *Lame, lame, lame!* But Mr. Jensen took her for her word and rearranged everyone, murmuring about how he'd just done a partner shake-up, but whatever.

The English teacher acted unconcerned, as if students asked to be moved into the front of the class every day. James was placed in the back, so as long as she arrived after him, she would be able to leave quickly without having to talk to him.

Relieved, Emma picked up her missed assignments and went in search of Keith. She really, really needed a trip to the beach.

Twenty-three

February 20th

147 days to departure

JAMES SPENT EVERY AVAILABLE MOMENT working for his uncle, hauling, cutting, and laying tile, and then mixing and spreading grout. Combined with basketball conditioning, the physically exhausting work went a long way to keeping his mind off Emma. He tried instead to focus on his bike and how quickly he'd have it running again once Ryan paid him.

Her cryptic text knotted his shoulders and pulled on his already tight muscles until his head ached, but he hadn't responded. Didn't know how. What could he even say? Best to take some space and get her out of his system. But no matter how hard he fought it, she crept back into his mind. He kept returning to the night and day he'd spent with Emma and fought the urge to call her, or to go over and talk to her, make her tell him to his face that she didn't feel anything for him, despite being busier than he'd ever been, with practically zero time to even think, let alone go see her. School, basketball, work. School, basketball, work.

This was his life. And if he was smart about it, kept his head in it, he might get to go to college—have a shot at a future he didn't hate. Then, if he still thought of her, and if she was interested, he could find time for Emma. Maybe by then she'd be better, healed from whatever demons currently haunted her. Maybe by then, she'd be ready for him. Maybe by then, *he'd* be ready for *her*.

Of course, he'd still think of her. Somehow, she'd managed to get under his skin like an infection that could only be cured by looking at her, touching her, experiencing that kiss over and over again in his head. And then all he could think about was how he wanted more of her. Thoughts like that were the reason he needed *not* to think of her. Best to avoid her altogether.

He told himself this again and again, until he didn't see her for four days that felt like a much-too-long piece of forever, and she became *all* he could think about, until nothing else mattered but finding out where she'd been and why. And what the hell that text was all about.

He ran into Heather on his way to practice on Wednesday and figured it couldn't hurt to ask. "Hey, is Emma okay?"

Heather scowled, her entire presence becoming fierce. "I haven't seen her much at all lately. And she's been mysteriously quiet when I have. Why? What did you do?"

"Nothing," he'd responded. "I haven't seen her either. Just wondering."

Finally, on Thursday, she showed up to biology looking alarmingly pale—sort of blue, thanks to the cheap florescent lighting—and so exhausted that he worried a gust of wind would blow her over. The hollows beneath her eyes were shadowed, and the rosy glow he was so fond of in her cheeks seemed to have disappeared. She didn't look at him as she took her newly assigned seat, but he wasn't sure she saw anyone else in the room either.

His concern grew when class started and she didn't open her textbook—though she had a stack of them—or take a single note. Emma always took notes in biology. What was going on? Something wasn't right with her. Maybe she was sick or something.

All through class, James fought to resist staring at her, and she continued to ignore him. Absolutely and completely. Her indifference shouldn't bother him—not after he'd been distant himself—but her ability to look and act like nothing had happened between them stabbed him in the stomach, hacking away like a hammer on a cold block of...

Ice.

The thought made him cringe. Mr. Jensen continued to lecture on who-knew-what, and James—having not heard a thing—lowered his head to the desk in shame.

Maybe she was angry that he hadn't chased her. Hadn't called, replied to her text, instant messaged, emailed, written on her wall . . . nothing. Neither of them had made promises, but still. Maybe she'd assumed or expected. Hadn't he pictured keeping her? Taking her on dates and to dances and seeing her cheering for him in the stands at his games? Didn't he still want that? He'd ignored the hundreds of communication options and waited for her to come to him. Deep down, he'd fully expected that she would. They all did, eventually.

But Emma was different. He'd known that from day one. No wonder she couldn't look at him. Mark and Lyle's accusations came back to him, echoing in his head until, unconsciously, he'd squeezed his hands into fists. The minute that bell rang, he'd corner her, talk to her, maybe even touch her for a second.

"Mr. Jensen?"

At the sound of her voice, James's head snapped up, heart sinking as Emma murmured to the teacher, then picked up her things and walked out. Every instinct screamed for him to jump up and go after her—to follow her and see if she was okay—but as he looked around the classroom, ignoring Lyle's grin and finally catching Mr. Jensen's eye, he realized that would be a really bad idea. Getting detention this week wasn't an option. Not with the new practice schedule, a game on Friday, and work besides. And Lyle was watching. If James left now, he'd never hear the end of it. Ever.

"Mr. Phelps?" Jensen's sharp voice cut into James's thoughts. "Why don't you tell us what genetics has to do with the makeup of a person's individual cells?"

"Oh, uh. Sure." He gulped, his brain sifting through all the information he remembered from last week and pushing Emma temporarily to the back of his mind. He'd track her down and talk to her after school, then he'd figure out what was what.

*E*MMA *FELT A LOT BETTER* after a swim, but it made her sad. Two months ago, she only needed thirty or forty minutes in the water every five or six days. Sometimes she could even go a full week. Now, she needed several hours every two or three days—and when she tried for three, she suffered for it.

She'd missed her last class and cheer practice, and was more than twenty minutes late getting home to meet Keith. The idea that he'd arrived to an empty house gave her the tiniest sick feeling in her stomach—he'd been acting so weird lately. The minute she let herself in, she knew he wasn't there. After looking in all the obvious places and not finding a note, she convinced herself that he was fine—probably just walking really slowly. He'd be upset if she picked him up halfway—he liked the independence—so she submerged herself in making up the school work she'd missed that afternoon.

An hour ticked by, and still no Keith. Worried, Emma walked over to Mrs. Hall's house to see if he'd gone to visit. No answer. Maybe he'd gone to the pizza joint where he'd been meeting his new friend to play the antique arcade games. Trying not to panic, she jogged back across the street and ran inside to grab her purse and keys, already composing another lecture.

I can't wait for Mom and Dad to get home.

A teenage employee who'd helped them the night they came with James swept the front walk. As Emma breezed past, she murmured, "Please be here."

The girl grinned. "You talking about that special needs boy and his hottie friend?"

Emma paused, folding her arms over her chest. "Yes, actually."

"Keith's a sweet kid." Sweat trickled down the girl's neck and she stopped sweeping to fan herself. "And he can bring his friend here anytime, with no complaints from me. Especially if Max never finds the shirt he always seems to have lost."

"Uh, okay." Emma felt her face scrunch into a confused frown as she opened the door and went inside. She found Keith sitting at a corner table by himself, drinking a soft drink—though she had no idea where he'd come up with the money to buy it. More relieved than angry, Emma shook her head and sat next to her brother. "Did you forget something today?"

Keith shrugged. She could tell from his expression that he knew exactly what she was talking about, but chose not to answer anyway.

"Can we talk about what's going on? You're hiding something from me, and I'm worried that it's something I really need to know."

"No, it isn't."

Um, okay. She tried a different tactic, and motioned to three antique gaming machines in the corner. "Where's your friend Max? I thought you two would be shooting up Asteroids over there."

Keith slurped up the last of his drink and then got to work on the ice. "He had to go. One-player games aren't as fun. And I don't have any quarters."

That's right—those games required an endless supply of quarters. "Do you usually have quarters when you come here?" She tapped his glass with a fingernail. "How did you pay for this?"

His frown deepened as he stared at the tabletop, refusing to respond.

"Keith, you can tell me. I promise I won't be mad."

"Max brings the quarters." He pointed to a woman behind the order counter on the other side of the room. "She always gives us free drinks because Max did something good for her a long time ago."

"Nice of her. Does Max expect you to pay him back for the quarters?"

Keith shook his head. "No, he just wants someone to play with, like me."

"Well, does Max have a last name? Maybe a cell phone so I can call him when you disappear?"

"Not telling." Keith shook his head. "I don't want you to call him. I'm in high school now. Big enough to pick my own friends."

Emma hoped the relationship was as innocent as it sounded. Unfortunately, her brother didn't have a good track record, so this guy Max seemed too good to be true. But for now, she let it go. Maybe Keith just needed some attention. She stood. "I was thinking about going to the mall, maybe seeing a movie. Wanna come with me?"

Keith set down his glass and stood. "Can we get a corn dog?"

Emma grinned. "Sure, if that's what you want."

Two hours later, they'd moseyed through all Keith's favorite stores in Westfield Plaza, and were working on the last of Emma's. While Keith wandered around the men's section, Emma took an armload of clothes into the dressing room, and came out with a sea-green blouse that matched her eyes.

She had absolutely nowhere to wear it, and that made it all the more important that she buy it. Keith met her at the register with a florescent yellow T-shirt that said, "Smarter than you think." "I need this," he said.

"Yes, you do," she agreed, and placed the items on the desk. She pulled out her wallet and handed Keith her purse. "Hold this for a second." Emma paid and they started for the exit. "You getting hungry?"

"Yeah." Keith scratched his nose, which, Emma noticed, had been twitching for the last several minutes. "How about, um . . ." He trailed off, eyes darting around like he was afraid.

What is up with him?

"Why don't we just go to the food court and see what looks good?"

"Excuse me." A man jogged toward them. "Ma'am, I need to ask you to stay where you are."

Emma's eyebrows creased. "Why?"

"I'm very sorry, but security needs to check your bag."

Emma handed him the shopping bag, grateful she was always careful to keep her receipts. "Oh, sure."

The man shook his head. "I meant your purse."

"Why?"

Keith fidgeted, his eyes bugging with fear. The man maneuvered Emma and Keith away from the exit and toward an office, where he dumped the contents of her purse on a desk.

There, mixed among lip gloss, gum, and hand sanitizer, was a loose white-gold necklace studded with what appeared to be either diamonds or expensive crystals. The man picked it up with a pencil, making it difficult not to see the hefty price tag—still attached. "Do you have a receipt for this?"

Emma stared, dumbfounded. Not only did she have zero clue how the necklace had gotten into her purse, she was positive she'd never seen it before. "No. I didn't buy that."

"Can you explain how it got in your purse?" He eyed Keith suspiciously.

Keith gasped, and Emma felt the blood drain from her face. *Was Keith playing the shopping game again? Should I try to explain?*

Not wanting to get her brother in trouble, her only response was to shake her head.

The man let out a slow breath, like what he was about to say caused him great pain. "I'm sorry, but I'm going to have to detain you for shoplifting."

Twenty-Four

JAMES HIT THE SHOWERS in the locker room and scrubbed off the sweat from practice. Might have been pointless—he was going to work, where he'd just sweat more—but at least he'd feel better on the way. Towel around his waist, he opened his locker just as his cell phone rang.

"Oh. Thank goodness." Emma's voice sounded frantic. "I'm so sorry to bother you, but I need a huge favor, and I wouldn't ask if it wasn't really, really important."

"Hello to you too." He pulled on his pants, leery.

"Sorry. Hi." She took a shaky breath. "I'm in trouble. Is there any way you could come get Keith at Westfield Plaza and take him home? Mrs. Hall, our neighbor, isn't answering, my grandma's half an hour away and can't drive, and Heather's at a movie with her boyfriend. There aren't very many people

I can trust with my brother, so I'm hoping . . ." Her voice trailed off.

James took the phone away from his ear to drag a T-shirt over his head, then cradled it against his shoulder so he could put on shoes. "I thought you weren't talking to me."

"Please. I wouldn't have called if I wasn't desperate." Her voice cracked on the last word, amplifying the worry James had felt when he saw her in class earlier.

Eyes closed, James leaned his head against the locker door. "I don't have a car."

A sniffle, shuffling in the background, and what might have been a muffled sob.

His growing concern gave him the ability to thrust aside his hurt. "Emma? You okay? I'll figure something out. Where do you want me to meet you?"

"Not me, just him. He'll be standing outside with a security guard." In a watery voice, she rattled off an entrance James was quite certain he'd never used, but could probably find. "He'll have my cell phone, so if you can't find him, call it."

"I'm going to have to track down some wheels, so it'll take me half an hour or so. That all right?"

"Yes, that's great." More sniffles. "Thank you. So much. You have no idea how much this means to me."

It better mean he was going to get some answers. And maybe another date. Including more kissing. Yes, kissing. "Do I need to stay with him, or . . ."

"Just take him home and make sure he gets in the house, and he should be fine. Maybe . . . could you remind him to call Mrs. Hall? She'll come stay with him if I'm gone too long."

James shoved his dirty shorts and jersey in his gym bag and zipped it, closing his locker while his brain computed something she'd said when he first answered. "What kind of trouble, Emma? Are you okay?"

She swallowed audibly. "I'll explain later. And now that I know someone will take care of Keith, I'm a lot better."

"Are you going to be long?"

Several heartbeats passed before she answered. "I don't know. Hope not."

After he clicked "end," James slung his pack over his shoulder and dialed his uncle. Not only would he have to skip work, but he needed to borrow a vehicle besides. This was not going to go over well.

Lucky for him, Ryan would never fire him as long as he had a good reason for not showing—and in his mind, helping Keith was a great reason. Also lucky, Ryan had an old beat-up work truck James could probably borrow for an hour. He'd have to work his ass off Saturday as payback, but that was fine.

A guy had to do what a guy had to do.

By the time he got the truck and drove to the mall, forty-five minutes had passed, and James worried Keith might have wandered away, or found another ride, or who-knew-what, and then Emma would never talk to him again. But as he pulled around an anchor store to the place where Emma asked, there was Keith, standing with a uniformed officer.

Rather than park against the red curb as he'd originally planned, James turned into a stall and got out, apprehensive to know what was happening with Emma. Trying for nonchalance, James twirled the keys around his index finger as he approached. "So, I hear there's this really awesome kid who needs a ride home. Thought maybe I could help."

"James! Hi." Keith made a show of looking both ways, twice, before running into the road to meet James halfway. "What are you doing here?"

James tried to focus on Keith rather than the officer, but it took effort. "Emma called me and said you were stuck. I figured I needed an evening off work anyway."

The officer held out a hand in greeting. "How you doing? I'm Officer McCarthy. Are you James Phelps?"

Accepting the man's hand, James nodded. "Yes, sir. Here to take Keith home. That is, if he's free to go." He glanced at Keith. "You are free, aren't you?"

"I think." Something in Keith's eyes told James there was a story here, but he didn't dare explore it right then.

McCarthy patted Keith's shoulder. "Yes, you are." His eyes traveled from Keith to James. "Drive safely, and have a good night."

Keith followed James to the truck, scrunching his nose as he climbed in the musty-smelling cab. James started the engine and backed out, glancing in the rearview to make sure McCarthy had gone inside. He had. After they'd left the lot and merged into traffic, James asked, "You going to tell me what's going on?"

Keith stared out the passenger-side window. "No."

Surprised, James turned his head to glance at the kid, then returned his gaze to the road. "Okay, let me rephrase that. Tell me what's going on and I won't make you walk the rest of the way."

"Humph." Keith folded his arms across his chest. "Humph."

"I'm serious. Either you start talking or you start walking. And I gotta tell you, I'm starving. Was going to drive through and grab a hamburger. Thought you'd probably like one too, but . . . if you're walking, guess I'll just get one."

"Emma's going to jail," Keith burst out.

James slammed on the brakes, barely avoiding a car that pulled out in front of him. "What? Why? What did she do?"

"I dunno."

By the way Keith stared at his shoes, James guessed he knew more than he was telling. "Keith. What. Did. She. Do?"

"Nothing. It was an accident." Keith looked up. "Can I get cheese on my hamburger?"

James swerved around a city bus, tapping the brakes when he thought he saw a police car in another lane. "Yeah, whatever you want. An accident?"

"And fries?"

"Yes, Keith. Fries. Tell me more about Emma."

"I think she likes you."

That made him pause, slow down. "Why do you say that?" They careened into the parking lot of a fast food joint.

Keith shifted in his seat, scanning the backlit menu. "She never used to let me hang out with Tom or her friends before. Only Heather, and now you. That means she likes you."

"Could've fooled me," James mumbled under his breath. He wondered if Emma being in trouble had anything to do with Keith's shoplifting history. "So does Emma need to be bailed out or something?"

"I-don't-know-I-don't-know-I-don't-know!" Keith covered his ears with his hands and hummed.

James gritted his teeth. This conversation was getting him nowhere. Once they had their food and were on their way, he made a decision. "Do you mind if I hang out with you until Emma gets home again? I was supposed to work, but I took the night off, so I don't really have anything going on."

"Yes," Keith said around a mouthful of fries. "We can play Xbox, and I'll even let you have the designer controller, 'cause it's the best."

Determined to figure things out, James agreed. "That, my friend, is a deal."

HUMILIATED AND EXHAUSTED, Emma dropped her keys on the counter and locked the door behind her. The mall closed hours earlier, but the police kept her until her parents could be reached, which took way too long.

A noise in the family room had her calling, "Keith, I'm home." She wondered if Mrs. Hall had come to check on him, or if he'd been alone all this time. Her stomach grumbled, and she opened the fridge to find a snack.

"He's asleep."

The low voice startled a squeak from her—had her clutching her chest. "Holy crap, James. You scared the daylights out of me. What are you doing here?"

"Looking after your brother. Where were you, anyway?"

She closed the fridge, wondering how best to explain in

as few words as possible. "Can we talk about this later? It's been a really long day."

He shook his head. "I've heard that one before. Still haven't had that talk, either."

She pinched the bridge of her nose. "I'm serious. I don't have the energy for this tonight."

"Fine." He folded his arms across his chest and leaned against the counter. "Just tell me where you were, then."

Whatever. She slammed her fist on the counter. "I was arrested, okay?" Her cheeks heated with embarrassment. "They had to detain me until they could track down my parents in Greece."

His jaw fell open, and the look on his face could only have been described as shock. "Arrested? For what?"

She turned away, reaching for a glass of water, partly to have something to do with her hands and partly because her throat felt like it was on fire. "Don't worry—it was a total misunderstanding. My parents' lawyer will get it all cleared up next week."

He leaned his elbows on the back of a barstool. "But why? What kind of misunderstanding gets you arrested at a mall, with your disabled brother in tow?"

Emma gulped her water, draining half the glass at once. "The kind where they think I was shoplifting."

"Were you?"

She shook her head. "No. Well, I mean, yes, there was an expensive piece of jewelry in my purse, but I didn't put it there."

He raised one eyebrow. "Then who did?"

More gulping until the glass was drained. "My in-tow disabled brother, probably. A souvenir habit left over from Jonathan. Or maybe his new friend, Max. I don't know."

"You took the rap?"

She leaned her head against the fridge and closed her eyes, let her whole body sag. "Nothing else I could do. He's done it before, so they probably would have taken him to jail, and I didn't think he could handle that. Besides, they probably wouldn't have believed me anyway. How many people in the world try to stick the blame on someone who doesn't know any better? Probably a lot."

"You look exhausted."

Her eyes popped open. "Thanks."

"Just an observation."

"A true one. I need sleep. And food. And sleep. Thanks for coming to the rescue today. I don't know what I would've done if you hadn't."

He stood upright, stretched his back, but kept his distance. "You do realize you owe me for real now?"

She nodded. "I figured."

He tapped the counter with his fingertip, his steady gaze mesmerizing. "And I intend to collect. Soon."

Collect what?

He hooked his leather jacket off the chair and around his shoulder. "Get some sleep. I'll see you at school tomorrow."

Emma watched him walk to a beat-up truck parked on the street, climb in, and drive away, then she locked the doors, turned off the lights, and crawled into bed, fully clothed, where she screamed all her frustrations into her pillow.

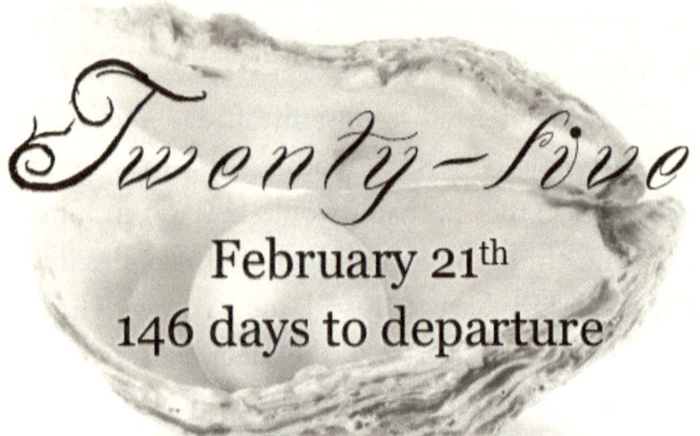

February 21th
146 days to departure

ON FRIDAY, SHE DIDN'T answer his calls or respond to his texts, though that was nothing new. He almost caught up to her after English, but Heather got there first, and before he could intervene, the two were swept up in the tide of students. When he hadn't cornered Emma by evening, James could hardly concentrate. He grabbed a taco at the fast food joint across the street and boarded the bus with the rest of his team, preparing for an away game. She was probably fine.

"Hey, loser." Mark stuck his foot into the aisle as James attempted to walk by. "Did you really leave the El Camino game with the ice queen? Even after we warned you off?"

James ignored him, as he'd been doing all week, and decided to sit in the very back.

"He better get his head together," Lyle announced. "She's starting to mess with his brain."

Mark hooted. "I doubt the problem's in his brain. Is it, James?"

He dropped his gym bag on the seat and leaned against the window, trying not to let them get to him. Mark was right. His brain wasn't the problem—except that he couldn't seem to push her out of it. The trouble with Emma was somewhere in his chest, between his ribs. Maybe, possibly, though he had no idea how, she just might have inched her way into his heart. And thanks to that little detail, he didn't know how to combat his sick worry. Where the hell was she? Why wouldn't she call him back?

Coach climbed aboard the bus, clipboard in hand, and stood in the aisle between the front seats. "Listen up. This game is every bit as important as the El Camino one. Don't go thinking we can have a one-lose-leeway and still get to State. There's no room for mistakes. Your name becomes Butterfingers, you warm the bench. We play as a team, or we don't play at all." Coach stopped talking long enough to squirt water from a bottle into his mouth, then he looked directly at James. "We're in this thing to win. Now, we have an hour drive to get where we're going. I suggest you use this time to eat some protein, rest your muscles, and meditate."

"Meditate?" someone crowed. James didn't bother looking to see who.

"You know," Coach slapped the clipboard with his free hand. "Concentrate and contemplate the meaning of teamwork and how we're going to win."

Several of the guys guffawed. The coach sat down, and conversations resumed at full volume as the bus began to roll. James put in ear buds and scrolled through his playlist to something heavy and hard—something that might help take his mind off Emma. He leaned against the wall and sprawled on the seat, then unwrapped his taco and dumped hot sauce over the top. The spice and crunch went well with his choice of music, and the heat gave him a burst of energy he hoped would last throughout the game.

As they turned onto the highway, a rank smell filtered through the bus, and James reached up to open his window. As he did, he caught a glance of a red convertible zipping past, a wave of red hair trailing behind the driver. "Emma!" he yelled. He hadn't meant to yell. She couldn't hear him anyway. But all eyes on the bus turned his way.

He slid back to sitting, refusing to meet Mark and Lyle's glares. It should have been beyond hope for him to think she might be coming to the game, yet he couldn't help but wonder where she was going. What was she up to, and how was she doing? Tonight he needed to track her down after the game— even if it was late. As he wondered what he'd say, Mark sat next to him, hooked a finger in the cord, and pulled the buds out of James's ears. "I thought you were smart. How many times do you have to be told fire's hot before you get burned?"

James cocked his head. "I thought you said she's an ice queen."

"Whatever. Ice burns same as fire. I'm telling you, she's trouble."

"So you keep saying. But far as I can see, the only reason

for you to say that is she doesn't give you a thought. You're jealous."

Mark laughed, clapping James's shoulder. "Is that what you think this is? Damn, James. You're funny. So let me ask you a question. Has she ever told you about her last boyfriend? Where he ended up or what happened to him?"

"I never asked because it doesn't matter." James shoved the rest of his taco in his mouth, chomping into Mark's ear. "Don't really care, as long as he's out of the picture now." Okay, it was only a half-truth since he hated every guy who'd ever touched her, but he wasn't about to admit that to Mark.

"You should care. Really. It matters in this case. And since I'm your friend, I'm going to tell you—because that's what friends do. They share vital information with each other."

It was James's turn to laugh. "Really? So we're friends now? That's news."

Mark ignored the jab and continued. "Last year, there was another guy on this team—played center. Maybe you've heard of him. Tom Rasmussen?"

James nodded, resigned to hearing the story whether he wanted to or not.

"So, Tom and Emma were a thing. Inseparable as salt and pepper for more than a year. And that girl was all over him. Everywhere they went, she had her hands on him, talking dirty, touching him, teasing the way those girls do, you know?"

"No, I don't know. Emma's not like that." He didn't like the way Mark classified Emma as one of "those girls." James now knew for certain he didn't want to hear the end of this story. "Tom treated that chick like a queen. Spent all his money on her, took her to expensive restaurants and concerts—even carried her books sometimes. The guy loved her, you know? And then came prom. We doubled—I took Lyla Remolds—and we shared the same limo. Emma shows up in this dress—I gotta admit, I thought my eyeballs were gonna pop right out of my face. Right then and there, I thought, if Tom wasn't my friend, I'd leave Lyla in the parking lot, and anyway, it was H-O-T. Deep green shiny stuff, molded to her like it was sewn to her skin, and a short train that followed behind her when she walked. Whole thing held up by thin little straps that crisscrossed all crazy in the back and showed skin in all the right places. We're at the dance, and she's moving like I've never seen a high school girl move—and I can tell Tom's itching to get her out of there. He's staring at her with this glazed look—like someone put a spell on him or something—and doesn't say a word to any of us. Just . . . just picks her up off the dance floor and takes her outside."

James blew out a long breath as tension snaked up his back. "Where'd he take her?"

"Home. He had a room at the hotel just upstairs from the dance. But she told him all through dinner that she wouldn't go—said she wasn't ready for that. And they never checked in."

"How do you know?"

"Because me and Lyla used the room instead." He cleared his throat. "So I spend the weekend wondering how things went, know what I mean? And all I hear from him is this text near the end of the dance, telling me that they got in a fight, and we'll talk Sunday. But then nothing. He doesn't answer his phone. No replies to texts, or email either. Monday, I'm expecting to see Tom at school, get some deets. But he's not there. Tuesday, I go to his house—find out from his parents he's in jail on some messed-up assault charge, and they're scrambling to get him a lawyer because that lying bitch claims he beat her up."

James felt the blood drain from his face. "He what?"

"So," Mark continued as if James hadn't spoken, "I go see him in jail, and he's scared to death, sobbing and telling me he didn't do it—says she's lying because she's mad he caught her naked on the beach with another guy. Claims the other guy did it." He paused to let that sink in. "Yeah. Don't know why Tom would even want her after that. Damaged goods. And the killer is, all this supposedly happened after prom. After Tom took her home."

"Some guy beat her up?" Nausea clenched James's stomach until he grabbed the window and yanked it down as far as it would go. He stuck his head out and inhaled a big gulp of air. Unsure he wanted to hear the answer, he turned back to Mark and asked, "What happened to him? Tom?"

Mark closed his eyes, swallowing. "Judge found him guilty of assault. Did six months, kicked out of school, lost his basketball scholarship to UCLA, and now—get this—because her dress got ripped, they make him register as a sex offender."

"Shit." James pressed the heels of his hands into his eyes, trying to wrap his mind around everything that had happened to Emma. No wonder she was so cautious. If even a portion of this was true, sounded like there had been more than punches thrown at her. Ashes, indeed. "You're kidding."

Mark slapped James on the back. "Nope, not kidding. Tom's life is ruined. Can't even get into a decent college now, and he was up for scholarships all over the place before. But Emma comes back to school two weeks later. Considering the supposed damage, she looked fine to me. Except now she doesn't want to talk to anyone because she's better than us. Dropped all her friends except Heather, who hated Tom from the get-go, and that 'tard of a brother. And now you. Don't become her next bootie call."

That explained where the rumors came from. And the stigma she'd mentioned the day they met. Even the panic attack that day they went to lunch. It explained a lot of things. But if Mark ever referred to Keith as a "'tard" again, James would have to break his nose. If it wasn't already broken by the end of this conversation. Maybe he'd have to break it twice. He'd see. "I can't believe you blame her. Did anyone ever ask her what really happened? Ever try to see it from her side? Did anyone offer her any kind of support?"

"Why? She wasn't the one in jail. She's not the one on probation for the next three years, or who had to leave town because of a bogus protective order. And now that I think about it, seems like that whole mess was about the time Emma's daddy bought her that shiny little toy she drives. Some kind of twisted reward for being a poor-sorry victim. How's that for justice?"

James shook his head. "What does her car have to do with anything? And it sounds to me like your so-called friend is shit-for-brains pond scum. How can you believe a crap story like that?" He scrubbed his hands over his face, needing to catch his breath. Needing Mark to back off and give him some space.

Mark's eyes narrowed. "Because I've known Emma since third grade, and because Tom would never lie to me. We're like brothers."

"You're out of your mind," James insisted, feeling his shoulder muscles tie into knots. "Out of your damn mind if you think something that messed up was in any way her fault."

"Believe what you want." Mark patted James's shoulder. "Your future on the line, not ours."

Though he hated both Mark and Lyle, and though he'd never trusted anything they'd ever said, James couldn't help wondering what had really happened. Before yesterday, he would never have believed Emma could do anything deceptive or wrong, but what if she was just a really good actress? The cops had kept her for a long time yesterday. But even so, could she be capable of destroying a guy's life like that? No. He couldn't believe it of her. Besides, why would she lie? She was clearly the one still suffering for the situation. She'd been right about one thing—these guys knew how to mess with his head. James shoved Mark off his seat, feeling like pond scum himself for even questioning her.

"You know what? It doesn't matter. I can't think about this right now. We're almost there, and I need to focus on the game."

"Yeah, that's right. Focus. Forget her. She's not worth it." Mark leaned closer. "Let's just get on the court and slam those guys into the wall."

James liked that idea way more than he was willing to

admit. It was good to have someplace to aim the rage boiling inside him, threatening to spew like a volcano at any moment. Was he mad at Emma for not telling him herself? Or Tom for doing such awful things to her? Or Mark for telling him when he didn't want to hear? Didn't matter. Too bad the strangers on the other team were going to be on the receiving end of his anger—and they had no idea just how furious he was.

T*HE WIND, CHARGED WITH THE ELECTRICITY* of an oncoming storm, pulled Emma's hair back and whipped her skin as she zoomed down the highway on the way to her cove. It had only been twenty-four hours, and already she needed to swim again. Her heart pounded, stomach cramping with anxiety as she drove toward the coast. This couldn't be happening now. Not now. Keith needed her. Her parents needed her. Heather needed her. Maybe even James needed her—maybe. But worse than them needing her, Emma needed them.

How was she going to survive Atlantis without them? How would she survive *life* without them?

She cranked a hard song on the stereo, hoping maybe anger would cover her growing sorrow, and gunned the engine to get around a bus, paying no attention to the district name on the side. As she passed, she thought she heard someone yell her name and glanced in the mirror to see if it was someone she knew, but by the time she looked, she was too far away to see who it was. Didn't matter.

All that mattered was her inability to change her body and stay human forever. Her car careened around a corner and screeched to a halt at the top of the trail that would lead her to the cove—her most favored and hated place in the world. She stormed down the path, dodging loose rocks and low patches of sand blown about by the strengthening wind, and into the shallow cave, slamming her beach bag onto the waist-high ledge she used as a shelf.

After all this time, she had the changing down to a science—clothes off and into her bikini in less than a minute. Emma strode to the mouth of the cave until her toes hung over the edge of the rock. The deepest entry point was only about eight feet, but it was better than the shallow end, where it was only three.

Poised to dive, she spotted a dark figure racing toward her and shook her head. Merrick. She sighed, a very human response, then dove in the water, darting in the opposite direction. Swimming may be something Merrick was born doing, but Emma had been good at avoiding people her whole life, and every time she came to swim, she felt faster than the time before. She skimmed around a coral formation, following it for about a mile before zooming into the open sea. Three miles later, her ab muscles tightened with a pleasant ache that tingled all the way down her hips and legs to her toes, and the gills in the back of her neck buzzed, filling her veins with what could only be compared to a sugar high.

A school of colorful angelfish paused to stare, then moved around Emma as if bored and annoyed by her blatant interruption of their formation. Not far behind, an enormous sea turtle bobbed, taking his sweet time getting wherever he was going. He seemed so content, so unaffected by his surroundings—including her—that Emma giggled, watching as bubbles floated past her head and then up, up, up to the surface somewhere high above.

"You cannot avoid me forever."

Startled, Emma darted away from Merrick, and didn't turn around until she'd gone several feet. "I can try." Under water, their voices carried a slow, sing-song quality that reminded Emma of music—only not. *At least I can understand.*

He inched closer, his eyes flashing with anger. "Your time is nearly here. When it is, we will mate, and you will no longer be allowed such freedoms as you now take."

Emma lifted her chin, clenching her teeth in anger. He had no right to demand that she become his. No right at all. "So you keep saying. Forgive me if I don't swim for joy."

"You should." He inched closer still. "I am a duke of Atlantis. If I wish, all you desire shall be yours once we are bound. We shall live in a palace that can't be broken, and I will decorate you with treasure far more beautiful than the trinket you wear now. I have been preparing for you since your hatching."

Since her hatching? No way. She let that thought go with a raised eyebrow. "Treasure? A palace? This is going to happen . . . how?"

"Tangaroa will allow you anything, as long as I will it. As king of Atlantis, he has much power and influence."

"Well, bully for you. And what will Tangaroa say when I tell him how you chased me into a school of sharks and left me there for hours? All. By. Myself, Merrick. You chase me around the ocean like I'm some kind of prize, but as soon as I actually need help, you bail? Yep, that's love, all right."

"Love is not why we mate," he said, clearly confused. "I helped keep the sharks away from you by leaving. If I had not left, they would have eaten us both. What do you wish?"

If only Merrick could comprehend what she really desired, the only thing she really wanted. Her freedom.

Her eyes traveled Merrick's solid form, from his chiseled face to his well-defined pecs and ripped abs, trying to force herself to feel something—anything—besides animosity toward him. If this was to be her life, if she were to have no other choice, at least she would be mated to someone who could provide her with everything she could possibly want in his world. But even that thought didn't help. Everything, everyone she loved lived on the surface.

Her parents. Keith. Gran. Heather.

She turned away, hands shaking.

James.

She'd stayed away. Avoided him as best she could, but her efforts had only served to make her miserable. Maybe he was better off, but she certainly wasn't. Her time was coming. And maybe it was selfish, but he could offer something she hadn't realized she needed until right now.

It would be a risk for them both. But she realized it was one she was willing to take, if James would give her a chance. And if he did, she'd be crazy not to take it—this was something she would never be able to do again.

But first she had to tell him. Everything. All of it. She

wouldn't ask more than he could give, not without making sure he had the facts. Another risk. And yet, somehow, she trusted him enough to share the secret even her parents didn't know. What did that mean?

She could feel Merrick following as she swam—without much speed—back toward the cove. "You know this isn't what I want, right?"

"I still do not understand," he responded, a strange cadence to his voice.

Emma sucked water through her gills and let out a stream of bubbles—the mermaid equivalent of a sigh. "I know. You probably never will. And I'm sorry, very sorry, but I think you should know that you're not *who* I want either."

"You will be mine soon."

It sounded eerily like a threat rather than a statement. Emma turned her head to meet his eyes—they blazed with a fire she couldn't comprehend, but that she'd seen once before. Her heart dropped into her stomach as she picked up speed, suddenly nervous.

A hundred yards from the cove, Merrick caught up, grabbed her wrist, and yanked her roughly into his arms, holding tight. "You will be mine soon," he repeated. "You are not a human, and thus cannot be bound to one." He fingered the necklace she'd worn for as long as she could remember. "This will also be mine. Valuable treasures are best hidden and protected. Do not forget."

She shook her head, blinking back tears and biting down on her lip to keep from crying out.

The skin where he held her wrist stung with the heat of

his temper, the throb reaching deeper and deeper as she watched, horrified, while the skin burned from bright red to deep purple. Merrick's eyes sparked with uncontrolled anger of which she hadn't realized him capable. A new kind of fear clogged her gills, leaving her struggling for air while Merrick held tight. Finally, she had no choice but to beg.

"Please, let me go. My gills . . . I need oxygen. Please."

He held tight, letting Emma struggle until she felt her lungs would burst, and only let her go when her movements became sluggish and weak. She kicked hard for the surface, wondering how she'd make it before she passed out, and glad that the excruciating heat in her wrist would at least keep her aware. When her head broke the surface, she gasped for air, relieved to discover they hadn't been as deep as she'd thought. Merrick had held her until her vision and judgment were impaired.

A shiver of terror coursed through her, bringing with it the strength borne of survival, and urging her to swim for shore with everything she had. Minutes later, she pulled herself out of the water, still gasping, and crawled to the farthest corner of the cave. Curling into a ball, she wrapped the towel around herself, shivering with adrenaline, and wondering why he thought her necklace had any value.

When her legs had dried enough, she wiped her nose and stood to dress, hyper-aware that Merrick was probably nearby, and terrified that he might come pull her back under now that she'd caught her breath. She never took much time dressing, but this time she did it doubly fast, sliding on her shoes as the first drops of rain fell outside the cave.

Cursing under her breath, Emma slung her bag over her shoulder and ran up the hill toward her car, wondering if Merrick was watching, and feeling her wrist sting with every brush of cool evening air.

Twenty-six

PAIN EXPLODED IN JAMES'S ANKLE as he fell, twisting it the wrong direction. He sat up and shook the hair out of his face, glancing at the scoreboard in despair. They were down by twenty-seven points with less than thirteen minutes left on the clock, and he'd just fouled out of the game. Another teammate, Braden, offered a hand to pull James up, and then helped him as he limped to the bench.

"Phelps!" Coach grumbled. "What were you thinking?"

James bit back a growl and shook his head, wondering how Coach would react if James admitted he wanted to kill someone. He'd played the entire first half and part of the second, and his fury still blazed hot and strong.

The red haze of anger coated everything he saw, reached into the corners of his mind and dragged out demons he'd long-since buried, causing an intense urge to hit or break whatever was in his path—including other people. The one thing he hadn't actually been able to hit was the basket—leaving his team in bad shape.

Mark had been smart enough to stay out of his way since their conversation on the bus. And that was fine, because James couldn't stand the thought of Mark at the moment. There were a lot of things he couldn't stand the thought of just now.

The minutes ticked by, and though the Pirates scored some shots, they remained woefully behind. He tipped his head back and dumped an electrolyte drink down his throat with closed eyes. Would Emma want him to know what happened? What should he say to her? Should he say anything at all? Could he? And how would he even approach the subject?

Braden slapped his back. "You awake?"

"Yeah," James answered, eyes still closed.

"Painful, isn't it?"

"Um-hm." He knew Braden was talking about the game. Or maybe the injured ankle. But James was thinking of Emma—had been, nonstop, all week. He'd only seen her for minutes last night, yet during that time, her presence had been an exquisite kind of torture to him. So much for trying to distance himself. "We might as well go home now—there's no way we're coming back from this."

Braden wiped the side of his sweaty face with a hand towel. "It would take a miracle."

James almost laughed, thinking it was too bad Emma

wasn't here—maybe it could happen. Then he caught a glimpse of Lyle, dribbling the ball into the key for an attempted lay-up—which he missed—and was glad Emma hadn't come. He was having a hard-enough time sorting through his thoughts and emotions without her here to cloud them.

They needed to have that talk she'd promised, and when they did, Lyle and Mark would not be within five miles of them.

The buzzer sounded and a cheer erupted in the bleachers, where fans of the San Diego Cavers had congregated. He opened his eyes, not wanting to see the damage, but unable to leave without knowing. The score ended in the other team's favor, forty-six to twenty-two.

"Humiliating," he told Braden.

"We're not completely out of State." Braden followed James to the team huddle. "We can come back from this."

James didn't answer. Did college recruiters come to watch players whose teams lost because he couldn't keep it together? He doubted it.

Did girls who'd been beat up by guys who supposedly loved them ever learn to trust other guys again? As he wondered, a little whisper of doubt crept in. What if she had lied? He couldn't think of a reason that fit with any type of logic, but so many people seemed to believe it. What if? Emma wouldn't lie about something like that. Would she?

Uncertainty ate away at him as he boarded the bus. By the time they pulled into the dark school parking lot, though his bruised ankle was iced and swollen, the idea of walking home was a relief, even though it was getting late. Maybe he'd walk off the last of his anger so he could get some sleep tonight. His head would be clearer in the morning.

Three blocks from the school, a car stopped along the curb, and someone yelled, "How was the game?"

James's shoulders slumped as he climbed into Uncle Ryan's car. "Bad. We got spanked."

Ryan patted him on the shoulder and put the car in gear. "Ah, man, I'm sorry. That's . . ."

"Go ahead—you can say it. The end of my hopes and dreams."

"Actually, it isn't. And saying those words is a sign of a bad attitude." Ryan turned away from James's street instead of toward it.

"Where are we going?" James asked, confused.

"Got to pick up an order. I need you to help me."

James sighed, feeling more exhausted with every streetlight they passed.

"I've never seen the loss of one game get you so down." Ryan peered at James. "Trouble at school? Girl problems?"

James ran his hands through his hair, relieved for the chance to unload on someone he trusted. "Where do I even start?"

Ryan shrugged, turning into an industrial area. "I'd tell you to start at the beginning, but I don't have all night to listen to you mooning over a chick you'll probably be over by next week. Why not just start with the problem? I can't promise to help, mind you. Just because I have a whole string of girlfriends doesn't make me an expert."

James glared—it was all he could do at the moment. "Oh, no?"

"Well, okay, maybe I am an expert. But I'm not proud of it."

"Whatever." In as short a version as possible, James relayed what Mark had told him on the bus, adding details of how much he truly liked Emma, and ending with her odd explanation of what had happened at the mall last night.

"I thought you seemed preoccupied this week." Ryan pulled into a parking lot and turned off the engine. The garage-style door of the business was closed, but light gleamed through a dingy window. "Listen, I can't tell you what's best. You're my nephew, and the idea of this girl and her history makes me want to tell you to run away as far and as fast as you can. But . . . I don't know her. You do. I think sometimes it's easy to take the thoughts and opinions of other people and make them your own. The problem with that is those people—whoever they are—don't always know everything, or everyone, or have all the answers, or even some of them. Unless they were directly involved, all they know is what other people have told them. Or worse, what they made up in their minds and decided must be true.

"If you really want to get the facts, you have to go straight to the source. Ask her. And if she can't or won't talk about it, you might have to make a judgment call based on instinct. What do you know? What do you believe?"

Resting elbows on knees, James dropped his head into his hands. "I don't know what to believe."

Ryan laid a comforting hand on James's back. "But you

like her. A lot. If you didn't, you'd be able to walk away—you wouldn't be so churned up."

"Ya think?" James looked up, biting off the rest of his sarcasm when he saw they were parked in front of a mechanic's shop. "Why are we here?"

His uncle grinned. "I know you're trying to save for college, but it's ridiculous for you to be walking all over town while that gorgeous bike rusts in your father's carport. My friend Matt owed me a favor, so I collected in your honor."

"What? What are you saying?" James let his hand hover over the door handle, not daring to get excited over a possibility.

"I'm saying your next paycheck is spent—so don't be waiting around for it—but you'll no longer need rides to work."

It was the best news he'd had in days. James's smile spread until he thought his ears would pop. "You got my bike fixed?"

"Well, she runs. Can't claim she won't still have problems, but she'll get you where you need to go. Work. School. And maybe to see that girl of yours."

James threw his arms around his uncle. "Thanks! Thank you, thank you, thank you so much."

"It's the least I can do for my sister's son." Ryan squeezed back. "You hear from your mom yet?"

James shook his head. "Don't expect I ever will."

Ryan sighed, pulling away from James. "I keep hoping someday she'll get help, get better, and then . . ."

"It's been two years. She's not coming back." James

stepped out of the car, and Ryan followed. "I know you want her to—believe me, I wanted that too, for a while. When she left, she told me she needed to start fresh, start over. Must be what she did. I hope wherever she is, whatever she's doing, she's happy in a way she never could be with my dad and me."

Ryan stared into the distance, his voice stained with disgust. "How could she abandon her own son?"

The old wound in James's heart splintered, and he swallowed. "Well. I'm still in school. Maybe she didn't have any other choice."

"Yeah." Ryan's smile was tight. "And you're going to be fine. I'll make sure of it." He got out of the car and knocked on the big steel door. "Let's go get your bike, yeah?"

James smiled—a real, genuine smile. His first in days. "Yes. Maybe I'll teach you how to drive her at some point."

"We'll see about that, kid. We'll see."

"WHAT'S UP WITH YOU THIS WEEK?" Heather didn't even bother to say hello when Emma answered her call.

"Nothing's up," Emma told her, exhausted by the very idea of even trying to explain. "Why would you think something's up?"

"Don't give me that crap. I've let it go for several days, but I know you. Something has you in a funk, and it better not be that guy, James. I might have to hurt him."

Emma stuck her pencil in the crease of her textbook and set it aside. *Of course it's James! And Merrick and the suckage that is my life.* "He hasn't done anything, if that's what you're asking. It's just—I like him. A lot."

Rustling on the other end indicated that Heather was either changing or lying down. "That's great. So why are you acting like someone is dying?"

Because I feel like that someone is me. "Because I can't go there, Heather. I really want to, but my life is just too complicated. I have too much baggage."

"That's the worst excuse I've ever heard. You've been watching too much TV drama. Emma, you're seventeen. I get that you have a past, but we all have crap. It's life. Get over it and move on."

Stunned at Heather's callous words, Emma couldn't even force herself to reply. *This is why I can never tell her.*

The intake of breath on the other end of the line was the only indication that Heather was thinking through her own words—after they spewed from her mouth. "I'm not saying you have to marry the guy. Just go out with him. Get a little action. It'll be good for you."

"Heather, he doesn't even know—"

"He doesn't have to," Heather insisted. "Just call him. I mean it. It's necessary."

Knowing Heather was right, Emma hung up and dialed James before she could chicken out. He didn't answer, so she forced herself to leave a short message. Relieved, she grabbed her English assignment and camped on the floor in the family room while Keith fell asleep watching a movie. Not wanting to leave him on the couch, Emma woke him and led him to his room, where she tucked him in bed, glad to have a quiet evening to herself.

She headed downstairs, closing the blinds and double-checking that the doors were locked. As she passed by the newly replaced window, she shivered, wondering who had really thrown the brick. Tom had a restraining order, but that didn't mean he wouldn't come after her someday, wouldn't find a way to exact his revenge.

I can't wait for Mom and Dad to come home.

Back door locked, dead bolted, and security chained, check. Garage closed, powered down, inside door locked, dead bolted, and chained, check. Blinds closed in the back of the house, blinds closed in front, check. Front door . . .

A tall shadow hovered on the porch, the face masked by a motorcycle helmet, peering into the skinny side window. Emma let out a shriek of terror, seizing the doorknob to be sure it was locked. She reached in her pocket and gripped her cell phone with shaking fingers as the shadow moved. The phone was flipped open, her fingers pressing 9-1 before the knocking registered.

"Emma, it's okay. It's me, James. Emma? Emma, look out the window."

The shadow moved again, pulling off the helmet, and she recognized the troubled eyes. She let out a sigh, relieved. "James."

"Yeah, it's me. Are you okay?" His voice was muffled, but recognizable.

Her fingers fumbled with the lock, but she managed to open the door, falling into his arms. "I thought you were an intruder. Scared me."

He squeezed her trembling shoulders and backed her

into the house, then turned to lock the dead bolt and secure the chain. "Sorry about that." He looked at his watch. "Whoa, it's later than I realized. Good thing your parents aren't here."

Emma didn't smile. "Actually, I was just wishing they were. I usually do okay when they're gone, but this time so much has happened." Her voice cracked on the last word, and she turned away rather than let James see her fighting tears again.

"I noticed." James cleared his throat. "Are you okay? It kind of freaks me out that I haven't seen you much at school all week. You've been avoiding me."

She took a deep breath and let it out, then took another one, needing time to figure out how to go about saying what she needed to say. "I have. I'm sorry."

He didn't look angry, but there was something there, behind his eyes. "Any reason in particular?"

Emma sagged, leaning on the banister, and pinching the bridge of her nose as she tried to collect her thoughts. "Sort of. It's complicated."

"Same old tune."

The venom in his voice surprised Emma, made little fingers of fear crawl up her neck. "Why are you here?"

James leaned against the door, fidgeting with his helmet. "I heard some stuff."

Her stomach pitched. Of course that's why he was here. Someone gave him their skewed, highly untrue version of events, and he suspected her of lying—or worse. She swallowed, disregarding the hurt that knotted her insides and fighting to compose herself before turning to face him again. "I'm sure you did. There's lots of talk going around."

His eyes narrowed. "Funny that I haven't heard any of it until now. And from you. I had to get it shoved at me secondhand."

She folded her arms over her chest, feeling exposed and vulnerable. "I guess you're out of the gossip loop. If you remember, I tried to warn you the day we met."

He stared, but didn't reply.

She'd already planned to tell him, but on her terms, and not under duress. Anger bubbled in her chest. "So, now you're here for details. You want me to tell you how Tom caught me on the beach with someone else and then put me in the hospital? He gave me three broken ribs, an eye so swollen I couldn't open it, and fifteen stitches in my head."

"Emma . . ." He stared at the floor, refusing to meet her eyes.

"The thing on the beach wasn't what Tom thought, but no one ever asks about that part. They just assume I was doing something horrible. That somehow I deserved what I got, even though everything that happened was out of my control." Her forehead pounded with the effort of holding back tears, and her eyes felt sticky. Her chest throbbed with the pain of a scar that had never completely healed. "Maybe I did deserve it. But not for the reasons everyone thinks." She sniffed.

"Emma."

James sounded more confused than angry, but Emma couldn't make herself stop now that the dam had broken. "You know what kills me? A couple of hours ago, I left you a message asking if we could talk. I wanted to tell you myself—

and just FYI, other than the cops and my parents, I haven't given anyone details. Not even Heather. But you know what? Just because you and I shared some fairly decent kissing doesn't mean I belong to you, that you get to be part of my life. It's entirely possible that our time together that one weekend is all we'll ever have."

"Fairly decent? That kiss was way more than fairly decent, and we both know it!" He finally looked up, his eyes blazing.

She straightened away from the wall, her jaw set, feet planted on the hardwood floor, determined to send him away however she had to. "I can't be with someone who could believe the rumors."

"I don't. I—"

"It won't be hard for you to find a girl who will give you everything I can't."

"What's that?" He straightened too, keeping his back to the door. "What can't you give me?"

A mix of emotions swelled like a balloon in Emma's chest. "It's time for you to go."

"I'm not leaving yet. Come on, Emma. I just—"

Memories of the night with Tom rushed in with surprising force, making the pressure in her chest almost unbearable. "I can't talk about this right now." Emma had to consciously unclench her hands. "Please. Just go. Leave me alone."

A muscle ticked in James's jaw as he stared her down. He shook his head. "I already tried that."

"Then you have some practice."

"It doesn't work."

"It will. It worked for everyone else I used to know—it'll work for you too. Eventually." She moved around him and unlatched the chain. "Bye, James."

He shook his head again, looking torn. Then, quick as lightning, he swooped her up in his arms and pressed his lips against hers. There was nothing gentle about it this time. He was rough, full of pent-up emotion he'd held back the last time they kissed. She could have fought him, or gone limp and non-responsive—Emma was fairly certain either reaction would send him running away in shame—but she met his assault with equal fervor, giving herself one last opportunity to experience what she wouldn't get to keep.

His arms around her tightened, and his fingers tangled in her loose hair, traced the curve of her shoulder and the outline of her birthmark. She leaned her head back, gasping for air, and James moved away from her lips to assault her neck, murmuring something she couldn't hear through the blood rushing in her ears. Fire danced along her skin, sent burning waves of pleasure into her core. She took a breath, closed her eyes, and kissed him once more—this time, softly— savoring his taste as she untangled herself from his arms and backed away. A tear escaped one of her eyes and rolled down her cheek. "That's enough. You've made your point."

James stood at the door, his expression horror-stricken. His mouth moved, but no sound came out.

"Go now," she said, bracing her hand on the wall, desperate to remain standing until he left.

"Emma. I'm—"

"Please. Just go."

He closed his eyes, his chest heaving, and nodded. "All right. I'll go. For now. But I'm coming back."

She shook her head, unsure if it was a good idea to see him again. Already, her heart felt like it was breaking to pieces, leaving her desperate for numbness to set in.

"This isn't over—not by a long shot." He slipped outside, looking dejected. "Lock up tight, okay?"

She nodded, closing the door on any more words and wondering again if she should—if she even could—close off her feelings for James. She turned the lock, secured the dead bolt and chain. A tap on the window had her opening the blinds to meet his eyes through the glass.

"Emma, I'm sorry."

She swallowed the ache. "I know."

"Please don't hate me."

The breath she took hurt—both going in and coming out—but her only reply was to close the blinds. *It's better this way. It's better this way. It's better this way.* She leaned against the door, listening as James started his bike with a loud rumble. When she could no longer hear the roar of the engine, she gave in to her emotions and allowed her body to slide down, where she curled up on the hardwood floor and sobbed.

EMMA HUGGED A THROW PILLOW to her chest and stared at the ringing cordless phone. She had purposefully left her cell phone off, afraid to turn it on and see that James had tried again to call, afraid that if he tried and she heard it ring, she wouldn't be able to resist answering. She thought he'd have stopped trying by now—it was nearly one a.m.

On the fourth ring, she couldn't take it anymore and snatched it up. "Hello?"

"Emma! Oh, Emma we've been so worried." Her mother's voice sounded frantic. "Why aren't you answering your cell?"

"It's out of power. I broke the charger," she lied, sadly disappointed that it wasn't actually James. "Haven't had time to go get a new one."

"Honey, you have to make time. You haven't replied to my emails all day, either. What's going on? Are you and Keith okay? We're worried."

"We're fine. Just busy."

"Tell me what happened with that incident at the mall. That police officer wasn't making any sense when we talked."

Sighing, Emma explained the situation to her mother. Again.

Cindy's voice turned business-like. "I called my office first thing this morning, and they're working on straightening the whole thing out. Expect to hear from either Lori or Ray sometime in the next few days."

"I already left them a message, but I'm sure they'll hurry faster if you call again."

Emma heard muffled talking and then her mother continued, "Your father wants to know if you and Keith are keeping up with your schoolwork, and I'd like to know about everything else."

Emma wondered if she should mention that she'd skipped several classes and one entire day since they left. "Yes, we're keeping up," she lied again. "And yes, we're getting enough to eat, taking care of each other, we lock the doors and set the alarm every night, and check in with Mrs. Hall once a day. At least."

"And how is Keith handling our absence?" Worry was evident in Cindy's voice.

"He's fine. Made a new friend, and they've been spending a lot of time playing arcade games at the pizza place. It's cute." Emma wound a lock of hair around her finger, wishing she could tell her mother everything, but unwilling to do it while the woman was half a world away. "I visited Gran the other day. She's doing so much better. The new medication must be working, because she got up and moved around while I was there."

"Oh, honey, I'm so glad you went. Your grandmother needs you right now."

I need her too. "I miss you both. Can't wait for you to get home."

It took Cindy a while to answer. "Actually, we should talk about that. Your father's getting a lot of research done, but I'm afraid he won't be able to finish by the weekend. There's really so much information to sift through. Do you think you and Keith could survive for another week if we changed our flight?"

Emma had to swallow a lump in her throat as she thought about how little time she had left, but answered, "Sure. We're big kids. We can handle things."

"How are you for groceries? I'm going to transfer more money into your account . . ."

Emma did her best to respond to her mother in all the right places, not letting on how depressed she was that they weren't coming home as she'd planned. It was hard to be cheerful as they talked at length, but if Cindy suspected how very much was wrong in Emma's world, she didn't mention it. When Emma yawned, Cindy heard it and cut herself short. "Oh, my goodness, it's so late. I should let you get to bed. Honey. I miss you so much."

A ball of sadness rolled up and down Emma's throat. The words made her feel completely and utterly alone. "Me too."

"I'm sorry if I woke you," Cindy said. "Make sure you pick up a phone charger tomorrow, and answer your emails, for heaven's sake. That's the whole reason we bought that expensive laptop."

"Sorry. I will."

Emma hung up the phone, sad. Rather than cheering her up, talking to her mother had made Emma feel more alone, more vulnerable, and needier. Now, more than ever, she needed to see her parents in person, talk to them about what was happening with her—despite what Gran said. She should've just said it. Blurted it out. They might not have believed her, but at least they'd notice that something was going on and come home. Then she could show them. Or maybe her father would research it, find her a way out. A cure for mermaid-ism.

If only the solution could be so simple.

Twenty-seven

February 22th
145 days to departure

EMMA'S HEAD THROBBED. She sat up. *What time is it?* The pain eased as she shifted, but the hammering continued. As her eyes cleared, she realized her head wasn't the source of the noise. She wrapped the blanket around her and hurried downstairs.

A glance at the clock told her it was ten fifteen in the morning. Whoever was at the door pounded hard, rang the doorbell, and pounded again. Emma peeked through the blinds and sighed when she saw who it was. She should've known.

"James." She cracked the door open—leaving the old-fashioned security chain in place—and allowed her eyes to take in his ripped jeans and a scarred leather jacket that accented the muscles in his chest and shoulders. His eyes mirrored both regret and determination. "What now?"

He swallowed, fidgeted. "I just want to make sure you're okay."

Emma finger-combed her tangled hair. "As you can see, I'm fine. You can go to work now. Guilt free."

He braced his hand on the heavy wood. "I can barely see you, and you definitely don't look fine. I mean, not that you look bad—you're gorgeous, as always—but . . . dammit. What's wrong with me? Why can't I talk?"

The distress on his face thawed Emma's insides, made her smile. Seeing his confidence shaken softened her faster than anything else could have. "Move your hand a second."

"Promise not to slam this thing in my face?"

She nodded, closing the door to unlatch the chain. When she opened it again, James still looked distressed. "I didn't mean—"

"I know what you meant." Emma tightened the comforter around her shoulders and gestured for him to follow her into the living room, where she dropped onto the love seat, resigned to moving forward with telling him. James surprised her by sitting next to her rather than in any of the available chairs. She scooted as far to the side as possible, needing space.

James sighed, leaning forward, elbows on his knees. "I'm not going to jump you. I'll never touch you that way unless you want me to, okay? I'm not . . . I'd never . . . I'm not like him."

Somehow, though she couldn't say why or how, Emma already knew that about James. It didn't change what he thought, or how he might let rumors and talk affect his feelings. But she felt safe with him, and that was more than she'd ever expected. "Why are you here?"

"I'm worried about you." He folded his hands together, staring out the large window at ripples in the pool. "I needed to make sure you're okay. I hate how I left things last night."

She tugged at a strand of hair and wrapped it around her finger, letting her eyes wander in the same direction as his as she tried to figure out where to start. "I'm fine. Was planning to take the day off and do nothing."

He turned his head and looked her over, nodded. "I got that much. You don't look like you're feeling so well—you sick or something?"

"Or something."

His gaze lingered on her face, and he scooted closer, rubbing a thumb on the soft part of her cheek, just under her eye. "Your eyes are puffy."

Her skin tingled where he touched, and the slight contact made her stomach jump with anticipation. She backed away. "Long night."

"Sorry for that," he murmured. "I'm sorry about, well, everything."

"Not entirely your fault." It was hard to admit, and even harder to ignore their proximity. She had to be strong, not let on how much he could affect her. If what she was about to tell him changed things, she would need to be able to walk away and still function. At least temporarily.

"Oh, so you're telling me someone *else* came over, about scared you to death, practically accused you of the unthinkable . . . and then forced you to kiss him?"

She smiled. "No, I can honestly say I didn't see anyone else after you left."

"Good." James blew out a breath. "Because, of course, if that happened, I'd have to track the guy down and kill him."

A giggle escaped her lips. "Is that so?"

"Yeah, it is." James picked up her hand, absently playing with her fingers. "I'm the only guy who should get away with something that . . . despicable." He brought her palm to his cheek, closing his eyes. "Can you forgive me?"

The gesture was so sweet, so sincere, it made her heart flip. She closed her eyes and drew in a strengthening breath. "James."

He turned his lips into the soft skin of her palm, closed his eyes again. "I like hearing you say my name like that. Like it has a whole other meaning to you."

This wasn't helping. Knowing she had to give it to him straight, she pulled her hand away and tried again. "I'm not mad at you. I'm just not sure it's wise for us to delve into a relationship right now. I can't give you what you want."

His face fell. "Can't or won't?"

"Does it matter?"

"Yes, it does." James recaptured the hand, pressing it between both of his. "It matters a lot, actually. You matter a lot."

She met his eyes, the blood pounding in her chest. "How can I matter when you don't know me? Not really. We haven't even gone on a real date."

"We can fix that today. Get dressed. I'll take you somewhere nice right now."

"I can't go right now," she sputtered. "I haven't even showered, and I have to . . ." She trailed off just short of telling him she had to go swim.

"Have to what?" He turned sideways, facing her.

"Never mind." The comforter slid to her waist as she stood, straightening her tank top to make sure the important parts were covered. "You matter to me too. Enough that it scares me." *More like, terrifies.* "And I don't want to hurt you, but if we do this—if we start something we can't finish—you *will* get hurt. We both will." She swallowed against the raw ache in her throat.

Looking bewildered, James stood and followed her out of the room. "Is this about him? Have you been avoiding me because . . . do you think I could ever hurt you the way he did? That I would?" He kept his word and didn't touch her, but reached out, his knuckles hovering near her cheek, caressing the air.

"No, he has nothing to do with this." Her every instinct screamed for her to lean in, to kiss him now, to at least close the distance between his hand and her cheek and feel the connection of skin on skin, the warmth of his touch, but instead, she backed up, one foot on the bottom stair. "I'm afraid. I don't want to be that prize you won and then regret."

"I hate when you talk in code." His voice cooled significantly as he leaned back, putting distance between them. "Why don't you stop worrying and let me decide what's best for me?"

She squeezed her eyes closed, the ache in her throat turning into a lump she couldn't swallow. "You don't know what you're dealing with—not really."

"So tell me. Let me make an informed decision."

Emma shook her hair back, hoping against her own judgment. "Is that really what you want?"

His "you-have-got-to-be-kidding-me" glare required no other response.

"Fine. Give me a few minutes." She pulled the comforter behind her as she tripped up the stairs, shaking with the knowledge of what she was about to do, the risk she was about to take.

James followed her to her bedroom, then talked through the door when she closed it. "You know I hate this, right? And I hate not having seen you all week."

She tossed the comforter on her bed, staring in the mirror at her disheveled hair and pale face. How did you go about telling the boy you're falling for that you're a mermaid changeling in the process of growing her fin?

She ran a brush through her hair and braided it, then straightened the cover on her bed. When the pillows were fluffed, and her trinkets all arranged, she dug in her closet for a fitted T-shirt and some cropped jeans and took her time getting dressed, still trying to decide where to start and how. Wondering how he would react, and what she would do if he ran away screaming.

When she opened the door again and found him still there, her heart did a little flip. *Maybe he can handle it.* "I thought you had to work today."

He followed her into the bathroom and leaned on the doorframe, watching as she lathered her face, rinsed the suds off with cool water, and patted dry. "Took the day off. I'm not in the mood. Bored with it."

"You must bore easily." She rolled her eyes, loading her toothbrush with paste. "One of these days, you'll realize you're bored with me."

"Baby, there's nothing remotely boring about you." His voice had a husky tone.

She ignored his comment—and the melting-chocolate sensation it gave her insides—while she brushed, spit, rinsed, and opened her makeup drawer.

"See that?" He pointed at the plastic containers holding pencils, brushes, lipsticks, and trays of color. "Even your bathroom isn't boring. What is all that?"

"Girl stuff." She sighed, feeling self-conscious. "Why don't you wait downstairs, let me get ready?"

"Can I watch you put it on?"

She pressed her lips together to keep from smiling. How did he manage to be both charming and creepy at the same time? "No. I'm serious. Go downstairs."

"But I like it better up here. With you."

"Now I'm getting annoyed." She shoved him into the hallway and closed the door, then leaned against the counter to apply mascara, allowing hope to wrap its strands around her. By the time she swabbed gloss on her lips, more pounding had her grinding her teeth. She flung the bathroom door open and stomped down the stairs, realizing belatedly that the noise wasn't coming from James. Someone else was knocking on the front door. "Does everyone in the world know I was planning to sleep in today?"

Keith met her on the stairs, showered and dressed, and looking guilty of something Emma couldn't even fathom.

And though she didn't see him, Emma felt James approach from the direction of the kitchen. Emma peeked through the blinds to see a uniformed police officer, and felt herself pale. At least this time she *knew* Keith was here.

Deep breath. She opened the door, forcing her voice to steady. "Lieutenant Peters. How can I help you?"

The lieutenant offered a reassuring smile. "Hi Emma, Keith." He raised an eyebrow and nodded. "James."

James nodded back.

"Are your parents around?"

Unsure if she should tell the police that her parents were now staying in Greece indefinitely, Emma hesitated. "Um. No. They're not back yet."

"Okay." He made a notation in his little notebook. "I have some information about your vandalism case, and I'd like to talk to them. When do you expect them?"

Emma's heart pounded. She'd always been a rotten liar. But what would happen if she told the truth? Keith answered for her. "Today my dad told me they're staying longer because of he loves researching, so now we don't know when they're coming home."

James cocked his head, eyebrows raised, but stayed silent.

"You can call them in Greece," Emma blurted. "My dad's cell phone has an international plan."

"Okay." Lieutenant Peters sighed, looking torn. "Look, I don't want to scare you, but seeing as how you're staying here alone," he glanced at James, then away. "I want to make sure you're taking extra precautions to be safe until we can figure this out."

The pounding in Emma's chest sped up, her shoulders tightening in anxiety. "What's going on?"

Lieutenant Peters met her eyes. "All the people on your list of possible suspects checked out. It's still feasible that one of them is our guy, but at this point, there's no evidence to indicate that anyone you named threw that brick through your window."

Her stomach pitched, because she knew there had to be more.

"However," he continued, "I noticed that you have a protective order against a Tom Rasmussen." Emma nodded, feeling her heartbeat in her toes. "In your statement, you said that Tom moved to San Diego last summer, but I think you should know that three days ago, he was stopped for speeding less than a mile from here. Told the officer he's moved back to the area because he got a job."

The knot in the pit of her stomach tightened, binding her in place, and making air feel scarce in her lungs. "But he's still not allowed to come near me, right? He won't, will he?"

"Theoretically, no. But for some people, a protective order is just a piece of paper. With your parents gone, I urge you to keep the doors locked at all times, be extra cautious, don't go walking alone at night, even to the neighbor's. And if Tom does come around, call us immediately."

What if Tom comes after me? What if he sees me swimming?

She couldn't breathe. No air, except the hurricane blowing in her ears. Lieutenant Peters' face swam in front of her eyes, and suddenly the house was hot. Too hot. If there was anything in her stomach, she'd have lost it. Even empty, the urge to throw up became so strong, she stumbled to the half bath, holding herself up with both hands while she dry-heaved over the toilet.

Someone said something, asked if she was okay, where she was going, did she need help. Emma couldn't answer, but someone else did. There were voices, lots of murmuring, then she heard the front door close. She squeezed her eyes shut, too scared to be embarrassed. She should send James away, make him go home so he didn't have to see her falling apart over an ex who would haunt her forever.

But then he was there, hand on her back, murmuring soothing words, offering her a glass of water and a washcloth, leading her out of the bathroom and back to the love seat. Sitting next to her and urging her to put her head between her knees and breathe.

Just breathe.

Before she realized what she was doing, she had his hand clutched between both of hers, using their combined fists as a support for her forehead. As a calm, steady anchor that would see her through a storm, she squeezed tight, wishing she could fix this, that there was some way to keep him without hurting him, without leaving him behind when she had to go. Wishing she could find a way to stay. To be with James and get over what Tom had done to her.

As James rubbed circles across her shoulders, she was glad she'd decided to tell him. Now. Today. Glad he'd understand why. Glad he'd know what was happening to her, and that she didn't leave on purpose. He needed to know he had a choice to avoid the pain she could cause him and move on.

"Emma? Emma, are you okay?" Keith sat on the floor in front of her, holding the water she didn't remember handing off or setting down. "Are you sick?"

She sat up, wiping her eyes with her wrist, and then drying it on her jeans, still holding James's hand. "No, just having a minor meltdown." She looked away from James. "I don't know why I reacted that way, but it was totally involuntary. Sorry."

"Why are you apologizing?" He leaned closer, lowered his voice to a murmur. "What did that guy do to you?"

Her whole body trembled—another involuntary response—and she let go of James's hand to curl her legs up to her chin and wrap her arms around them. "He broke me."

James clasped his hands together, squeezing hard enough that the veins in his arms rolled over the rippling muscles. He clenched his jaw, grinding his teeth while Emma told him everything that happened that night last spring as she came up from the beach. How Tom had broken two ribs on one side, and one on the other, displaced her shoulder, blackened both her eyes and slammed her head on the ground as he lay on top of her. He ripped her clothes, and might have done so many more unspeakable things. And how the shouting homeowner saved her.

Needing something to do with her hands, Emma sipped the water, then gently set the glass on an end table.

Keith leaned back on his hands and crossed his legs at the ankles. "The police took Mom and Dad to Emma at the hospital, and I stayed with Mrs. Hall, and Emma didn't come home forever, and then when she did, I didn't know it was her except because of her curly red hair."

James dropped his head in his hands, letting loose a stream of swear words Emma could barely hear. She knew he wanted to know what she was doing on the beach that late at night. And she was determined to tell him. But not in front of Keith. She had already talked about too many details in front of him today.

Her hands trembled when she picked up her glass again and finished off the water. "Keith, weren't you and Mrs. Hall going to the animal shelter to volunteer today? You should probably get ready for that. It's eleven."

"Oh, no. If I'm late, maybe they won't let me walk the dogs." Keith popped up off the floor and scurried to his room, and Emma watched him go, unable to look James in the eyes.

"There's more. Are you sure you want to know all this?"

James had been staring out the window, but turned his head, eyes blazing with too many emotions for Emma to identify just one. "Can't be worse than what you just told me, right?"

She struggled to find her voice in the thickness of her throat, more terrified by what still remained than by what she'd already told. "Yes, it could. But I'll let you decide that one yourself."

Footsteps pounding on the stairs announced that Keith was ready to go. Emma found her purse and handed him some cash for treats, then called Mrs. Hall to find out the approximate timeline before sending her brother across the street. James stayed relatively silent until after the front door slammed. "Right now, there are about a hundred different scenarios going through my head, and I hate every one of them. I'm kind of dying here. What could possibly be worse than having an ass beat the shit out of you?"

It wasn't fair to him, but nothing in *her* life had been fair lately either, and though it couldn't last, she needed him to be hers. Really, truly hers, unlike Tom. Needed to know that he was here for her, just her. She wanted the reassurance of having his arms around her, even if she wouldn't torture him with a kiss, however badly she wanted it.

Closing her eyes, she leaned into him, wrapped her arms around his waist, and rested her head against his chest. He took her in, arms around her back, absorbing her fear, strong and safe. So safe. His sigh was so soft, she didn't hear it, but felt it shiver through his chest and tickle her ear as he rested his cheek on the top of her head. "I may never understand you," he whispered. "But I wish you'd let me try."

"You're better off without me, you know."

"Don't." He cupped his hand under her chin and tilted her head up. "Dammit, Emma, don't keep doing this to me. It isn't fair. I don't want to keep this up for the rest of the year."

"What?"

"Pretending. Pretending I'm not looking at you during class, pretending I'm not searching for you at lunch. Pretending I can't feel you nearby at school every day, even when I can't see you." He loosened his grip on her and pulled back so he could tilt his forehead against hers. "Pretending I'm interested in other girls when the only girl I ever really see is you."

Emma felt her whole body go warm at his words. Why

couldn't he just get angry with her and yell and scream and swear? She knew how to handle anger. But this softer side, this honest admission, threatened to break her apart.

There was only one thing left now. But where to start? Maybe this part of the explanation would be best told from the very beginning.

"*TELL ME AGAIN* where we're going." Struggling to be patient, James fiddled with the knobs on Emma's stereo. He scrolled through the digital playlists, not really looking for anything specific, and settled on one Emma had labeled as "awesome songs," pleased when the first one was on his "tops" list too.

"I want to show you something." She flipped the blinker and curved toward the coast.

"Can I at least have a hint? Is it good, like, a favorite restaurant? Or bad, like where something bad happened?" His gut told him it was the latter, and if so, he wanted to be prepared. Although, when he thought about it, there was no way to prepare for anything when it came to Emma. That was the biggest problem in their relationship.

"Both, actually. Always both." She parked the car in front of a large house. On one side of the street, through a grove of citrus trees, wound a narrow foot path. The other side was a cliff with a steep drop-off. Emma slung a beach bag over her shoulder and led him into the trees. "I've never brought anyone here before, and I should probably warn you that whatever you suspect I'm going to show you right now is wrong. Or, at least, not right in the way you're thinking. But. I don't know how else to be sure you understand, so. Yeah." She raked her hands through her hair. "Why am I so nervous?"

He reached out, laced his fingers through hers, trying to hide his own nerves. "Because this matters to you, and having you share it with me means that I do too."

She stopped to face him. "You do matter. More than you should. That's part of the problem. I don't know what to do about you, and I'm afraid you might hate me after this." She tried to tug her hand free, but he held fast, and she relented.

He wanted to promise not to hate her, promise that he'd deal with whatever she told him. But he didn't. Because of Mark. And Lyle. All the things he'd heard, and what she'd already told him. Yes, it was stupid to make assumptions, but for now, assumptions and rumors were all he had. Fortunately, all the rumors in the world couldn't stop him from hiking that path, going down to that beach to find out everything he could about her. From knowing the whole truth.

As they emerged onto a rocky beach, the short patch of sand gave way to sharp, jagged rock littered with tide pools. To their right, the cliff rose straight up, and on the left, the trail wound through the trees to where they'd parked. Behind them, a school of fish swam in and out of the reeds and plant life growing in a pond about the size of a backyard swimming pool. The couple continued along the sand, and then onto rocks, until they reached a narrow ledge suspended between cliff and water. When James thought they'd run out of walking space, Emma pulled him into a small natural cave.

By the way she tossed her bag aside and flopped onto the sandy ground, James guessed she came here often. "This place is cool. How'd you find it?"

"I've always known where to find it. Maybe it found me." She patted the sand next to her and motioned for him to sit, so he did. Emma curled her legs up to her chin and wrapped her arms around them. The position made her look small, like a little girl. "I used to love the beach. Came every day for as long as I can remember. I had this thing for sitting on the sand with my toes in the waves, even in the winter when the water was like ice. Something about it just made me feel calm, whole. My parents didn't understand, but they humored me, you know? Probably had something to do with Gran. She used to threaten that if they wouldn't bring me here, she would. Sometimes she did." She rested her chin on her knees, staring out at the ocean.

"Anyway, when I was fifteen, my gran brought me here for a picnic, even though her house was on a beach. I used to think it was so funny that we had to get in her car and drive here, but even so, I knew this place was special, significant somehow. Anyway, I splashed and played and got soaked, and the whole time, *the whole time,* she watched me with this strange look on her face. On our way home, she asked, 'Emma, how do you feel when you're in that water?' and I told her it made me feel alive. She asked if it made my skin feel funny, which was a strange question, but I told her that my skin felt just fine. Then she warned me that if my feet ever felt itchy or tingly when I stepped in the ocean, I was to get out and go home and never come back."

Emma turned to meet his eyes, her expression mischievous. "Of course, that made me curious. And I blew it off, because Gran has never been the most stable person on the planet. In fact, not much later, she voluntarily moved into an assisted living facility. We invited her to move in with us, but she refused. Didn't want to be a burden. She's been there ever since.

"Just before I turned sixteen, I came to the beach—I came here—and put my feet in the water, and just like Gran's warning, they itched. No, that's not accurate. My skin burned so badly, it felt like fire scorched up the veins in my legs, and the pain was so distracting that next thing I knew, I was falling in the water. It wasn't that deep, but I couldn't figure out which way was up, couldn't get to the top to catch my breath. I swam and swam. Eventually, I surfaced and turned toward the beach, only to discover I was farther from shore than I realized, too far for me to have been able to swim back. I got scared, screamed and screamed, but no one could hear me. So, I started swimming again.

"In circles, apparently, because no matter how far or how hard I swam, I never made any progress. Then I met Merrick."

At the mention of another guy, James felt his chest tighten. "Who's Merrick?"

She sighed. "The second part of the story. I'm getting ahead of myself. Obviously, I made it back to shore alive." She reached out, squeezed his hand, her eyes pleading. "James. You can't tell anyone what I'm about to share with you. No one. For any reason. Swear it."

He turned his hand over, laced their fingers together and squeezed, feeling nervous in a way he never had before. Could he keep her secrets? Should he? In most cases, the answer would have been absolutely not. But he sensed this was big—for both of them. And it was Emma asking. If that's what it would take, he thought maybe he could. "I do. I swear."

She held his gaze for several long seconds. "Thank you. Okay, turn around."

"Why?"

"Just do it. And no peeking until I say."

He did as she asked, staring at the wall and listening to the crash of waves and something that sounded like rustling clothes. *Is she . . .?* "Um, Emma? Don't take this the wrong way, but it kind of sounds like you're taking your clothes off. Gotta be honest here, much as I'm dying to see you naked, I didn't realize we're in that place yet." As he heard his own words, he found himself wishing he could take them back. What guy in his right mind would tell a girl who looked like Emma he didn't want to see her naked? Killer was, he did, and not just see, but touch. Hold. But he wanted to go slow with her, easy, make it special, because she mattered to him. More importantly, he needed to matter to her. "Although, if you are, I can be too. But, you know, maybe just warn me first?" It would be strange timing, but he could go with it, adapt.

"Relax. It's not what you think."

The war of relief and disappointment inside surprised James. "That's, well . . . now I don't know what to think."

"Neither do I." Her giggle was of the nervous variety, and

it gave him a perverse amount of pleasure. "Don't turn around yet, but I'm ready. I'm going to jump in the water. I want you to wait ten seconds, then come out of the cave."

"Uh, okay. I guess I can do that."

"And James?"

"Yeah?"

"Promise me one more thing." He didn't answer, so she continued, her voice sounding small. "No matter what happens, whatever goes through your head, please, please promise you won't leave until you give me the chance to explain. Please." Her voice cracked on the last "please," and James's heart hammered with anxiety. "Please." Then. "I'm jumping in. Ten seconds."

He heard the splash, smaller than he'd expected, and it took all his willpower to give her the time she'd requested. When he finally dared look, it took him a minute to find her. She was underwater, swimming so fast she looked more like the blur of a fish than a human girl. He watched her move, fascinated with her speed, feeling disoriented because something about her felt wrong, different. Then she slowed, swam closer, brought her head up out of the water with her hair cascading down her back in waves of liquid fire that clung to her skin and the pink bikini top covering her breasts, and he realized what had changed.

Two tiny slits had opened up on each side of her neck, just above the necklace she apparently never took off. And though her legs weren't connected in the way he'd seen in storybooks, the skin on them had grown scales that, with the help of her swimming style, made them appear to be a fin.

Twenty-eight

JAMES STEPPED BACK, mouth hanging open with an emotion Emma couldn't quite gauge.

She approached slowly, leaving some distance between herself and the rocky ledge where he stood. Here, the water wasn't deep enough for swimming, but was too deep to sit in and keep her head above water, so she glided to the edge, careful to leave him some distance, and lifted herself up to perch on the rocks.

He continued to stare, clearly shocked, but didn't run away. Emma twisted the water out of her hair in silence, studying the bane of her existence—scales on her legs, webbing between her toes—while giving him time to process. Even though she'd started "the change" just before her sixteenth birthday, she refused to go naked, the way Merrick claimed all mermaids did. Being at least partially covered made her feel slightly less vulnerable, and after what James said earlier, as she felt his gaze drilling holes in her back, she was glad for her choice. Emma didn't look up or offer further explanation, and he didn't leave. The silence between them continued to stretch like taffy, thinner and thinner until there was nothing left but for it to break.

"Are you wishing you hadn't come back this morning?" Emma's throat felt hot, scratchy. James still didn't say anything. A hole opened up inside her chest, growing wider and wider with every unspoken accusation, every unshared thought. "Well. This is me. This is what Gran was trying to warn me against—not that either of us could have stopped it. This is why I both love and hate the ocean, why I couldn't go to Greece with my parents, and why I can't be with you."

His mouth moved, like he was trying to form words but had the sound muted. Finally he managed, "You're . . . you're a mermaid?"

"No, I'm an electric eel," she shot back.

He took a step toward her, tentative, holding out a hand as if he wanted to touch her but was afraid. "How did . . . when? How?"

She closed her eyes, preparing herself for the inevitable end, and trying to remember that it was for the best. "I started changing when I was fifteen, not long after that picnic with Gran. At first, it came as a driving need to go to the ocean, get wet. Swim around. No big deal, because I didn't understand what was happening, just that I was semi-obsessed with being at the beach and playing in the water. As time went on, the need grew into an addiction, and every few weeks, I'd have trouble breathing—felt a lot like pneumonia—until I could get to the water, dive in. Then I started *needing* to swim, and things happened to my body. Changes." This was the hard part, and Emma took a deep breath. "Now, I have to split my time between water and land, or my skin and lungs start to shrivel. The way things are going, by the end of summer, I won't be able to stay on land for any length of time. I'll have to stay in the water or die."

James made a choking sound, and Emma glanced up, but couldn't read what was in his eyes. Swamped with the pain of losing him, she almost couldn't speak. "I'd stop it if I could, but I don't know how."

"I don't understand," he croaked. "Is it . . . like a disease?"

Emma shook her head, staring at her shiny webbed feet. "I was born this way, James. Adopted. Raised by humans who don't know I'm not one."

His chest heaved, eyes wide with the enormity of what he was seeing. "Who's Merrick?"

She took another shaky breath. "The merman who first discovered I was changing. He brought me back to shore, explained what was happening to me, and how eventually I'll have to live permanently in Atlantis."

"You said you didn't have a boyfriend." His voice was incredulous as he lowered himself to sit cross-legged three feet away.

It took discipline for her not to be encouraged by the pain in James's voice. Pain meant he cared. "I don't. I don't even like the guy."

James squeezed handfuls of sand from a dip in the rocky ledge until it pressed between his fingers, then let go, and then squeezed again. Finally, he said, "Atlantis. So . . . what? It's inhabited by mermaids and located off the coast of California, rather than somewhere in the Greek Islands?"

Emma started to answer, but didn't know how. Instead, she changed the subject. "I'm what Gran calls a changeling. When she was a girl, there were legends of mermaids who would come ashore to hatch their young, but couldn't stay to care for them. In the stories, the mermaid mother would leave her baby on the doorstep of an unsuspecting family that was expected to raise the child until he or she was naturally forced to return to the sea, sometime around their eighteenth birthday." Unconsciously, she kicked her feet, sending a wave of water out toward the arch, and some of her despair floated away with it. "Gran believed the stories were nothing more than local fairy tales—until I showed up on her doorstep with a note pinned to my blanket. Something like, 'Must return to the sea in her eighteenth year.' I mean, it said more than that, I think, but that was the gist of it."

"She knew what you were, and kept you anyway." James scooted closer, making Emma shiver with more nerves. Hope could be a dangerous thing for her right now.

"Well, my parents had struggled to conceive for over ten years, and my mom was suffering a severe bout of depression because of it. In Gran's eyes, I was an answer to all their prayers."

"Weren't you?" One at a time, he pulled off his shoes, then stuffed his socks in them, and rolled up his jeans.

"Yes," she said with confidence. "I was. I am. And they're mine. I have never wished for anything the way I wish to stop the changes in my body so I can stay with them."

"Why do you think they picked your Gran? Wasn't she old to be raising a newborn?"

"We're not sure," she murmured, wondering if she would ever have the answers to all her questions. "But Gran thinks my birth parents might have lived or swam near her house. She thinks they picked her because she was close. Or because she was nice to them at some point. Or because they knew she would turn me over to my parents, and my dad is obsessed with Atlantis. I just think it was fate. But we'll probably never know."

James lowered his feet in the water and inched closer still. "If you'd listened to your Gran—stayed away from the water—would it have changed anything?" He looked up, meeting her eyes for the first time since she'd shown him her true self.

"No. I don't think so."

He cleared his throat like he had something stuck in it, and his voice was low and hoarse when he said, "How long do you have?"

Emma stared at the arch. It seemed so much smaller from this distance. "August if I'm lucky; June or July if I'm not."

The tension between them had become palpable, thick like fog and just as impossible to grasp, to break. She swallowed, wanting, needing, but no longer sure of what she wanted—what she needed. Everything and nothing. Nothing and everything. The world, the water, the land, the sky. Oceanside and Atlantis. James and her freedom. His arms around her, comforting, protecting, his lips on her face, in her hair, roaming her skin. More. So much more.

Time. It all boiled down to time.

James squinted into the distance, swinging his legs back and forth as he thought. "So. The night that guy beat you up. You came to swim, and he followed you and saw the other guy, Merrick? And then he thought . . ." James shook his head, his eyes flickering to her and away as he slid the pieces together in his head. He inched closer, close enough so they were only an arm's length apart.

"Yes." She wanted to reach out, touch him, tell him how sorry she was that they couldn't have more, that she couldn't be more for him. Tell him how much it meant to her that he was still here, how hard it had been to bring him in the first place, what it meant that she'd taken this chance at all. But the words wouldn't come. "So that's it. The story of me, the reason I keep telling you no, and why you should probably run away as fast as you can."

He sighed, loud and long. "If I was going to run, I'd have done it fifteen minutes ago."

Between the sea breeze and the last rays of sunshine, her legs were drying fast. Needing something to do with her hands, Emma scooped handfuls of water and poured them over her exposed scales, watching the water bead up and roll away from the contours, wishing he'd say something more, give her some indication of what was going through his head.

"Does it hurt?" James's voice was so low she had to strain to hear him.

"Which part?"

"You know, when your legs . . ." He waved his hand at them.

"It itches. Definitely an uncomfortable sensation, but I'm getting used to it."

James dug his fists into the sand, squeezing, but didn't take his eyes off her scaly legs.

"Look, I'm still me, okay? Just . . . more than you expected." She heard the quiver in her voice and cleared her throat. "Do you want to touch them?"

He raised an eyebrow. "Can I?"

"Unless you're afraid it's contagious." She took hold of his wrist and worked at loosening his fist until the sand drained away. The veins in his forearm stood out, flexed with tension, and his pulse jumped. Emma brushed his hand clean, then cupped it in both of hers and placed it on the curve of her lower thigh.

His intake of breath could've meant a hundred different things, but she tried not to speculate. His fingers stroked, nervously at first, but then more bold, down toward her knee. When he got there, he hooked his hand under and lifted, so Emma scooted back, pulling both legs out of the water and perching her feet on the rock. James continued down her calf to her heel, across the bottom of her foot to the webbing between her toes on that foot, then moved onto the other, until his hand ran up the length of her other leg, coming to rest on the hip opposite from where he'd started. He moved closer, sitting so they were hip to hip, facing each other. His eyes searched hers, exploring, hoping.

Desperate for his approval, Emma leaned toward him, resting her hand on the side of his neck.

It was all the encouragement he needed. James pulled her onto his lap and wrapped his arms around her, his lips crashing down on hers, hungry, demanding, needy. She could feel him searching for the Emma he'd kissed before, the human one he knew already. Determined to prove she was the same person, Emma kissed him back, finally giving him everything, the emotions, the fear, all the love she'd been withholding.

One of his hands roved over her back, found the bare skin on her stomach, drew a trail down the side of her waist to where soft skin transitioned to smooth scales. That hand rested there, pulled her closer while his other stayed busy, trailed up her arm, around her bare shoulder—he traced the fin-shaped birthmark—and stilled near the thin string knotted at her neck. He played with the tie, a mischievous glint in his eye, and Emma gave a half-hearted swat at the naughty hand. "Be good."

"Trying." His voice was breathless, throaty. He trailed a line of kisses down the side of her neck to her shoulder, then back again by way of her collarbone.

A new kind of tingling zinged through Emma, starting at each new place James touched and expanding until her whole body trembled. He kissed her like she was air he needed to breathe, like she was life and death and everything in between. Trouble was, the moment he'd touched her scales, she realized that James wouldn't be the only one whose heart would bleed when this was over.

When she tried to pull away, he tugged her back. "I'm not finished yet."

"James." She rested her forehead on his. "My legs are drying and it's really uncomfortable. I need my towel."

He nodded, cradling her in his arms as he stood—wobbling on the uneven surface—and carried her into the shelter. With one arm holding tight around James's neck and her lips occupied, Emma searched blindly for her bag, finally coming up with a handful of thick terrycloth.

She'd been fully removed from the water for several minutes, and Emma could feel the sensation of her scales smoothing back into regular, hairless skin, her gills closing and drawing under her delicate membranes. Gasping with the change, she pushed against James's chest, more firmly than before. "You have to put me down. I need to get the salt off. It burns."

He groaned against her lips, but didn't argue, and set her gently on the sand. She pulled the towel out of her bag and dried off, then draped it over her, leaning against the wall, eyes closed, while she caught her breath. She would never recover from losing him. "You couldn't just let me go, could you?" Her voice cracked as emotion threatened to drown her. "Had to stay long enough to torture us both."

The sand beside her shifted, and she could feel heat radiating off his body as he settled next to her. "I tried."

Her stomach wrenched in agony as she thought about what her life would be like in a few months. "Maybe it'll be easier after I'm gone."

His breathing paused, and she opened her eyes to find him glaring at her. "What do you mean, easier? Hell, no—it won't be easier. Especially not now. Don't tell me that after all this," he waved his arm around, pointed at her legs, now dry under the towel, "you're going to keep pretending this isn't happening. That you're not falling for me just as hard as I've already fallen for you. I don't buy it."

Her mouth fell slack as she shook her head. "No. No pretending. No more lies. I don't . . . I won't. But, you have to understand. I can't stop this process. In a few months, I'll be gone. And it won't matter who I love, or how little time we've had—I'll have to leave you all behind."

He banged his head against the cave wall, his throat working like he was trying to swallow something large, and closed his eyes. "You should get dressed, then, before I'm tempted to move this relationship at Mach speed." He scrubbed his hands over his face. "I hate not knowing what I'm up against. Or who. But I don't know what to do with the things I do know, either."

Her hand stilled in the process of gathering her clothes. He knew there was more, others involved, and she owed it to him to be straight about Merrick. About Keith and her parents. Tom. She would hold nothing back. Not now.

James didn't move, not even a flicker of his eyelids, while she changed. Considering how active his hands had been only minutes ago, this worried her. Once she'd pulled on a shirt and buttoned her jeans, she tickled the bottom of his bare foot with her toes. "All clear."

His eyes popped open, and he watched silently as she rubbed her hair dry with the towel, then brushed it out and plaited it in a loose braid down her back. "What are you thinking?" he asked.

Wishing I hadn't stopped you kissing me just now. Considering climbing back into your lap to pick up where we left off. Wondering how I'll ever live without you. "Trying to figure out what else I need to tell you, and how."

He nodded, catching her hand in his and pulling her knuckles to his cheek, eyes closed. "Still determined to get rid of me?"

She stroked his lips with her thumb. "No, but I don't know how to keep you, either."

The corners of his lips turned up as he stood and brushed himself off. "Guess that's a step up from where I was when you answered the door this morning."

She narrowed her eyes, trying to flirt, but only managing to blink the salt out. "More than a step. And I'm tired of pretending, too. Tired of lying. Tired of fighting."

"Agreed." He grabbed her wrists and pulled her to him, sliding her arms around his middle, then draped his arms around her back. "It would all be so much easier if we just gave in to it."

"Why don't you let me tell you the rest? Then, if you still want to stick around, take your chances with me, we'll go on an actual, real-live date. I'll pay."

"Are we back to that again? Who gets to pay?"

She sighed, exasperated. "Fine. You can pay if you want. Whatever. I'm just saying—"

"We can go public?" His smile was slow and easy, and so full of warmth she wondered how she'd ever be cold again. But she still worried about the possible repercussions of what her reputation—however false—could do to him. Especially once she was gone.

"Are you sure you want that?"

In answer, he leaned down and kissed the tip of her nose. "Babe, there is nothing in this world that would make me more proud than to claim you in front of the whole entire school. They could hold an assembly about it. Tell everyone else I'm permanently off the market. Or whatever."

"I don't think we should go quite that far, but . . . okay." She took a breath, knowing that the hardest revelations were yet to come. "I haven't dated anyone since Tom. He tried to . . . and it scared me. A lot. More than all my other injuries, I was just scared."

James squeezed tighter, his arms shaking, but his heartbeat soothing.

"They charged him as an adult, so he actually went to jail for a few months, and when he was released, my parents got a protective order so he couldn't come near me. And then he moved, so I stopped being so scared and—"

A splash and the slap of webbed footsteps were followed by a gasp. Emma and James whipped their heads around to catch Merrick at the mouth of their little cave, looking flabbergasted and disgusted. "Human, what are you doing with my mate?"

Twenty-nine

"MERRICK." EMMA TRIED TO PULL out of James's arms, but he held fast, trying to gauge her level of guilt. If she didn't like this guy, why would she worry what he thought? What was between them, really? "I was swimming. Showing James . . ."

Merrick glared at Emma, and the possession in his eyes made James wonder exactly how well Merrick knew her. He glanced down, then away after confirming his suspicion that Merrick was, in fact, buck naked. Nauseating and annoyingly so.

"You should not have brought him here." Naked or not, Merrick stormed toward them, hand extended as if he intended to yank Emma out of James's arms. Not sure whether to tighten his hold or let go, James didn't move. Though she could've pulled away now, Emma shrank into

James's chest. Merrick paused, head tilted to one side in confusion, and James was rewarded with a smidgen of satisfaction. *Two points for the human.* This was the most awkward situation he'd ever been in. Although, when he thought about it, had Merrick shown up just five minutes earlier, or if Emma hadn't made him slow down, the discomfort would've been compounded by about a hundred, considering how he'd pretty much lost himself in her.

As Merrick glared, seething over something, the drunken euphoria James had felt when kissing Emma drained away, replaced by a heavy, leaden sense of dread that felt like a brick in his stomach. The merman was more than angry. He was jealous.

And James had no idea what angry, jealous mermen were capable of. Nor did he understand why Merrick would have reason to be jealous.

"There's nowhere else," Emma said to Merrick, her voice rising. Her hand absently gripped James's T-shirt, twisting in anxiety. "This is the only place I know where I can swim and not be discovered by people. The only protected place. You know that."

"Yeah. Don't really like the idea of my girlfriend becoming a lab rat." James piped up, loosening her grip. "And dude, could you like, cover up or something? I find it beyond creepy that you're waving the jewels around."

"Girlfriend?" Emma bit her lip, looking uncertain, and James felt his heart sink lower. He dropped his arms from around her and tried to take a step back, but she still had hold of his shirt. "Are you sure . . .? Do you really want . . .?"

"Yeah, I thought we were just discussing that," James heard himself murmur.

"Emma wears the jewels," Merrick interrupted, indicating her necklace. "And she cannot be your mate. Tangaroa has promised her to me. When she returns to Atlantis, we will be joined."

"Emma?" James looked at her face, expecting her to deny any such thing, and found only utter despair. "He can't be serious." Still, no denial. "I thought we . . . but what about—"

"That's what I've been trying to tell you, James. The sea king made a deal with Merrick, and I don't know what other choices I have, because I've never met the sea king, but I'm trying to find a way out. I'm *not* his."

The word "*yet*" echoed in his head, and something inside him ripped open, gushed so hard, he almost couldn't breathe. Emma finally let go. Shrank back toward the cave wall like she was afraid. "But you will be."

Her voice shook. "No. Not by choice. I would never—"

"But you knew. All this time, you've known you're going to go with him, run away to Atlantis with him, and you let me fall for you anyway."

"Yes. No. I wasn't . . . I tried to stop you." Her hiccup sounded more like a sob. "And I'm not running away with him. I don't *want* to go. Who would run away to a prison?"

"You said no more lies, Emma. No more pretending." Pain, hot and sharp, stabbed through him at the very idea that she and Merrick had a thing. A romantic thing. A companionship thing. An intimate thing. They'd never discussed this part of her past before, and he had no idea how deep her connection with Merrick went, or how intimately it had been explored. The idea of Emma and this guy, of Emma and any guy—merman or human—boiled his blood until he worried he'd burn up. Self-preservation kicked in, and James reacted the only way he could. "Damn. I must be the stupidest guy on the planet. Here I am ready to dive in and take on your past, attempt to heal your scars, while you're busy squeezing me in before you get—what did he say? Joined. So, I'm what? The other man? Your last fling? Dammit, Emma." Heart aching with loss, he let loose a long string of profanities to which he would never otherwise expose her.

Both hands flew to her mouth, muffling a mewling sound, and tears trickled down her cheeks, but James ignored the twist in his gut. Already, he was fighting the urge to sweep her up and carry her off like a caveman. Even when his mother left, he hadn't felt so betrayed. This was not part of his plans for future happiness.

Shaking with a mixture of anguish and pent-up rage, he pushed past Merrick, pausing long enough to rake his gaze up and down the merman with a mirthless chuckle. "Dude. Seriously? You should learn to cover up. Not exactly a set to be parading to the masses, if you get what I mean. Especially the competition." He grabbed a handful of loose rocks off a ledge and hurled them toward the water, wrenching his shoulder and taking strength from the pain.

"James. James, wait. Please, let me explain." Emma sobbed as he snatched his shoes and headed out of the cave.

The sound hurt just enough to make him pause, slowly turn back. "You were right, Emma. It's all too much. I think

I'm going to say good-bye now, before I sink any further over my head."

A keening wail followed him out of the cave, but he ignored it, jogging as fast as he could barefooted over the uneven rocks. He stopped where the trees met the sand at the bottom of the trail and sat on a fallen log to put on his shoes. Might as well not cut his feet into the same shreds as his heart. He pulled on his socks, fighting the instinct to look back toward the cave and wonder what was going on in there.

A tiny voice in the back of his head whispered that he shouldn't go. That leaving her alone with that guy was probably not the best move he'd ever made. She told him there was more to the story, made him promise to stick around, so maybe he should've stayed. But another voice, the one that formed lumps down his throat and all the way into his toes, told him to go. Get away before he lost it and did something else stupid. To put her out of his mind and never think of her again. His life would be so much simpler without her.

Yet, so lonely.

From the cave, high-pitched arguing echoed off the sandy hills. James tied his laces and stood to leave, but at the last second, he ducked into a denser part of the wooded area. He had no idea why he should wait. It made no sense. Except that deep down, he wanted to make sure she came out safely.

At the moment, he cursed his chivalrous side. Over and over again. Thoughts and visual images of what could be going on in that cave made him want to vomit. He closed his eyes and rested his forehead on a tree, licking his lips. He could still taste her. Still smell her on his hands, his clothes. She was everywhere. And that was the problem, wasn't it? He couldn't just leave her there, because whatever else she was, or had done, or was planning to do, her safety mattered to him.

But why? His heart thudded, bleeding harder, the knife twisting deeper with each beat. Love. That's why. He was in love with her. And he didn't know how to turn it off. So, he hugged a tree—literally—and waited, every second a new lesson in agony that seemed to drag into forever and ever and always until he couldn't wait anymore. Until he had to leave or drown himself or storm into the cave and snap Merrick's neck.

He peeled his arms away and disconnected his forehead from its resting place, ready to hike up to the road. He'd gone less than a dozen steps when he heard her voice, shouting. Full of hatred, anguish. "Go. Get out of here! Take it. Take my necklace and just *leave!*"

James turned back in time to see Emma run out of the cave—still fully clothed, to his relief—and throw something shiny way out into the ocean. Merrick shouted back at her, but the wind ate up the words before James could decipher them, and then Merrick dove into the water, with Emma shouting profanities at his back.

She stormed back into the cave, and was out again seconds later wearing her sandals and carrying her beach bag. Not wanting to be caught spying, James slunk farther into the lengthening evening shadows, taking shelter behind a particularly wide rubber tree. Minutes later, she crunched past, sniffling, hiccupping, her usually confident steps uneven.

Guilt. He'd hurt her on purpose, even though he was positive that if he lived to be two hundred and kissed a girl every single day, he'd never again experience a kiss like the one he'd shared with Emma.

When he could no longer hear her footsteps, James stood and followed slowly up the trail, unable to process the span of emotions he'd experienced in one day. Too much. Too many. And all he could feel at the moment was pure and utter numbness.

WHEN SHE REACHED THE SIDEWALK near her car, Emma half hoped to see James waiting there, wanting to talk, needing a ride—something. Stark reality stung more tears from her eyes when it hit her just how much damage had been done. To James, to her, maybe to Merrick—not that she cared. Okay, she cared a little. He already scared her, and there was no telling what he'd be like the next time she saw him.

She hated him for once again being at the center of her most heart-wrenching problems. He had the worst timing of anyone alive.

Despair, tall as a building and overwhelming as fog, settled over her as she opened the car door, still trembling. A cold breeze blew under her hair and down her shirt, effectively turning her trembling into a fit of shivers. She slammed the door and started the car, cranking the heater to full blast. She should've put the top up, but found she didn't have the energy. Her lungs struggled to pull in air as she leaned both arms on the steering wheel and rested her forehead there, allowing the tears to wash her eyes clean. Maybe she should stop fighting and just give in. She was pretty sure that once she embraced what was happening and crossed the threshold of Atlantis, her change would become complete. Go to Atlantis, give up life as she knew it, her plans and her ideas and her hopes for the future, and let fate take her where it would.

Why was she still fighting the inevitable?

Mom. Dad. Keith. Gran.

Emma glanced at the clock. It was dinnertime. As long as Keith was still okay with Mrs. Hall, it wasn't too late to go visit Gran. She needed someone to cry to.

Her whole body felt hollow. Empty. Spent.

Her relationship with James was over before she'd had the chance to embrace it. He'd walked away. She'd finally accomplished the thing she'd meant to do from the beginning.

Why did success hurt so badly, she could hardly breathe? She gulped. Wasn't this what she'd wanted? To protect both of them from inevitable heartache? Well, too late for that, because now she couldn't remember why she'd fought against loving him in the first place.

Emma wiped her eyes on the sleeve of her sweatshirt and put the car in gear. One thing she knew for certain. No matter what happened, even if she did end up staying in Atlantis, she would not be with Merrick. Not after today. Not when he'd so thoroughly succeeded in ripping her heart to shreds. Even if she could have tolerated him before, he would forever be a constant reminder of everything she'd lost, especially James.

A breeze rustled the leaves in some nearby trees, and she glanced at the trail, wondering if she'd ever again be able to come here and not feel an overwhelming resentment for the place she'd grown to love.

Another tear fell before she peeled away from the curb, feeling absolutely and completely lost.

SEEING HER LIKE THAT—curled over the steering wheel, gasping for air—did something to James, ripped another hole in a place he thought was already wide open. He hung back in the shadows, leaning against his tree and watching through the web of leaves and vines.

If Emma wanted to be with Merrick, she had the ability. Obviously, he wanted her, was waiting for her to come to him. He even had a plan for her future as a mermaid of privilege. Yet, she was still here. And minutes ago, she'd kissed James as if he was valuable and important to her. The idea caught in his chest, made him pause and hold his breath. He licked his lips again, trying to find another taste of her. He'd kissed a lot of girls. More than he cared to admit. Done a lot more than kissing with a couple. But none of them, not a single one, had ever felt so completely his as Emma had down there in that cave. He'd felt the shift about the time he'd pulled her into his lap, the shift from curiosity and lust into something more substantial. More meaningful and important. It was the reason he'd gone so far with her, and also the reason he'd stopped, knowing full well she'd probably give in if he pushed the right buttons. And he knew those buttons well.

How could he have imagined a connection like that? But then Merrick came and things got all confused. James banged his head against the tree. What was wrong with him? He shrank into the shadows when Emma turned to look back. A tear rolled down her cheek before she drove away.

When she was out of sight, he left the grove, realizing for the first time how dark it had become. He glanced at his watch, swearing viciously. As if this day hadn't been bad enough, he now had fifteen minutes to get across town—on foot—to basketball conditioning.

THE GOOD THING ABOUT BEING late was that James didn't have to worry about avoiding Lyle and Mark in the locker room because they were already on the court when he jogged in. He'd been lucky enough to catch a bus not far from the beach, and managed to be only ten minutes late, but ten minutes was enough.

Riding the bus had given him time to think. He regretted not sticking around long enough to hear the rest of what Emma had to say. Or what Merrick was going to say, for that matter. Maybe it was just wishful thinking, but the way Emma clung to James when Merrick got possessive hadn't escaped his memory. And Merrick had seemed confused and angry when he'd caught them together, but strangely calm. Jealous, yes, but maybe there was a difference between "I'm-in-love" jealous and "she's-my-property" jealous. Had the situation been reversed, James didn't know how he would've reacted, but calm was definitely not it. More likely, he'd have pounded Merrick black and blue first and asked who he was later.

Emma couldn't love Merrick. James would've seen it, would have felt it in her kiss, in the set of her arms around his waist. So. What was it, then?

He jogged onto the court just in time to be thrown into the scrimmage game on the side opposite Mark and Lyle. An hour later, James's side was up by eight, the whole team good and sweaty, and Coach called practice.

"That's it for today, guys. You played well—now go home and get some rest. Don't forget early practice Monday. We can't afford to lose this week." Chatter and team spirit rippled through the gym. "Phelps—stick around."

James held back as the rest of the team hit the showers, knowing he was about to be lectured. "Sorry I was late, Coach."

Coach frowned as he stared at the scoreboard. He cleared his throat, turning to James. "Hope you have a good excuse, or I might be forced to bench you next game."

"Uh, I had an appointment." It was true. Sort of. He and Emma *had* agreed to have a talk.

"What kind of appointment?" Coach glared now, and James knew he was in for it.

"The personal kind, Coach." He wiped the sweat off his forehead with his already-soaked jersey.

"Your parents going to back that up when I call them?" Coach poked James in the chest with his clipboard.

James stood his ground. "My dad will, if you can get a hold of him, sir. Or I can have him call you on Monday."

"Do that, Phelps. I find out you skipped in late because you were diddling around with a girl or something, you're benched, got that?"

James nodded and leaned over to gulp a mouthful of water from the fountain. He would need to give his uncle Ryan a heads up.

The coach made a harrumphing noise under his breath. "Since you missed the first ten minutes, I want twenty laps—two laps per late minute."

James groaned. Sometime between driving, blocking, and shooting, he'd made a decision. He wouldn't be able to sleep until he talked to her—she probably wouldn't, either. They might as well hash it out tonight. Better to get it over with. She didn't have enough time left for him to waste any.

"But first, drop and give me a hundred push-ups. You do the math."

When did Coach become so harsh?

"Get going, boy," Coach growled. "I want to eat dinner sometime before tomorrow."

James dropped on the floor, not bothering to hide his scowl, and put the last of his strength into a serious workout. He was going to be a while getting back to Emma's. Fortunately, he was pretty sure she'd still be up.

Thirty-one

EMMA KNOCKED ON THE DOOR as she pushed it open and was pleasantly surprised to find Gran rocking away in her recliner, engrossed in a TV show. "Hi, Gran."

"Back already. You catch that James Dean look-alike yet? Get him to take you out properly?"

Emma tried to smile, but a sob climbed up her throat instead, and she gasped, momentarily struggling to breathe.

Gran clicked off the TV and pushed herself out of the chair. "Here, now. What's all this about?"

Emma sank onto the edge of Gran's bed, not realizing she was shaking until it creaked. "Why can't I just have a normal life? Be a normal girl who likes a boy and goes to dances and movies and bonfires, and who doesn't have to swim every few days just so she can tolerate regular air?"

Gran sat next to Emma, stroking her hair. "He rejected you."

More miserable than she'd ever been, Emma shook her head. "No. Well, yes, he did, but not at first. Not the way I expected. It's my fault. I pushed him away and kept pushing until I couldn't anymore, because I need him. I tried to let him go, like you said. I promise I tried. But he kept coming back, and now I've ruined it. It hurts. It hurts so much. I think I'm in love with him, Gran."

"That's nothing to be ashamed of, honey. Love is a beautiful thing. You should experience it as it comes. Don't let a crazy old woman's advice keep you from it."

More sobs settled in her chest, so Emma buried her face in her hands until she could talk again. "It's too late. I told him. About me. My changes, my future. Thought he'd run away, you know? I took him to the cave, swam so I could show him my scales, my gills. I trusted him with things my own parents don't even know. And he was okay with it, I really thought he was okay with it, until Merrick showed up. And now . . . James probably hates me, Gran. Merrick told him about the deal with the sea king. James was so angry, and he left me there. He wouldn't even let me tell him that I don't want Merrick. That I have never wanted Merrick."

Gran took Emma's face in her hands, her steady eyes searching Emma's. "I doubt James hates you. Not for being truthful. He's just processing. Tell me everything. We'll figure it out."

So Emma explained about James and how he'd managed to weasel his way into her heart, even after she'd tried so hard to avoid it, how Merrick messed up everything, and how she'd given him the necklace she'd had since birth just to get rid of him. Gran listened, frowning, shaking her head, and holding on to Emma whenever her voice cracked or tears broke loose.

When Emma was sure there was nothing more to explain, she lay back on Gran's bed, wishing she could spend the night. Gran lay on her side next to Emma, singing a familiar childhood lullaby, stroking Emma's arms and hair and forehead.

After a while, Emma sat up. "Guess I should get home, check on Keith. Go to bed so I can pretend today never happened."

Before Emma could stand to leave, Gran gripped her wrist and stroked her cheek. "Honey. If that boy of yours is worth an ounce of the heartache I see in your eyes, you should go to him, tell him you love him, make him believe you."

"He won't listen, Gran. I tried."

"Give him a chance, darling. He was hurt. Probably shocked. Definitely confused—you would have been too. My guess is, after he's had time to cool off, to think it through, he'll be back. It's up to you to make sure he understands what's at stake. Your safety depends on it. Chances are, it will be too much for him, but at least you'll know he isn't going to go spouting off to the media or sending university scientists after you out of spite."

Emma nodded, not even wanting to consider those possibilities.

"And baby, next time you see Merrick, get your necklace back. It's important somehow, or he wouldn't have wanted it in the first place."

When Emma got home, she ignored the pain that surfaced when she saw James's bike in her driveway—they'd taken her car to the cove—and went inside to relieve Mrs. Hall. Keith had eaten dinner, and he was happily engrossed in a TV show by the time their sweet neighbor said good-bye. Darkness had long since fallen, and Emma wanted nothing more than to crawl in bed and stay there indefinitely. Or at least until her parents came home. She wandered the house aimlessly, ignoring the plastic-wrapped meal left in the fridge, courtesy of Mrs. Hall, and eventually begged Keith to call it a night so she could as well. When he did, Emma stumbled up the stairs, where she peeled off her sweatshirt and fell into bed, exhausted.

Why did she feel like she needed to swim again already? It didn't make sense.

Tomorrow. Tomorrow she would track down James and tell him . . . what?

She sighed, snuggling deeper into her pillow. The truth. She could offer him nothing more than her heart.

Thirty-Two

JAMES CURSED HIMSELF the entire walk home. His muscles ached, his head swam, and his shoulders knotted with frustration and anger over the way his night had gone. Added to everything else, he'd left his bike at Emma's.

He went home anyway, took care of dinner—it was his turn, after all—showered, and pretended to go to bed early. Soon after ten o'clock, he heard the TV in the living room switch off, and his dad's laborious breathing as the man trudged down the hall. James removed the screen from his window and climbed out, creeping along the side of the house, cut through the neighbor's yard to the sidewalk around the corner.

Half an hour later, he stood at the base of Emma's front porch, heart sinking. The house was completely dark—without even the smallest hint of light shining through the closed blinds. "Please be here, Emma, and please be awake." His first knock was soft, and brought no sign of movement from inside. He knocked harder. Still nothing.

"You gotta be kidding me." James swore, trying to decide what to do next. How could she possibly sleep after everything that had happened today? He was exhausted after practice, but knew he wouldn't be able to sleep until they cleared things up, so he'd walked—*walked!*—the two-plus miles to her house. Maybe she wasn't as upset as he'd thought.

Maybe she wasn't home.

He tried the doorknob, and when it turned in his hand, a shiver of worry had him opening the un-chained door, murmuring, "Emma?"

No answer. More worry.

"Emma?" he said louder.

Nothing. Something wasn't right. Why was the house unlocked? A faint sound—was it a whimper? A gasp?—had him moving up the stairs toward Emma's room. He paused by her door, listening, wondering if he should knock, wondering if she was asleep, wondering what she was wearing. What if she slept naked?

He knocked softly, turning the knob with caution—just in case. "Emma? Are you awake? It's James." The room was dark, except for a ray of moonlight spilling through the uncovered window. The light fell over half of Emma's face and the arm she'd flung over her head, turning her skin a light shade of blue, and her hair dark like the skin of a plum. She looked like a painting—ethereal and angelic.

She was wearing the same clothes from earlier, minus the sweatshirt. Her shoes lay on the floor near the side of her bed, the bag she'd taken to the beach dumped next to them, specks of sand still clinging to the sides. Like she'd come home and fallen in bed.

He couldn't move. What was he doing? Spying on her while she slept. Should he wake her up or leave a note? Did he even want her to know he'd come back?

She gasped again, turning on her side and curling her knees into her chest with a shiver. James crept to her bed and pulled the comforter up to her shoulders.

He closed her door with a quiet click and headed into the family room where he'd once spent the night, plopped onto the couch, and dropped his head in his hands, threading his fingers through his hair. He couldn't go home. With his luck, he'd probably get busted, then he'd really have a problem. But what was he doing here? Waiting for her to wake up? To find him . . . what? Asleep on her couch? Waiting to talk? To yell at her again?

What he wanted most was to finish what they started in that cave—the first part, more than the last. But that was just a bad idea all the way around. Why did he come back again?

"What are you doing in my house?" Emma croaked.

Startled, James jumped to his feet. When had she come in? "Emma. I . . ." What? How could he give her an answer when he'd just been asking himself the same thing? "I didn't mean to wake you. Sorry. I came to talk."

"So you broke into my house?" She padded into the room and perched on the arm of the couch with a heavy sigh. "You already said good-bye. What more is there?"

"I came to say I'm sorry for the way I reacted. And for the record, the door was open. Well, it was closed, but unlocked. It worried me." Her hair was rumpled, her face free of makeup, and she had a sleep mark on her cheek. James caught himself staring and glanced away, trying to focus.

"Why would you worry?"

"You mean something to me. A lot of something. I care about you, Emma, and it scares the hell out of me. I wish I knew what to do about it." He knew what he wanted to do about it, but doing *that* would definitely complicate things a whole lot more. And it wouldn't keep her here.

"Me too." Shaking her head, she slid onto the couch and leaned back, wide awake now. "What do you want from me, James? I can't change what's happening to me. Believe me, I would."

"I want . . ." What? How could he tell her when he didn't even know himself? He settled on the other end of the couch, careful to leave a full cushion between them. Again, he leaned his elbows on his knees and pressed his forehead onto his fists in frustration. "Look. I don't know, okay? I just . . . can't seem to stay away."

Emma rested her feet on the edge of the cushion, her arms wrapped around her legs. "Not for my lack of trying."

"A fact that hasn't escaped me." She'd been pushing him away since they met, and it wasn't like him to pursue a girl the way he'd had to pursue Emma.

She sighed. "It'll get easier. The longer you stay away, the easier it will be."

"So, it's a mermaid thing? Like, a siren call or something?

Is that why I can't get you out of my head?" It would make sense. He wanted it to be true, just to feel like there was an explanation as to why he was such a wreck over her.

"More like common sense. When people are apart, relationships tend to fade. I mean, yes, when I've been swimming, I probably put off extra pheromones—I don't actually know for sure—but the rest of the time I'm pretty sure I'm no more special than anyone else."

"Oh. Right." James took a deep breath, deciding to just spit it out. He had to know. "That guy in the cave. Merrick. What's the real story with him? He acted possessive, like he had a claim on you. But before that, I was under the impression . . . I felt like I did, too. Unless whatever happened between us was purely physical. It wasn't for me. But. Maybe for you?"

"James."

He closed his eyes, his heart thudding with a dull ache.

"How can you want this?" She nudged his thigh with her toes until he turned his head, met her steady gaze. "I'm a mess. And that's not going to change. In fact, it only gets worse from here."

"Why do you do that?"

"What?"

"That push/pull thing you've been doing since we met. You push me away, then reel me back in. It's driving me crazy."

"Who's reeling who, James? I've been doing just fine on my own, but then you show up and never seem to go away. You just keep coming back." She picked up the TV remote and lobbed it at him. Reflexively, he stuck his hand out and caught it before it could do any damage. "I have enough to worry about without you adding more. I didn't even want a guy in my life."

"So call the cops." James tossed the remote on the floor, inching closer to her. Reeling her in, the way she'd continually done to him. "I broke into your house in the middle of the night. Go ahead, call them."

"I should."

"But you won't. Why?"

She dropped her forehead onto her knees, pulling in a long, slow breath. "I don't know. Maybe I've had enough of cops this week. Maybe I just want to finish this conversation so we can both move on with our lives."

"Or maybe you lo—" He stopped himself before voicing the "L" word. Somehow, he doubted saying it would do either of them any good right now. Part of him believed it was true—that she did. But there was no way to be sure, and he didn't think his heart could take a denial right now. "Fine. Fine. Let's finish the conversation then. I want to know the rest."

"The rest of what?"

"The rest of everything. All of whatever you were going to tell me before that pretentious prick showed up and interrupted us."

"He is kind of a prick, isn't he?"

The look he gave her felt like response enough as he leaned back, running a hand through his hair to keep from touching her. "I think I must have a masochistic need to understand why you continually crush my ego."

"Crush your ego? That's what you're worried about?"

"Wait, that's not what I meant." He pounded the cushion with his fists, feeling tongue-tied and nervous all over again. "I just meant . . . I need . . . Ugh. What's wrong with me? My brain isn't cooperating with my mouth."

She snorted. "Why don't you do us both a favor and be quiet while I tell you about my family." She sobered. "And Merrick."

James closed his eyes, nodding as nerves caused his stomach to gurgle. "Okay. But can you promise me one thing?"

"Depends on what it is."

"If I open my big mouth before you're finished, please smack me."

"Done." Her fingers grazed his and he took them, laced their hands together and squeezed.

Emma started. "My parents—my brother—they don't know what's happening to me. I haven't told them. But not long after I started to change, my grandmother—who had, apparently, been watching for signs—figured it out. She came to me, explained how I was adopted, how I was left on her doorstep by neighbors who disappeared. She told me that my mom and dad didn't know she suspected I was a changeling. She never told them about the note. I wanted to tell them then, but Gran and I both worried about how they'd take it. Seems like this is how it would feel to tell them I had a terminal disease."

James felt his heart skip, and squeezed her fingers tighter than he meant. Emma manually loosened his grip and stroked the top of his hand.

"Don't worry—mermaid-ism isn't terminal. Merrick claims they live a lot longer than humans. At least, I think. Maybe they keep time differently in Atlantis. Who knows? The point is that soon I'll be forced to leave my family, and I won't be able to come back—ever."

This time the squeezing happened in his chest. But—as promised—he didn't say anything.

"So I've written letters to each of my family members. Gran will deliver them when I can no longer come back myself. And she'll explain why, so they'll know I didn't leave by choice. But also that I can't come back."

"But that guy, Merrick, came ashore." James slapped a hand over his mouth. "Sorry."

Emma shot him a warning glance. "I know. And there are hundreds of other mermaids and mermen in Atlantis who can't. He's an anomaly." She shifted, turned her head toward Keith's room. "Keith is having issues—trying to be independent, but going about it all wrong—and I can't stay to help him through them. Can't stay to ease the strain on my parents, which is why I felt so strongly that they should go to Greece while they can. I guess I hope my dad will uncover some kind of miracle method of saving me from my fate—even though he doesn't know. Now I really want to tell them, but it feels like it's too late. And Tom's back in town, and my guess is he's probably stalking me—which means he'll eventually catch me swimming." She blinked, her eyes bright with fear. "That terrifies me too."

Wanting to reassure her that he would never let that happen, never let Tom near her again, he traced her knuckles with his thumb, moved his arm closer to her so their forearms touched, so he could feel the pulse jump erratically in her wrist. This situation was one he could help with—one that didn't leave him completely powerless.

She hid her eyes behind her knees, but kept talking. "Merrick wasn't lying. Tangaroa—the sea king—let him have me. Like a prize he's earned for guarding the entrance to Atlantis for the last fifteen years."

He couldn't stay quiet anymore, had to ask, had to know. "Are you . . . will you go through with it? Do you love him?"

She lifted her head, her eyes fierce. "No. I don't know how binding his agreement thing is, but I keep telling Merrick I'm not going to do it, and he seems determined to force me into it." Her voice quivered. "He burned me yesterday. Some mermaids have an electric pulse—like eels—and he was mad because he was tired of trying to catch up every time I swam away. So when he caught me, he grabbed my wrist and burned me with a shot of electricity."

James sat up straight, alarmed. Furious. "He burned you? Let me see." She held out her wrist. It looked fine at first glance, but upon closer inspection, he could see a pink line all the way around. "I don't want him near you anymore. Can you find somewhere else to swim?"

She breathed deep again, then exhaled through her nose. "I've looked, but haven't found anywhere that feels private and protected like the cove. Besides, I don't know how to survive on my own in the ocean—I might actually need Merrick's help when I complete the change."

James closed his eyes, hating the thought. Despising the

thought. Damning the thought. "If he ever hurts you again, I'm going to beat the hell out of him." Her intake of breath had his eyes popping open again. "In fact, the next time I see him, I'll probably do it anyway."

"What about when I have to go permanently? I have to learn how to defend myself, how to take care of myself. I have to learn how to stand up to Merrick and the sea king and anyone else who tries to force me to do something I don't want to do."

She was right. He knew she was right, but the whole situation made him feel absolutely helpless. Not a feeling he liked. She didn't belong in Atlantis. She belonged here, with him, where he could keep her safe and protect her from anyone who would even try to hurt her. He glanced at Emma, who stared at her knees, hand over her mouth. Was it just him, or was her skin a light shade of green?

James wanted to growl in frustration, but instead leaned forward, elbows to knees, and knocked his fists together. He'd spent his life finding ways around impossible situations, but this one—it looked like there was no way around this one. "I hate knowing that every time you go there, he might hurt you." Or worse. He had to force himself not to think about the worse—it would drive him insane.

She lifted her head, rested her cheek on her knee, still folded into a human ball. "I hate it too. Feels like Tom all over again, only compounded by my lack of choice. I *have* to go there. Physically, I can't stay away. Do you have any idea how scary that is for me?"

"You're the bravest girl I know." Grinding his teeth,

James debated whether or not he should ask for more details about Tom. What she'd already told him had been difficult enough. But she'd survived—escaped what could have been the worst part of the attack—and he had to know so he could find a way to help her. Though the situations seemed unrelated, his instincts screamed that there had to be some kind of connection that meant something. If nothing else, her experience with Tom could help him teach her to defend herself against Merrick. "Tom was convicted, right? Because there was a witness? Maybe if we talk it through, we can figure out a way to—"

"What? A way to what?" Her eyes glistened with unshed tears. "To prevent the inevitable? Even if Merrick went away forever, I'd still be what I am. That's not going to change. Not ever. I still have to go, James."

He sucked in a breath. "I know. But at least you'd be safe."

"Only from Merrick. What about the hundreds of other mermen? What about the sea king?"

"Dammit, Emma," James exploded, crazy desperation threatening to undo his threads of control. "I'm trying to help. Can we just focus on one problem at a time? Because I'm seeing red right now, and the only thing I can think about is that I. Do. Not. Want him anywhere near you. So let's try to deal with that, and then we'll move onto the next thing, okay?"

A tear trickled from the corner of Emma's eye, but she wiped it away with her wrist and cleared her throat. "Why are you putting yourself through this when it would be easier to walk away?"

Because I love you! He sat back, swallowing a lump in his throat. "Because you matter."

She met his eyes, hers a confusing jumble of misery, awe, and determination—pretty much what he'd been feeling since the cave—and sniffled. "I wasn't going to go with him. To prom, I mean. I'd gone out with him on and off for the whole school year, and it had become apparent that we were very different. Wanted different things. But by the time I decided I shouldn't, he'd already rented a limo and bought tickets. I couldn't back out. There was too much guilt involved."

James reached over and grabbed her hand, held it against his chest, anchoring them together. Offering her strength he wasn't sure he had.

"It wasn't terrible. We were with two other couples, went to a nice restaurant for dinner, made it to the dance at about the perfect time. And then . . . I don't know. One minute, we were dancing and laughing, the next he was angry because he'd paid for a hotel room and I didn't want to go there."

James had to remind himself that her hand was breakable, and rather than squeezing, opted to press his lips against her knuckles.

"Tom was scary when he was mad, so I made him take me home. By the time we got there, I was so worked up, it was hard to breathe. Even my eyes felt too dry. So I changed out of my dress and headed for the cove. Tom must have followed me because when I got back to my car after the swim, he was there." Her body convulsed, and she drew a shaky breath.

"It was dark, and he didn't come all the way to the beach, so I don't know how much he saw, but it looked bad. I can't deny that. Me, going into that cave, and Merrick following. Naked."

James cleared his throat, an uneasy sensation crawling up his back. He'd had similar thoughts himself. Even as he'd held Emma in his arms, just seeing Merrick had given him the urge to break something. Or someone.

"Tom waited for me."

She didn't say anything else for a long time, and James wondered what was going through her head. He wanted to tell her to stop, that it was enough. He knew the rest. But he couldn't find his voice, and the problem solver in him believed the answer might be written into the question. Gently, James draped his arm around her and pulled her close enough to lean her head on his shoulder.

"He hit me," she whispered. "A lot. Accused me of using him. Called me things I will never repeat. And then . . . then."

James squeezed his eyes shut, clenching and unclenching his fists. He'd known how this story ended already. But hearing the anguish in her voice made it so much worse. He closed his eyes, trying to block out the images her words put in his head, but no matter how hard he tried, he could see it like he'd been there—a witness who was helpless to stop the injustice. Circumstances didn't matter. Only facts. That guy had hurt her—in about a million different ways, more ways than James could know. The idea had his muscles shaking in fury, and his mind whirling. Would she ever get over this? Get past it? Could he?

"If he hadn't been interrupted . . ." Another tear rolled down the side of her cheek and into her ear. James pulled her into his lap, wrapping his arms around her shaking form to let her cry into his chest. The sound of her weeping cracked something inside him, and emotions he'd never experienced rose up to choke him. "Shh," he crooned. "It's okay now, baby. You're safe. I won't let them hurt you again."

Her arms wound around his neck. James squeezed her tighter and ran his hand down her hair, wishing for the impossible, needing to protect her from everything bad that had ever happened, or would ever happen in her future. Protect them both from the heartaches of things they couldn't change.

When her sobs calmed, he kissed the top of her head. "It's okay. It's all going to be okay."

"How? How will anything be okay? Whether or not I can get rid of Merrick, when I complete the change, I'll have to go."

James didn't reply to that, still caught up in what Tom had done to her. "What made him stop? Do you remember?"

She wiped her wet cheeks with the tips of her fingers. "There was a witness. A homeowner who heard me scream came to check things out. He called the police. Handed over the digital footage from his security cameras. Lawyer made Tom take a plea. Six months plus probation, and a protective order to stay away from me."

There was so much to process. So much to think about. Sorting it all would require a kind of clear thinking that was impossible while he was in Emma's house, holding her in his arms, feeling her pulse race, her scent hypnotizing him, assaulting him. It had been hours since he'd kissed her, and yet, he could still taste her in his mouth. She surrounded him. Overwhelmed him.

As if she'd read his mind, she leaned back, her face close to his. "Thanks."

"For what?"

"For coming back. For listening. For not judging . . . or, well, at least for thinking it through and realizing there was more to me than appearances would allow you to see."

"Ha. I figured that out the first time I met you," he murmured. Her face was so close, her body so warm. He could barely think straight. They were alone. Could be alone all night. It would be so easy to give into temptation. To lose himself in her, right here in the family room. Or. He wondered how she'd react if he picked her up and took her in the bedroom.

He'd never wanted anything more.

He had to leave. Had to get out before he lost all his willpower. "I should get going."

"Probably smart." She reached out, grazed her fingers down the side of his face, whisper soft. His heart raced as she threaded her fingers into his hair and pulled him closer. His body wanted so badly to comply, but his brain screamed for him to think it through—go slow. Take care.

Because strong as she tried to be, Emma was still fragile. Especially this part of her. Fragile enough to break. And he wouldn't be the one to shatter her.

Her eyelids fluttered closed, and his willpower took another hit. After all his pursuing, she was ready to give in now?

"Emma," he whispered. He removed her hands from his hair, then pulled back, lifted her off his lap and set her on the couch so he could stand. "I have to go. You've been through a lot, and I don't want to screw this up. And I work early in the morning. Really. I just have to go."

She stared at him, eyes wide with surprise. And . . . was that hurt? She nodded, swallowed. "Okay."

His hands shook as he ran them through his hair again, watched a hundred different emotions at war in her eyes. She didn't understand. But he couldn't explain it to her, either. Not now. Not until he figured it out himself.

"Sorry," she murmured, closing her eyes like she was embarrassed. "I thought . . ."

"No." He crouched down, tipped her chin until she looked at him. "Don't be sorry. We'll get to that point soon enough. When you're ready, and that's not tonight. But we will. I'll see you soon." James kissed her forehead—it was all he could handle at the moment—and stood, backing out of the room. He ran down the stairs, stopping only long enough to turn the lock on the doorknob as he closed it. So much for thinking he'd sleep better if they talked. No way was his brain going to shut down now.

Thirty-three

February 23th
144 days to departure

AT TEN THIRTY ON SUNDAY morning, Emma awakened in the silent house, confused about how it could be so late, and why Keith hadn't dragged her out of bed to help him with his tie. Maybe she would swim while he was at church. She felt like she needed it again already, and the sensation frightened her.

She padded to the bathroom, and then down to the kitchen, hoping Keith hadn't left a huge mess and wondering what he was doing. When she found no evidence of cereal bowls or other breakfast makings, a niggle of worry crawled up her spine.

"Keith? I'm up." She veered into the living room, then back upstairs to the family room. "Keith? Sorry I slept so long. I . . ." He wasn't there, either. Nor was he in his bedroom. "Keith?"

Nothing. Moving faster than she normally did in the morning, Emma raced into her room and snatched her cell phone. "Mrs. Hall, did Keith come to your house earlier than his usual Sunday time?"

"Why no, honey, I haven't heard from him. Isn't he there with you?"

Emma shook her head, knowing the woman couldn't see and not caring. "He's not. He was planning to go to church with you, wasn't he?"

"As far as I know, he was planning to keep our regular Sunday routine. I'm sure he's fine, but if he doesn't show up soon, you might check at the pizza place where he plays video games with that boy, Max. Seems to spend a lot of time there."

"Thanks. Have fun at church. I'll let you know when I find him." Emma disconnected. When she found Keith, he was in so much trouble. She pulled a sweatshirt over her head, and yanked on her jeans, brushing her teeth as she ran a brush through her hair. By the time she revved the engine in her car, she figured the restaurant would be gearing up for the lunch crowd. She hoped Keith and Max would still be there.

She screeched to a halt and left her car parked near a red curb so she could dash into the little joint and attempt to sift through the people to find her brother. Unfortunately, when she tried to yank the door open, it was locked. Emma pounded once, frowning, then looked at the sign in the window that read, "Closed for Maintenance."

That brought her up short. Where would he be?

Not willing to give up yet, Emma went into the shop next door and asked the gray-haired clerk if she'd seen two boys hanging around, and took time to describe Keith. The lady frowned. "Not today, I haven't, but I have seen a boy matching that description around quite a bit. Hangs out with a tall blond. Mid-twenties, walks around shirtless, like he's a gift to us all. Catch my drift? Bad news, that one. Got a temper on him, from what I've seen. Course, I don't know much about it except what I see, but I see a lot through my little windows."

"But you haven't seen them today?" Emma pressed.

The woman scrunched her wrinkled nose. "No, ma'am, I haven't. I'd know, since that Max boy owes me some sweeping to pay for things he broke a while back. Like I said, got a temper on him."

At the word "*temper*," all Emma could see was Tom winding back his fist, getting ready to hit her. What if Max was a fake name? What if Tom had befriended her brother and was planning to use him to get back at her? They'd only met once, so maybe Keith hadn't recognized her ex.

Not wanting to waste another minute, Emma waved at the woman and raced to her car, needing to check at home again. James pulled into the driveway behind her as she opened the garage, and Emma jumped out, not giving him a chance to speak. "I can't find Keith. Will you please help me look for him?"

James looked alarmed. "How long has he been gone?"

She shook her head, on the edge of hysteria. "I don't know. Before I woke up."

They scoured the house until they were sure he wasn't hiding, and met at the bottom of the stairs. Without another word, Emma slid the phone out of her pocket and dialed the number for Lieutenant Peters. She needed to talk to someone who knew about her brother, as well as her history with Tom.

EMMA'S HAND FELT LIKE ice when James took it between both of his, feeling helpless to do anything but comfort her when no comfort could be found. Three hours had passed since she called the police, and he worried that they were bound to wait several more while officers attempted to locate Emma's ex. In the meantime, the two of them had been instructed to stick around the house in case Keith came home.

James understood why, but the whole sitting-around-doing-nothing thing wasn't in his nature.

Emma's hand flexed in his. He glanced at her still form, curled up on the loveseat and staring out the window at dark clouds rolling across the sky, her breathing uneven. Her intensity worried him. "You cold?" he asked.

She nodded.

Wordlessly, he left the room and took the stairs—two at a time—to the family room. When he didn't see a blanket in there, he headed for Emma's room, hesitating at her door. Why he should be nervous to go in was a mystery. He'd been inside once before, though it had been very dark. Shaking his head, he pushed the door open. Light blue walls, soft pink-and-white bedding, prints of fish and sea life, knick-knacks made of sand and seashells. Everything about the room screamed "Emma."

He snatched the comforter off her bed and returned to the living room, where Emma remained, as still as if she'd been carved from stone. James sat next to her, pulling the comforter around her and drawing her close enough to lean on his shoulder. "They're going to find him. He's going to be fine."

Emma still didn't respond, other than to clutch his shirt in her fisted hand.

"Have you eaten today?" Maybe food would bring her out of this stress coma.

"No," she murmured. "Not hungry."

"You still need to eat." Once again, he left her on the couch, this time to root through the kitchen cupboards. In the fridge, he found a plastic container with noodles covered in a white sauce and baby shrimp, another with lettuce topped with mini-fish-looking things. Both looked like entrees Emma would choose. One way or another, he was going to make her eat. He returned to the living room with a steaming plate of pasta and cold fish-thingy salad and two forks. "Dinner is served."

Emma accepted a fork—her movements wooden—and didn't bother to look at what he'd brought in. "I told you, I'm not hungry."

James stabbed a piece of shrimp and waved it in front of her. "Eat anyway."

"Why?"

"Because you need the protein. And carbs. And whatever else. Emma, you have to snap out of this funk. It's not helping."

"But they won't let me do anything. I can't even go look for him."

James acknowledged this with a nod, prodding her lips with the forked shrimp. "Maybe not, but eventually they're going to come back here with news, and when they do, you're going to need your strength to do whatever needs to be done. Eat."

Reluctantly, she opened her mouth and took the shrimp off his fork. "Happy?"

"Nowhere near, but it's a start."

The knock on the back door brought both fear and relief until the knob twisted and Heather let herself in. Upon seeing James, she paused. "Uh, hi."

"How you doing?" James asked, setting aside the food Emma refused to eat, and lacing their fingers together.

Heather raised an eyebrow at their clasped hands, but didn't ask. "I've driven every route he's taken in this neighborhood. He has to be with someone. I know Keith. He doesn't go new places by himself."

Emma jerked as if she'd been slapped. "I know. Just wish we could figure out who."

Heather crouched next to the couch to meet Emma's distant gaze. "We'll find him, sweetie. I promise."

James continued to try force-feeding Emma, but gave up when he realized she was too distraught to swallow. They didn't hear from the detectives until long after dark. By then, Emma had snapped out of her catatonic-stare-out-the-window phase and had begun pacing the house in a pre-hysteria panic. Out of ideas, James let her pace, strangely relieved to realize that Heather didn't know how to help any more than he did. But when the knock came, he somehow managed to be the first to the door. "Tell me you found him. Emma's on the verge of a meltdown." *And I'm right behind her.*

Lieutenant Peters didn't look like a man with good news.

"We found Tom. But he claims he hasn't seen Keith since he was dating Emma."

James shook his head, backing away from the door so the officer could come inside. Emma grasped James's arm from behind, and Heather's on her other side. "Maybe he's lying," she said.

Peters took a breath. "Maybe. But it's not likely. Tom is staying with his parents for the time being, and when I questioned him about the protective order, he seemed to be well aware of his limitations. He has an alibi for where he's been all day—and it's solid. I checked it out myself."

"But . . . what about . . . then where? What happened to my brother?"

James could feel Emma falling apart, and reached back to hold her up.

"There are a lot of possibilities, and my officers are checking them all," Peters said, clearly trying to reassure them, and failing. "Does Keith have any friends whose houses he might have gone to visit? Any special places he hangs out where he might have lost track of time?"

"Keith doesn't do things like that," Heather started.

"Actually, he does." Emma told him about the pizza parlor and about Max no-last-name, eyes downcast, shuffling her feet as she admitted to not having met the kid. Something about the situation struck James as odd, made his nose itch like he was on the cusp of a sneeze that just wouldn't come.

"You're going to keep looking tonight, right?" Emma's plea sounded on the verge of a wail.

"Yes, we will. And again, I'm going to encourage you to stay here, see if he shows up. Answer every phone call, even if you don't recognize the number. But I suggest you get a hold of your parents, let them know what's happening. If we don't find your brother by morning, they'll need to cut their trip short."

Emma nodded as tears ran down her cheeks. "I called them after you were here earlier. My mother is already looking for flights."

After the cops left, Heather wrapped Emma in a death-grip hug. "I'm so sorry, sweetie. I promised my mom I'd look after the twins tonight. Let me go home long enough to explain, and I'll be back."

Emma shook her head. "Don't cancel. There's nothing more you can do right now."

"I can stay with you—make sure you're not alone." She glanced at James, and then away.

"She won't be," he said firmly, ushering Heather toward the door. "I'm not going anywhere tonight." Heather fixed him with a look similar to the one she'd skewered him with that day after the game, but James stopped her before she could utter threats or warnings. "Don't even say it. I'm not that big of an ass."

Pressing her lips together, Heather hugged Emma once more. "Call me as soon as you have news."

After Heather left, James—keeping Emma on her feet when she would otherwise have melted into a puddle on the floor—grabbed Emma's phone and helped her upstairs. He paused at the landing, unsure what to do next, but Emma took the lead, straight into her bedroom to curl into a ball on her bed. "I wish I could go to sleep and wake up to discover this was all a dream."

"Me too." James spread her comforter over her more evenly, then crouched closer to her face. "I'll be on the couch in the family room if you need me."

By way of reply, Emma reached out and grabbed his wrist, tugging him toward her. "Stay here. Please. I don't want to be alone."

Not knowing what else to do, James slid onto the bed. Emma curled around to lay her head in the crook of his arm, a hand on his chest, fisted in his T-shirt. On any other day, under any other circumstances, he would have been beyond happy at this development. But today, anxiety eclipsed every other emotion. He pulled Emma closer—finding comfort in having her here, in his arms, where he knew she was safe—and she spread her quilt over him.

They might be in for a long night, but at least they'd pass it together.

Thirty-Four

A *LOUD BOOM OF THUNDER* woke Emma from her restless sleep. James tightened his hold on her, but when she moved her head to better see his face, she could tell he was out cold. Rain battered the window glass, its eerie music playing a haunting melody that only added fuel to her worry. She slid out of James's arms and padded to the window to watch the storm.

Where is my brother? Why hasn't he come home yet?

She fingered the spot where her necklace used to be, wishing she hadn't thrown it away. Without it, she felt way too vulnerable, exposed, and since she'd given it to Merrick, like she needed to swim again. It was stupid, really. Just a thing made of twine and pearls and the flat, open face of a seashell. But it had also been part of her identity, and not wearing it felt strange in the same way as not having Keith in the house in the middle of the night. If only she'd paid closer attention, learned more about Max.

"He'll be back," James croaked from behind her. "Probably sleeping over at that kid's house and has no idea we're all frantic over him." His hands rested on her shoulders as he pulled her backward into him.

"If so, he's never been in so much trouble. Ever. You might have to spring me for murdering my own brother."

James rested his chin on Emma's shoulder. "I'll do better than that. I'll show up with a key to the jail and my bike all packed for a trip across the border to Mexico."

"And how would you propose to keep me breathing?"

"They have oceans in Mexico. Gorgeous ones. Doctors, too. I bet one of them could figure out how to keep you breathing on land. If we paid him enough, he probably would even keep your secret."

When his arms came around her waist, Emma rested hers on top of them. "If stopping my change was that easy, Gran would have already taken me there, done it."

His lips found her neck, the soft spot just above her closed gills. "If that guy Merrick can come ashore and breathe, there has to be a way for you to do it too. I refuse to believe he's a fluke."

Merrick. Keith. Max. Merrick. Keith. Max. Something.

Keith always had to go to Max, rather than the other way around. He claimed they only ever met at the pizza joint, and Emma had never asked if Max ate, or what, but Keith *had* once commented on Max liking the same foods as her. And then that woman in the shop had said Max never wore a shirt, that he was in his twenties. And when she'd asked, Keith had been unwilling—or maybe unable—to supply a last name, address, or phone number.

What if . . .

Emma stepped out of James's arms and faced him. "It's Merrick."

Looking confused, James ran his hands down her arms, linking their fingers. "I know, babe. He's different. But we'll find a way to—"

"No, James. Merrick is Max. Has to be. And if he's really the friend Keith calls Max, he's the one who has my brother. Why didn't I realize this before?"

James blinked like he was trying to keep up. "What?"

Emma buzzed around the room, grabbing the things she'd need and shoving them in her beach bag, shaking her head at her own stupidity. Just because she hadn't *seen* him come into town didn't mean he couldn't. Or wouldn't. She tugged a sweatshirt over her head and slid on her shoes, belatedly realizing that James was still staring at her. "I have to go get him. Are you coming?"

He shook himself out of his trance. "Course I am. Yes." He followed Emma down the stairs, grabbing his shoes and jacket.

The windshield wipers worked furiously to keep up with the downpour, but didn't do much to improve visibility, and water sloshed in the streets. The storm cut their speed by half of the normal limit. Emma banged her hand on the steering wheel, frustrated with her luck. Why hadn't she figured this out earlier today? What if it was too late? What if Merrick had taken her brother under water and he drowned? What if—

She slammed on the brakes just in time to avoid hitting a poor, drenched little dog. James clutched the dash, looking shaken. "Want me to drive?"

"No," she said, starting again. "Let's just get there."

"Emma, I think we should call Lieutenant Peters, let him know what you're thinking. Maybe they can help us."

"No way. No, no, no, no." She shook her head adamantly. How could she ever explain about her change? About how she knew Merrick?

"Just hear me out." James lowered his voice, giving Emma the impression that he was trying to convince her. "We don't have to tell them about you being a mermaid. Or Merrick, for that matter. All we have to do is ask that same guy for his security tapes, see if Keith is on there. We tell the police Keith sometimes likes to go there when he's pouting or some crap like that. If he is, and it looks like he's going willfully, we'll probably be on our own anyway. But if not, if it looks like Merrick forced him, the police will come haul that sorry mer-dude to jail where he can rot."

It wasn't a horrible idea. "But he would, James. If the police took Merrick to jail, eventually he wouldn't be able to breathe, and he'd wither up and die."

James shrugged, seeming indifferent. "Least I know he'd never touch you again."

Emma raised her eyebrow, fighting the inklings of what felt like a sacrilegious smile. "Death might be the only way for me to convince him I don't want to be his mate."

James swore, shaking his head and running a hand through his hair. "And if the death thing doesn't work out, here's another idea. After we save Keith, it's you, me, and the backseat. Or the sand, or your bed—whatever works. Maybe if I claim you in every way, he'll figure out who you really belong to and leave you alone."

A giggle worked up her throat. "Are you serious?"

He reached over the middle console to squeeze her thigh, the desire in his eyes leaving Emma with no doubts about his intentions. A tremor shook her shoulders and made her voice breathy as she parked in the same spot she'd been parking in since she'd started her change. "Okay, but I have to save my brother first."

Another squeeze, and then she was out of the car, running down the steep path toward the beach with James on her heels.

FOR A LITTLE THING, Emma could run fast when she had to, especially considering the rain. James barely managed to keep stride, and he was in pretty damn good shape. She danced around the tide pools and sharp lava rocks like a water nymph, disappearing into the cave several feet ahead of him.

He entered just in time to see Emma—with her back to him—strip off her wet sweatshirt and tie on a bikini top. There was no sign of either Keith or Merrick. Eyes round with surprise, James cleared his throat. Emma didn't turn, but he could hear the devastation in her voice. "I know Merrick has him, James. I know it. I have to find out where they took my brother, even if he's . . . drowned."

Adrenaline kept his blood pumping so fast, his hands trembled. She would blame herself if Keith was dead. James wanted to take her in his arms, comfort her. But he stood back, wringing out his shirt and averting his eyes while she finished changing, if for no other reason than to keep his head straight. "How can I help?"

"You can't." Clad only in a bikini, hair drenched and sticking to her skin, Emma marched to James and handed him her keys. "I don't know how long I'll be, and if . . . if something happens, I don't want the police investigating you. So." She clicked an app on her cell phone, then turned it so the camera was on her. She stated her name, the date, and that she suspected her little brother might have tried to go swimming in this cove and she was going to look for his body. When she was finished, she handed James the cell phone too.

He clutched her hand as a terrifying thought swept his heart into overdrive. "What if you don't come back?"

She pulled her hand from his and used it to draw his face to hers. "Move on. Get your scholarship, go to college, and get out of here—the way you've been wanting."

He shook his head. "I don't want that. Not anymore."

"James—"

"Shut up. I love you, okay? I don't want to go anywhere if there's a possibility that you might find a way to come back someday."

She sucked in a breath. "I . . . You love me?"

"Yes. I do. I'm completely in love with you. Why else

would I have kept coming back?" Desperate, he swooped her into his arms and kissed her, drawing her up onto her toes and closing any remaining space between them until he thought his chest would burst with feelings he'd never experienced for anyone else. She matched his ferocity like she believed this kiss could be their last. A clashing of teeth and tongues and lips and hands that left them both breathless and warm, despite the chill in the stormy air.

When their lips parted, she buried her face in his neck. "I love you too. I'm sorry it took so long for me to realize it. And I'll do everything I can to come back so we can go on a real date. Without my brother."

It took all his willpower to let go and watch her dive in and swim away. All his life, he'd waited for someone—anyone—to say those words, and had never heard them. At least, not in reference to him. Not his mother, or his father. Not even his uncle vocalized the words James knew to be true. He finally got them from Emma, the girl he'd once considered out of his league, completely unattainable.

Thunder rumbled in the sky, and his heart ached with loss. How would he survive when she was gone?

Thirty-Five

February 24th
143 days to departure

THE REFRESHING COLD of the salty water kicked her adrenaline into high gear, allowing Emma bursts of speed that rocketed her across more than a mile of deep, dark sea. Even before her eyesight adjusted, she became ultra-aware of her surroundings, of the possibility that she could be swimming into an ambush (though by whom, she wasn't sure) or worse, that she could happen upon her little brother's body, floating aimlessly.

She shuddered, trying not to think about what predatory fish could have done to a body in the amount of time Keith had been missing. The familiar area felt eerily different tonight, a distinct lack of sound or movement giving Emma the impression that something was definitely amiss.

She wanted desperately to be wrong, but her every instinct screamed that she was right.

She'd been in the ocean for more than a mile, and Merrick—who always guarded the entrance to Atlantis—was nowhere to be seen. Tonight, the sea felt exceptionally imposing, the usually clear water dark like ink. Her momentum shot her past schools of multi-colored fish, coral formations, and bits and pieces of sunken humanity until she'd gone another mile and a half from shore, and two miles down. By now, Emma could see the pulsing blue light she'd always avoided—the one that would lead her into the home she would have to learn to love—or at least where she would someday live.

Atlantis.

The glowing light stood out in stark contrast to the murky water surrounding it, making it difficult to distinguish anything more than the vague shapes of what may—or may not—be buildings. As she approached the radiant circle of blue, Emma had the impression that she was surrounded by thousands of eyes that watched, waited. She wasn't at all sure if her uninvited entrance into the underwater city would be looked upon as friendly or threatening.

Doesn't matter, as long as they give me back my brother.

She dove deeper and deeper toward the light, doing her best to avoid fish and other sea life—a brightly-colored eel, a shining jelly fish, a baby squid she almost didn't see—any creature that might impede her progress. Something brushed past her, bumped against her leg, and Emma looked back expecting another fish, but her heart dropped into her toes as she came face-to-face with several hostile-looking mermaids.

A stream of bubbles flowed from her mouth as Emma

screamed and spun in the opposite direction, instinctively propelling herself up. When mermaid hands didn't grab for her, Emma paused, looked back. The green-haired female cocked her head and stared at Emma through wide, violet-colored eyes, and reached out, running a long, curved finger over the fin-shaped birthmark on Emma's shoulder. The mermaid made a noise that sounded like something between a screech and a croon, but didn't attempt to capture Emma or come any closer.

"Where is he?" Emma asked, her voice sounding slow to her ears. "Where's Keith?" The mermaid made the noise again, louder this time. Her body shook as her fin—as true a fin as in legends, unlike Emma's separated legs—swished, agitating the water and causing a current to swirl Emma's hair into knots around her face. Before she could see again, she was grabbed by the wrists and pulled forward.

Other mermaids joined the first in pulling Emma toward the narrow tunnel through which the light glowed, and which she assumed must be the entrance to Atlantis. After what felt like an hour without surface air, Emma's head spun, feeling light, yet heavy at the same time as she was propelled farther and farther away from any chance of breathing that way again. Spots danced in front of her eyes—or maybe it was microscopic fish, she wasn't sure—but even as her brain told her she needed to kick for the surface, her lungs adjusted, equalized, and she could breathe again.

Relieved, Emma yanked her wrists free, startling the blue-skinned mermaids who'd kept such a good grip on her, and dove toward the light, into the passage. The tunnel glowed with bright grasses in yellows, greens, and reds, interwoven with colored seaweed that seemed to give off the very light by which she was able to see. This far from the surface, the temperature plummeted, and Emma felt her blood slowing, thickening, changing. The human part of her should have been cold, but she wasn't. Though she continued moving, Emma slowed to take in her surroundings, and was incensed when one of her mermaid captors bumped her from behind, jabbed her in the back with pointed, talon-tipped fingers.

Go away, you stupid fish.

As they continued on, the blue became brighter, reminding Emma of sunlight, only softer. And obviously, not yellow. All around her, sea life glowed in rainbows of perfect colors that were considerably brighter than anything she'd ever seen above the surface, and lent to a surreal, somewhat fake atmosphere that cranked her anxiety up a few more notches.

The tunnel opened into a cavern that reminded her of pictures she'd seen in one of her father's books about the ruins in ancient Greece, stone floors and walls, parts of which were carved with shapes that—at some time—had probably been symbolic of an era long passed, and all of which had grown barnacles, sand formations, and kelp. She continued toward the light, watched by at least a hundred pairs of eyes, staring from every rock, turn, and crevice as their party swam lower and lower along the uneven sea floor. Eventually, her mermaid captors shoved her onto a solid slab of rock, leaving two sentries behind while the rest continued down a corridor.

With nothing else to do, Emma leaned her head back to

better take in her surroundings. Glowing walls of ice—different from the stone ones she'd first seen—towered over her, looming so high, she wasn't sure if they ended below water or above. They pulsed with energy, as though the very power given off came from between the thick layers. In some places, coral formations and seaweed vines covered the ice, giving this room a garden-type feel that surprised her. And though it made no logical sense, she would swear she could smell the flowers that bloomed on the vines.

Emma ran her hands along her bumpy, sand-covered ledge, trying to decide if it was natural or creature created. She hadn't yet decided if it was coral, stone, or ice when the mermen guarding her grasped her upper arms and forced her to follow them.

From somewhere ahead—or maybe behind—a melodic voice sang a tragic song about lovers going to their deaths. Emma whirled, searching for the source, and came face-to-face with the female she'd originally met, and whom she now recognized as a leader of sorts. Underwater, her voice was beautiful, hypnotic, mesmerizing, and Emma could see why the rest revered her. It was definitely not for her looks. While Merrick's skin—like Emma's—was smooth and fair, the mermaid leader's was an odd shade of blue-green, with patches of reddish scales that spread like a rash across her shoulders and down her torso. Her hair looked like seaweed that had been hastily glued on, matted along the scalp.

Yes, the singing. A feeling of euphoria enveloped her, causing her veins to buzz with a pleasant numbness, not unlike what she'd felt the last time her dentist gave her laughing gas. She tried to keep calm, keep her thoughts straight, remember what she should be doing. Something. Something. An incredible bouquet of sensations poured into her, heightening her senses until she experienced a brand of pleasure she'd never imagined existed. The euphoria compounded, building into a cyclone of vibrations that originated in her core. The cyclone built, expanded, filled her up. Everything, everything about her felt alive, free.

Powerful.

Mechanically, Emma followed the mermaid leader, surrounded by twenty or thirty others—all female—through another bright tunnel. They passed a natural-looking cave that must have connected to a blow hole on the surface because Emma could see several human-sized pockets of air. She had a vague, distressing thought that she needed to look in there. Find something important. Something she should remember. She paused, wondering why a human face passed through her mind—blue eyes, messy blondish hair, glasses, enormous smile—but continued on when another mermaid nudged her from behind.

They emerged into a large city of towering ice and coral buildings topped with sharp points and jagged edges. Faint blue light pulsed within the walls, the source of which seemed to originate from a point not far away, and which lit the city with an otherworldly glow. She passed homey dwellings made from a combination of rock, shells, and sand, and some she assumed were shops or markets. One place in particular caught her eye, as it appeared to have been crafted entirely from mother-of-pearl, and gleamed luminescent, its surface rippling in the glow of light and water. She turned to ask who lived there, or what was sold, but the mermaid behind her nudged her on, and Emma remained silent, taking in more of her surroundings.

A pattern of waterways that resembled streets were lined with sandy shells and colorful plants, and occasionally separated into narrow intersections. There were more merpeople now, as well as other sea creatures, mingling together in their daily routines. She tried hard not to stare, but found it difficult. There was so much to see. Not unlike the big cities above the surface, the variety of merpeople was unbelievable. Each one such an individual in skin, hair, fin colors and features, build, shape, voice—the list was endless.

She also noticed that certain merpeople had distinguished themselves by adorning their bodies with ornamental decorations. Many of the females wore strings of shells and coral so thick that they layered over one another front to back, draping them in the way human women wore clothes.

Well. Now Emma could see why artists tended to cover mermaid's breasts with seashells. Maybe it wasn't only a human sensitivity to nakedness. From what she could see, mermaids had their own version of fashion. She made a mental note to get her hands on some of those drapes for herself when she was forced to stay. Her bikini would only last so long.

With the help of the city noise, her head began to clear, and something fluttered in her chest. Something she should be worried about? Again, a human face came to mind, but this time a name came with it. *Keith.*

The name sparked a memory of the two of them sitting side-by-side on a couch, watching a movie. Keith wrapped his arm around her and told her she was his best girl. Her chest moved with a familiar sensation—one she liked, that felt right, natural. Love. That was it. Love. She loved Keith. Keith loved her.

Where was he?

She shook her head, forcing her brain to function, to remember the important thing she had forgotten.

A merman broke through the wall of mermaids that had gathered on either side of Emma and came to swim next to her. Throughout their trek in the city, none of the merpeople had been allowed near her, except her guards, but this one was granted access. Emma glanced over and found she recognized the face.

Merrick.

Merrick was her friend. Wait, no. That wasn't right. Was he her enemy, then? That didn't seem quite right either. It frightened her not to know. She let out a whimper of dismay. Merrick ignored it, reaching out to take her hand.

When their palms touched, what was left of the singing mermaid's spell broke. Facts rained down on Emma like debris from a shipwreck. Merrick had taken Keith, forced him into Atlantis, she was sure.

She met Merrick's uneasy gaze and read not only guilt, but intent in his eyes. Without him saying anything, she knew Merrick was taking her to see Tangaroa, the sea king. He was going to try to force her to become his mate. Right now.

Anger seethed in her cool blood, and electricity zinged

up her spine as she wrenched her hand away. She wanted to slap Merrick, to swim away and find Keith, but without her consent, her body continued going with the flow of other mermaids. A sob worked up her throat as she struggled against the unfamiliar instinct, fighting to free herself as the pod led her closer to the center of town, to the ruins of an ancient castle from which the blue light originated. Merrick glanced at her, something that resembled sympathy in his eyes.

She glared back. *I'll hate him forever.* They came to an enormous set of double doors made from millions of pearls. Two guards nodded at the singing mermaid—whose name Emma still didn't know—and ushered the entire pod inside. When the others crossed the threshold, Emma stopped, tried to turn, swim away, and managed to get nearly twenty feet before the guards caught her and forced her back into the formation. Merrick shook his head, as if trying to tell her to be good.

Her eyes stung with tears that could not fall here, and her shoulders shook with the effort of holding in her sobs. Her body and mind completely at odds, the only thing Emma dared trust was her heart. As Merrick and the mermaids led her into the sea king's lair, Emma allowed herself one broken cry. "Keith."

Thirty-six

JAMES PACED THE CAVE for a good hour, torn between waiting for Emma and going to get help. If he did the first, and something happened to either her or Keith, he'd never forgive himself for his impotence in the situation, or for sitting around waiting while they struggled for their lives. If he did the second, who would he even call? Who would believe him? And really, how could they possibly help?

If only I could breathe underwater, the way Emma does.

He stayed long enough to wear a distinct back-and-forth line in the sand, wringing his hands and yanking at his hair, and then he had to do something. Something. Anything. The downpour had turned into a light drizzle, and the black sky seemed a lighter shade of gray when he picked his way around the edge of the cave and started up the trail, fingering Emma's car keys in his pocket and turning back every few seconds to make sure there was no movement below. When he reached the street, he stopped. What was he doing? He didn't even have a plan.

Craning his neck, he peered down the trail, but the trees and shrubs blocked his view of the beach near the cave. *Think, James, think.* Emma's car was parked at the edge of a property line, and James started toward it, pausing at a mailbox. He turned his head, squinting at the shadowed house. If Merrick was walking around in public, he couldn't be strutting around naked the way he did in the cave. These people would have seen him and called the cops. He would have been arrested a long time ago.

If Emma was right, and Merrick was also the Max who had been playing video games with Keith, he had to at least own a pair of pants. There had to be more to the story. Heart pounding into his throat, James started down the trail again, this time determined to find evidence of Merrick's secret clothing stash.

AFTER FORTY-FIVE MINUTES of searching, James worried that he was wrong about the pants—that Emma was wrong about Merrick being Max. He'd scoured the tiny forest and searched the cave from top to bottom and found nothing. Frustrated beyond belief, he left the cave again, ignoring the now-drizzling rain, and stepped in exactly the wrong spot—the one where the slippery surface of the rock sent him sprawling straight into the nearest tide pool. Swearing in ways he'd never want Emma to hear, he cursed everything about his current circumstances and grabbed the nearest large boulder for balance as he pulled himself out of the water.

He didn't think much of the movement of the stone and would have continued on his way if the moon hadn't chosen that exact moment to peek through the clouds and reflect off something silver. It was probably a gum wrapper, but he had to be sure, so he slid his hand between the boulder and the side of the cliff, half expecting to be bitten by a snake or pinched by a crab, and was rewarded with two shiny quarters. Grinning, he stood, eyeing the boulder to decide on the right angle, and then put all his strength into moving it.

A COLLECTIVE MURMUR ROSE as Emma and her guards entered the throne room. She lifted her head in time to catch a glimpse of one stately merman gliding above the rest. Like hers, his skin was pale, translucent white, and smooth. His fiery red hair curled around his ears and along the nape of his neck, tendrils of it floating inches above his scalp as he moved. Though he swam several feet above the rest, the others created a wide path for him and his attendants as he wound around the room and settled into the throne.

An incandescent tank stood, tall and majestic, just behind and to one side of the enormous, jewel-encrusted chair. When Emma saw what it held, she felt a nearly uncontrollable urge to vomit.

"Keith!" she screamed. "What have you done to my brother? He can't breathe down here. I—"

Merrick slapped a hand over her mouth and held it there, one arm around her waist, forcing her to be still. "Do not disrespect the court of the sea king or he will take away the tank keeping the human alive."

Emma sobbed into Merrick's hand, unable to keep her eyes open, and hating to close them and miss what was happening to Keith. He looked so pale, suspended in the water like that. His eyes were open and he seemed alert, thanks to the long, black tubes running from his mouth to a silver cylinder suspended above. Once she'd calmed herself, Emma rationalized that at least he was alive—for now—and that maybe she could save him if she was careful, used the right words and bargaining tools. Maybe.

On the other side of the throne, one of the king's attendants, a dwarfed merman with triangular hair on his chin and bulging muscles in his arms, leveled a curious, but steely gaze on her. Uncomfortable, she glanced away, focused again on Keith.

When he recognized her, his face animated, and he pressed his hands against the walls of ice, trying to reach her.

Even in the cold water, Emma's blood heated with fury. "Let him out," she croaked. "Please, let him out." She thrashed around and broke away from Merrick, shoved past the startled merpeople until she could touch the surface of the tank. "Are you okay?"

Keith pressed his hand just opposite Emma's. He had a cut above his eye, and some bruises on his face, but looked otherwise fine. For now. "I'm going to try to get you out of here, okay? Just hang on. I'm sorry," she cried. "I'm so, so sorry."

Before she could say more, Merrick's hands came around her waist, and he pulled her back into the crowd as the sea king's court was called to order.

"I present King Tangaroa of Atlantis." The rippling and bubbling of conversations calmed as the king's aide glided forth and saluted the crowd with a fist over his heart and a double tailfin swish. The mermen mimicked the salute while the mermaids swayed in a sort of dancing rhythm. The aide turned back to the king. "Duke Merrick of Atlantis has brought you a gift, sir."

Tangaroa hadn't taken his eyes off Emma from the moment he'd been seated, staring through her with a penetrating gaze that made her uncomfortable. "I see her, Glan."

Emma lifted her chin defiantly. "I'm not a gift. My human brother was kidnapped, brought into your city against his will, risking his life, and I've come to take him back to the surface."

"Ever feisty. So much like Prince Caspian." The king's gaze didn't waver. "Against his will or not, the human has brought you home."

Um, no. Not even close. "Respectfully, sir, my home will always be on the surface."

The king frowned. "That you've grown gills and a partial fin should be proof enough. *This* is your home."

"Sir, home is not a place, but the feeling I have when I

am with the people I love. And in this entire city, the only person I love is that boy in the tank. He cannot live here. Please, let me take him back."

Merrick interrupted before the king could answer. "You will make a home with me."

Emma whirled on Merrick. "You just kidnapped my brother and tricked me into coming here. Why would I want to be anywhere near you? I hate you right now, Merrick. I'll hate you forever for putting Keith through this. Besides, I'm not nearly old enough to get married. Or joined. Whatever you call it here. I'm not even eighteen yet."

Tangaroa made a noise that, on land, would have translated into a sigh. "A mermaid comes of age upon the development of her fin, which, for you, was nearly twenty-four moon-cycles ago. It is unusual for a mermaid of royal blood to remain unmated at your age. Merrick has paid a handsome maid-price for you."

Royal blood? "What's a maid-price?" Emma asked.

Keith stirred again, banging on the ice wall to get Emma's attention. He waved his arms and pointed at Merrick, as if trying to tell her something. Emma shook her head, confused. She wished Keith could communicate underwater the way she could.

Merrick? She nodded to assure Keith that she had figured out about Merrick being Max.

"It is customary in Atlantis," Merrick answered, "for a merman to pay a price for his intended mate."

She couldn't stop her sound of derision. "A price, Merrick? You paid for me? How? What kind of price?"

His eyes skittered away, and guilt hunched his shoulders.

Emma glared at Merrick as everything added up in her head. Mrs. Hall's missing bracelet. Her necklace. The jewelry Keith had tried to steal from the mall. She turned to the sea king. "That price was not paid by Merrick, but by my human brother, Keith. I believe Merrick has tricked him into taking things that didn't belong to either of them. It's caused us both a great deal of trouble."

"Is this true?" The king frowned at Merrick. "Did you trick the boy? Did you lie to my granddaughter, princess of Atlantis?"

Granddaughter? Emma's head swirled with the implication of that one word until another piece of the puzzle clicked into place. *Princess? So that's it. Merrick has an agenda.*

Merrick replied, "I did not lie to her, sir. She has always known who I am. She has known I asked for her hand, and that you have consented. It is the human boy to whom I lied, and humans are of no consequence to us."

The king frowned as Merrick continued. "Only the boy could help her understand that Atlantis is where she truly belongs."

A long stream of James-words went through Emma's head, but she didn't utter them for fear of causing more trouble. Merrick had used her brother, and now he was using her. He probably wanted to inherit the throne. That's what this was about. Not her. Not Keith.

She turned pleading eyes on the king. "If I'm your granddaughter, how did I come to live on the surface? Who were my parents?"

Tangaroa shook his head with a hint of sadness. "My dear Emmalina, your father, Caspian, was a difficult merman. Hated being confined to the sea, a feeling which never made sense to me. Land is such a small place, yet it was where he most wanted to live. Just before he was to come into his full power and inherit my crown, I created for him a pendant that would allow him to breathe while he spent lengths of time on the surface. I hoped this would be adventure enough and that he would get over his obsession. Instead, he mated with a human girl, and together, they hatched a youngling, a secret they kept hidden from me and the people of Atlantis.

"Then Caspian's mate became ill and died, leaving my merman son alone with the squalling youngling. Caspian visited a trusted friend who was guardian of the gate, confessing all and requesting to come home. This is how I discovered your existence. Because you are half human, you could not be brought to Atlantis, and Caspian refused to leave you on the surface alone. So he tied his pendant around your neck as a last gift and left you in the arms of a human he believed would love you as he did.

"Then, rather than return to Atlantis, Caspian—who no longer had the ability to breathe ashore for long periods of time—trekked to the grave of his human mate, where he stayed until he became as part of the dry, shifting soil."

My birth mother was human. And I threw away my father's pendant—the one thing that might allow me to go home later. "If the pendant helped my father breathe, why have I continued to struggle?"

The sadness in his eyes gave Emma a touch of empathy

for this merman who claimed to be her grandfather. "Your fin was not fully developed, and you had never passed through the gates of Atlantis."

His words pressed down on her like heavy, heavy weights. "Like my father, I prefer to live on the surface. Please. I gave Caspian's pendant to Merrick in anger, not knowing what it was. I'd like to have it back."

The sea king's brows knitted together as he steepled his fingers against his lips. "I know nothing of the pendant. But the betrothal has been sealed, the maid-price paid. You are to remain in Atlantis and become a mate to Duke Merrick."

She scooted farther away from Merrick, panic clawing in her throat. "Merrick, please."

"It is too late. Your treasure is stored among the king's possessions until you assume your rightful home in the palace. You belong here."

"I don't want to live in a palace!" she shrieked. "That necklace belonged to my father. I demand that you give it back. Why do you even need it? How do you breathe on land? How can you have both legs *and* a fully developed fin?"

Merrick turned away, fingering the seaweed strap on his wrist. "I am Guardian of the Gate, a humble servant to the sea king, and have received just rewards."

Rewards. Like a title. A bride / hostage. And Emma suspected a magic token of some kind.

"Atlantis has not had a queen for many, many years. But we will have one now." Merrick's voice sounded more earnest than she'd ever heard, but Emma wasn't buying it. Not anymore. "You must stay here and become my mate. The king has ordered it so."

Shaking her head in denial, Emma looked at the king, who appeared to be deep in thought. This couldn't be happening. She had to get Keith out of here, had to get back to James. "Let my brother go so I can take him home," she demanded in a voice that sounded much stronger than she felt. And then, thinking of James, of the words they'd exchanged before she left him behind, she said, "I can't be mated to Merrick because I'm already mated to a human."

A shocked murmur created bubbles that floated high above them.

Glan clapped his hands and a ripple of water popped most of the bubbles, causing the merpeople to fall silent again.

For the first time since he had arrived, Tangaroa glanced at the tank. "You cannot be mated without the consent of the sea king."

"Customs are different on the surface, and I didn't know about you until recently. I'm bound to James." Knowing it was risky, Emma pushed on, hoping they would believe her. "Merrick has seen the proof. He lied to you, sir."

More ripples, and once again, Emma felt a mass of attention center on her.

The king spoke. "Bound. In what way?"

Emma's voice quivered. "Love. We're bound by love. I love him."

"But you and the human are not joined. You have not joined?"

Not wanting to give him a straight answer, Emma remained silent.

"This match can and will be broken." Tangaroa swiped a

hand over the top of his head, brushing back his wild mane. "You will stay in the palace until the question of your mates can be sorted out. As for the human in the tank, he shall stay—"

"No!" Emma shouted, interrupting the king. "He'll die. Please, let me take him home. If you must put me in prison, please let me take Keith back to the surface first. The oxygen tank will run out soon. Please."

The king raised an eyebrow as if to remind her he wasn't finished speaking, then tapped his trident on the floor to restore order. "Once your surface binding is successfully severed, you will honor my wishes and be bound to Merrick. This binding shall take place on the day of the moon celebration." For Emma, he clarified, "The day humans call solstice. There will be no more waiting, no more stalling, and no more games. Enough time has already passed."

"You can't do that," Emma shouted indignantly. "You can't force me to be bound to Merrick. I haven't even completed the change. I'm still part human."

A collective gasp, more bubbles, and the tittering voices swelled to a dull roar. Once again, Glan attempted to restore order, but this time, the controversy must have been too much because he was largely ignored.

"Young maid." Tangaroa's eyes flashed with tiny bolts of lightning as he arose from his throne. "I have tolerated a great deal of impertinence from you. I am king here, and there will be no more lenience for disrespectful behavior." To the guards, he bellowed. "Take her to the servants' grotto, and keep her there until she learns the laws of the Atlantis court. Glan."

At the short aide's gesture, two burly mermen approached Emma, one grabbing her by the wrists, the other the ankles near her webbed feet. Fear gripped her throat, but Emma struggled, squealing in fear as the men angled through the crowd and down a long, dark tunnel. Here, the walls didn't pulse with light, but were instead lit by strategically placed glowing stones. The guards took her to a cave that reminded Emma of a TV show she'd seen about deserted prisons, and she shuddered. By a complete stroke of luck, the first guard let go of her to find a key, and the second, not paying attention, loosened his grasp enough so Emma could swim through. She darted up, far enough so the dark enveloped her.

Both guards stared into the inky darkness, but refused to swim up to find her, both looking frightened.

Interesting.

While they conversed in hushed tones, Emma inched away, trying not to disturb the water and alert them to her position, and headed back to where she'd last seen Keith.

The throne room was empty when she entered, and she found Keith already fighting to free himself. Emma grabbed the oxygen container and leveraged it under the thick ice top of the tank, pulling down against the opposite edge. Encouraged by the loud crackling sound, she continued to work at weakening the rest of the walls. She was so intent in her work that it was several minutes before she realized Merrick was attempting to help.

Emma didn't say anything. As badly as she hated Merrick, she would accept help in whatever form it came until she could get Keith safely home. She'd wait until after that to give Merrick a black eye. Or maybe two.

Eventually, the opening was large enough for Keith to squeeze his body through. But getting out of the confined space didn't free him from the oxygen tubes, which were still tethered to the ice by thick seaweed ropes. Together, Emma and Keith pulled, yanked, and picked at the weeds to no avail. Merrick swam away, returning minutes later holding a long, rusted sword, lifted it high, and brought it down on the rope. It didn't cut through. But as Merrick hacked away, the threads began to unravel. Emma grabbed hold of the oxygen tank, tugging in the opposite direction until she heard a snap and felt it break free, then she swung the straps over Keith's shoulders and fastened a clip around his waist. Having no other choice, the two of them followed Merrick.

He'd better be taking us out of this infernal city.

He led them down narrow halls, made of both stone and ice, past rooms filled with fish of every variety, and merpeople that differed in appearance every bit as much as the colorful fish. They wound around corners, down corridors, and past an amphitheater filled with what Emma guessed to be hundreds, maybe thousands of merpeople watching some kind of show or other entertainment until they swam through a small, dark opening. There were fewer fish here, and no merpeople. Very little light shone inside what appeared to be a small cave about the size of a bedroom. Merrick swam to the end of the cave, pointing out a narrow hidden tunnel, and offering to let them go first. Emma shook her head. She didn't trust Merrick.

"I am sorry they locked you up," Merrick said to Emma. "That was not my hope when I presented you to Tangaroa."

Yeah, I'll just bet.

"How do we get out of here?" she asked Merrick. "Keith can't have much oxygen left." To prove her point, she tapped the metal with her fingernail. It made a ping that sounded frighteningly hollow.

"This way. We must hurry. I do not wish the human you love to die." Merrick led them into the tunnel for such a long way, Emma wondered if they were lost. Eventually, though, they pushed through a door that led out of the city and into the clear blue water. From here, Emma thought she could find the way back to the cave where she'd left James. Keith lagged behind, exhausted from the swim, so Emma pulled his arms over her shoulders and kept going.

Merrick swam ahead, and Emma allowed herself to relax as if she were swimming with just Keith. But she couldn't let go of the dread that ate at her insides as they rose toward the surface. As they approached the tall white walls of coral near the arch, she slowed significantly, and pulled back twenty or so feet below the surface. *This has been too easy.*

"Come. We must hurry," Merrick urged.

"Merrick, something's not right. Why hasn't anyone come after us?"

The merman frowned, his large eyes seeming to take in everything around them. "No one has noticed that you are missing yet. Let us not waste time, or your human will run out of air."

She pushed Keith ahead of her and put on a burst of

speed. Just before their heads broke the surface, an eerie screech sounded from the city. Merrick's face went gray. "Swim! Head for shore as fast as you can. They're coming."

"Who's they, exactly?" Emma shouted, wanting to know exactly who the sea king would send as she dragged Keith behind her, her webbed feet beating at the water.

Merrick's pressed his lips together, grim. "Tangaroa's army."

Thirty-seven

JINGLING A HANDFUL OF QUARTERS, James decided that this second cave didn't really classify as an actual cave. More like a hole in a rock. But it was protected and hidden, as if it had been created precisely so Merrick could hide his stash of human-type trappings. If not for James's momentary flash of klutz, he would never have found it.

He dropped the quarters back into the huge pile of them (probably three hundred dollars' worth—at least) and forced himself to pinch the hem of the cotton shorts between two fingers and toss them out onto the boulder. An unworn navy T-shirt with tags and stickers still attached was next, followed by first one, then the other flip-flop. "Let's see what happens when you try coming ashore without any clothes," he ground through his teeth.

Having their suspicions confirmed should have been a relief, but now that James knew Emma was right, his fear and anger multiplied, amplified until his head spun. He didn't know what to do. There was no way for him to help Emma save her brother, if he was even still alive. So James did the only thing he could. He scooped the quarters into the T-shirt, preparing to haul the entire stash to Emma's car and leave the hiding place empty.

When the shirt was full, he reached for the shorts, and felt a crunch inside one of the pockets. Setting aside everything else, James stuck his hand in the pocket and retrieved a small slip of paper on which was written a phone number.

Hands shaking with dread, James pulled out his phone and dialed the number, not caring that it was nearly four a.m. As he'd hoped, the line rang straight to voicemail, inadvertently giving him the answer he most needed. "Hey, it's Tom. You know what to do."

Finally understanding where Emma's haunted look had come from, her every action cautious and her every reaction preceded by fear, James dropped his phone into the sand. Her ex-boyfriend had a wide streak of psycho.

W*ITH THE SOUND OF THE ALARM*, a school of mermen guards streamed from the city gates as bees from a hive. Emma clasped tight to Keith's arm, dragging him like deadweight. He tried hard to kick, to swim, but his human body wasn't

meant for swimming, not the way her mermaid body was. It made them slow. Too slow.

The guards picked up speed, closing in on the three of them until they were surrounded. Still, Emma continued swimming for shore. Regardless of what they might do to punish her, she had to get Keith to where he could breathe.

A rather beefy-looking merman with a purple tint to his skin barreled straight at them, catching Emma around the waist and squeezing the breath out of her before she even realized what was happening. Another grabbed hold of her hair, twining it around his fingers and yanking hard until Emma screamed. Tears threatened again as she lost her grip on Keith's hand. "Swim," she yelled. "Go. Head for shore— James is waiting to help you." She didn't dare tell him she'd meet him later because she knew that as soon as Keith was safe, she would end up a prisoner of Atlantis.

It didn't matter, as long as Keith was safe.

But Keith didn't swim away when their hands disconnected. Instead, he turned and came back for her, wrestling with the merman who had her in such a tight squeeze. Even as they wrestled, the other merman wound her hair harder until her eyes felt unnaturally narrowed and the skin on her forehead tightened to the point of pain. She struggled, but rather than loosen his grip, he managed to drag her head back so her neck curved unnaturally. She couldn't see Keith and the other merman, but she could hear grunts and bubbles of sound that meant her brother was putting up a good fight. Or, so she hoped.

And then, a loud grunt left them in eerie stillness. Her

eyes popped open and she strained her neck to see what had happened, dreading what she might see. Before she could find her brother drifting to the bottom, she felt the guard's hand in her hair loosen, and Keith came out of nowhere, his fist connecting with the blue-tinted skin of the merman's nose. Blood—an odd mix of blue and purple—swirled in the water near his mouth and chin. Electricity shot from the guard's hands as he released Emma to go after Keith. He snatched her brother's ankles and pulled him down, away from the surface. She raced toward them, watching in what felt like slow motion as Keith kicked at nothing until finally, one well-aimed heel slammed into the merman's forehead.

Two guards were down, but during the fight, the rest had closed in, and once again, they were surrounded. Emma searched the faces, but couldn't see Merrick. She took Keith's hand again, and together they climbed up.

They hadn't made it far when one of the guards grabbed hold of Keith's oxygen, wrapping his arms around the metal container. Keith fought to remove the merman from his back, but the fishman had latched on tight. While they struggled, Emma continued pulling the battle toward the surface. Just below, she reached down and unhooked the tank from Keith's waist, helped him slide his arms from the straps.

He spit out the mouthpiece, and Emma shoved the tank into the merman's chest, propelling him away. More and more guards had gathered. There was no time left. She grabbed Keith's hand again, and together they broke the surface. Emma did her best to keep her brother's head above water and swam for shore with everything she had.

Out of nowhere, a tall, thin guard with yellow-green hair grabbed Keith around the ankle, pulling him down and almost causing Emma to lose her grip on his hand. Keith kicked and struggled, but the merman kept a tight hold. Keith thrashed about as Emma fought to help free him, and then his eyes went wide with fear.

He needed to breathe, and there was nothing she could do about it.

Out of nowhere, Merrick barreled through the army of mermen, catching the offending guard in the chest and causing him to let go of Keith. They wrestled, and Emma grabbed Keith's hand and pulled him up, steadily picking up pace as she was able. She glanced down in Keith's face, expecting to see relief, since he seemed to have stopped struggling, but his eyes were closed, his body limp.

Before panic could consume her, Emma sucked in a mouthful of water, forcing her body to convert it to air, then she pressed her lips to Keith's, transferring the air into him, pressing it into his lungs, begging him to take it. Another breath, then another, until finally Keith started coming around. His arms flailed in confusion as she pushed him above her until his head broke through the fragile waves and he was able to gulp air into his lungs—real air. She surfaced with him, knowing they needed to move fast. "You okay?" she asked.

He shook his head, coughing and sputtering as water came up and air went down. "Emma!" he wailed. His breaths were too shallow, his lips too blue. She had to get him out of there.

She blinked the salt out of her eyes, squinted to find her small, private beach. From this distance, it resembled a dollhouse toy rather than an actual beach. Keith sputtered and cried, his words disoriented and disjointed, making no sense at all. She slid her arm around his waist. "Hold on to me. Tight."

"Emma," he wailed again. "I want Mommy and Daddy."

"Big breath," she demanded. "I swim faster under water. I'll try to keep you above, but just in case." She arranged his arms around her middle until she felt secure that he wouldn't slip away. And then they were swimming, Emma's fin-legs pulling them through the ebbing current, gliding with the flow over swells, avoiding the breaks, and skirting rocks and coral formations near shore until she worried Keith would need another solid breath. She didn't want to stop, but didn't dare to keep going. She slowed, curtailing the direct path as she paused again, to ask, "You doing okay?"

He gurgled water out of his mouth and cried again, but his breath didn't rattle in his chest this time. Improvement. "Someone's following us."

She nodded, focusing again and diving under, more determined than ever to get Keith to shore. James was there. If she could get Keith to land, James would take care of him; they could get away. She'd distract the merpeople. It wasn't Keith they wanted—it was Emma. Never in her life had she swum so hard. Even with her body being built for this, giving her great bursts of speed no human could match, she felt the strain of overuse and under-conditioning.

Soon, they reached the shallow, and Emma slowed to

avoid the outcroppings of sharp, volcanic rock. A loud splash brought her to an abrupt stop, and she surfaced to find James half-wading, half-swimming toward them. "Emma!" he screamed. "Keith. I was so worried."

She braved a look behind them, and seeing no guards nearby, let James scoop her into his arms. He kissed her neck, and then let go, leading her and Keith to the rocky ledge of the cave, where they all fell into the sand, exhausted.

Keith curled into the fetal position under Emma's towel, sobbing for his parents, and refusing to let either of them touch him.

Helpless to do more for her brother, Emma leaned her head against James's soaked chest. The cold breeze stung her wet skin and whipped ropes of her hair into James's face, but she was too tired to brush it away. "Thanks for helping that last little bit. I was afraid we wouldn't make it."

He shook his head and glanced at Keith. "I feel like I didn't do anything except sit in this cave and wait for you. I've never felt so helpless in my life." His hands stroked her hair, traced the birthmark on her bare shoulder. "Are they coming? Don't you think we should move? Get out of here?"

She opened her eyes and peered at the still water. They knew she'd be back, and they'd wait. "They won't come ashore."

"Except Merrick."

Emma closed her eyes and buried her face in James's neck. "He's busy fighting off an army."

She felt his grip tighten around her, but he didn't say anything.

"I'm sorry," she murmured. "I did warn you I was trouble when we first met." But the joke fell flat.

"Stop. Just stop, okay? That's not funny." His hand traveled down her back and up her other arm. "You're not trouble. Not to me. Even if your original warning mattered, it was already too late. I've had a thing for you since I laid eyes on you, and no matter how hard I tried, who I tried to focus on, you were always there."

"But. I was—I was awful to you. And you were so occupied with Nettie and all those other girls—"

He shook his head, threading his fingers into the dripping hair at the nape of her neck and pulling her closer, speaking quickly, like he had to get it out before it was too late. "No. Nettie. The others . . . they were . . . just a way to distract myself from you. Because I thought there was no way in hell you could ever love me. Ever even look at me in that way and I . . . it hurt. It hurt, Emma, because it feels like I've been in love with you for as long as I can remember."

His fingers stroked the back of her head. She leaned into him, pressed her lips to his shoulder, her body shaking with exhaustion, and fear—and something else. The inability to breathe. "I love you too. And for the record, I hated—absolutely despised—every one of your girlfriends."

He groaned. "I wish I'd known sooner."

"Me too." She squeezed her eyes shut, fighting the sinking feeling, and trying to force herself to convert oxygen the way she had been able to do before going after Keith.

"I searched the area—found Merrick's stash. He had a couple hundred bucks' worth of quarters. And get this—the guy owns pants. Or, he did. I took them, along with a shirt he never wore, and shoes and the quarters."

She sat up straighter. "I figured he must have some kind of clothes if he was coming ashore. The question is, how and where would he get them?"

James shifted her in his lap, wrapping his jacket around her when she shivered. "Baby, I don't know how to tell you this, or if I even should. There was a phone number in Merrick's pants pocket. I called it."

Her chest tightened. "And?"

"It was Tom's."

She gasped as her lungs constricted again. "How do they know each other?" She leaned back, searching James's face, knowing that the answer didn't matter anymore because it wouldn't change anything. Her surface time was over.

James wiped a drop of water from her forehead. "Just a guess, but I'm thinking Tom saw more than you thought that night. He probably came back and made some kind of deal with Merrick. I don't know. But babe, Merrick is not a nice guy. You need to stay away from him."

Emma swallowed. "Wish I could."

"Don't." James's voice lashed. "Don't tell me you're going to keep letting him near you—not after this."

"Oh, I'm not. But." She sniffled. "I think I have to go back."

James pulled away, looking shocked, hurt. "What? Why?"

She lifted her face, memorized James, all his lines and dips and curves. His dimple. She had to tell him. Be honest. Because it was time. "We've been out of the water less than ten minutes, and I'm struggling to breathe." Her chest tightened. "James, I can't breathe."

SSTUNNED, JAMES COULD ONLY STARE at her. She couldn't breathe? It couldn't be true. "No. No, you haven't completed the change yet. You're just upset. Overworked. Scared." He stood, took her hand to pull her up with him, help her dress.

But she didn't stand, and she didn't reply except to let two errant tears draw tracks down her cheeks.

He kept her hand in his. "Emma, we have to get out of here. What if you were followed?"

"We were." She turned her head, looked out toward the arch. "Merrick fought them off so I could get Keith back here. They're probably waiting. I think they know."

He crouched to her level. "I'm not letting you go back."

She took his face in her hands, running her thumbs across his cheeks. "You have to. Let me go, James. Because if you insist on my staying, I will. But I won't be alive tomorrow."

His insides swelled like an infected balloon. "Yes, you will. I'll figure it out. Find a way. I'll . . . fill my bathtub with salt water. Something."

She let out a sob. "I can't live in your bathtub, James."

"Better than going back to . . ." *Him.*

She wiped her cheeks with her wrists, steeling her face. "I'm not. I won't. They can't force me to marry Merrick. I'll run away first. But I have to stay near the water. And I have to go back to Atlantis to try to retrieve my pendant if I ever want to come ashore again. Do you understand? It was my father's. If I can get my pendant back, it might help me breathe here." She told him about her biological parents, her connection to the sea king.

Then she gasped, coughed, gasped again.

The balloon inside James popped, breaking into so many pieces, he wondered that he didn't melt into the sand. Her lips touched his, sweet, yielding, and he sat, scooped her into his arms and kissed her, and kissed her, and kissed her, tangling one hand in her hair and letting the other roam where it would, each caress a new point of pain to add to his agony. Emma's hands were busy too, assaulting his shoulders, neck, chest, while their lips and tongues wrestled in a battle he wished would never end. They were both damp, but he wouldn't have been surprised if their bodies created wisps of steam. James tried to capture it all, remember every sensation like a gift he could take out and remember later. He knew her brother was only feet away, but all that mattered was this one last chance to drink her in as they intermittently murmured promises and declarations they'd waited too long to make. When he could feel her gasping for breath between kisses, feel her chest constrict as she pressed against him, he couldn't deny the truth. Emma had to go.

She pulled away, sandwiching his hands between hers. "Take my car and get Keith home. Mrs. Hall across the street will look after him until my parents get back. Use my phone to call Gran. Tell her who you are, and what happened. She'll deal with my parents. The school. And if anyone gives you any trouble about me disappearing, she'll help deal with that too. Okay?"

He leaned his forehead on hers. "I can't say good-bye. I don't know how."

"I'll love you forever."

Grief swamped him in such an overwhelming torrent that he couldn't have cried if he wanted—all he could do was shake. "I love you. Now. Forever. Always. Only you. Ever."

"Don't say that." She sniffled. "Don't waste your life pining for someone who probably can't come back."

He felt a breath inflate in his chest, and opened on a single nugget of hope. "Emma Harris. I'll be here, in this cave, waiting. Every day. As often as I can, for as long as I can, until I find you again. This isn't over, so don't you dare let them make you marry a stranger. Promise?"

She nodded, more tears falling. "I do. I promise. I'll do everything I can to get back to you."

Keith still wouldn't let her touch him, so she kissed him through the towel and whispered, "Love you, bud. Be good."

James pressed his lips together as he helped her to the edge, held her hands as she lowered herself into the water with a sob, and kissed him once more. "Don't wait for me."

James leaned farther over the edge, his chest skimming the water as he clasped her hand, feeling her skin slide through his fingertips, his life slide through his fingertips, until there was nothing left to hold but empty ripples in the deep, dark water. "Every day. I'll be here, Emma. Every day."

And then she was gone.

Thirty-eight

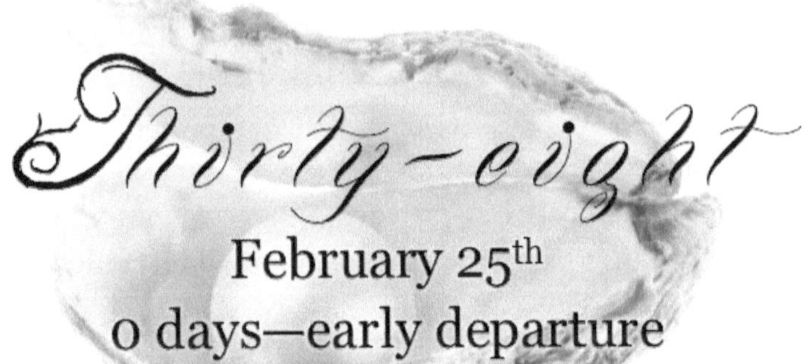

February 25th
0 days—early departure

"KEITH." JAMES LEANED TOWARD the boy, prepared to carry him if necessary. They had to get out of here—now. James couldn't stand being here without Emma. Movement at the mouth of the cave had James snapping his head, hoping Emma was coming back.

His heart sank again when Merrick lifted himself out of the water and onto the rocks. "You should not come here again. She will no longer be allowed to visit ashore."

James placed himself protectively between Merrick and Keith, grief and anger burning a black hole in his stomach. "Shut up, fishman. We both know you have an ulterior motive. Probably several. If Emma's the sea king's granddaughter, she stands to inherit a throne, doesn't she? Big motivator."

Merrick lowered his eyes in shame. "That is not why. None of it matters any longer. I loved her before—long before, when she was a tiny human toddling on the sand in the summer. I've never wanted any other for a mate."

"Sure have a funny way of showing it. Kidnapping her brother?" Merrick's gaze dropped, cementing James's hatred. "Great way to win her affections, dude. Although, I must applaud you for your attempts at eliminating your competition by forcing her to complete her change."

"That was not—"

"She doesn't want you!" James shouted, fists aching to take his pain out on Merrick. "She'll never want you. She wants me. Emma may be forced to stay in the water for now— but if you lay a single hand on her, if you ever again harm her in any way, I swear, I'll hunt you down. Under water. On land. Anywhere you go. And I. Will. Destroy you."

"Stop." Keith stood on wobbly legs, Emma's towel bundled around him. "Stop fighting. Max, I hate you. You hurt me. You hurt my sister. I never want you to come back here again."

The shallows rustled with a flurry of activity as the first rays of sun crested the horizon. "They come," Merrick said. "Go, humans, before it is too late."

James snatched Emma's keys and cell phone off the ledge, gently picked up her wet clothing as if it was glass, and slipped everything in Emma's beach bag. He glanced at Keith. "Time to go. Now."

"But what about Emma?"

His throat felt like it was crammed with peanut butter. "Already gone. Don't argue. Just get to the car."

"But what if she comes back?"

"She won't. If I thought there was any way, I wouldn't leave. But she won't. Keith, we have to go. Now." Guiding Keith ahead of him, James picked his way up the rocky path to the trail, grateful that the rain had stopped. Grateful Keith had been there to keep him from killing Merrick on the spot. Grateful for the numbness that was starting to take over, and that would help him do what had to be done. He opened the car door for Keith, still clutching Emma's things to his chest.

Merrick dropped a hand on James's shoulder, startling him. "I'll take care of her—she will befall no harm in Atlantis."

The merman's words twisted the knife of despair deeper into James's gut. Unable to either breathe or speak, James shrugged the hand off and climbed in the car, gunning the engine and peeling away as the sky behind them turned pink. He would get her back. He would. Even if it meant buying a boat and learning to scuba dive.

He wouldn't rest until he had her in his arms again.

JAMES HELD HIS SHOES with two fingers, stepping across the sharp ground and tide pools on his way to Emma's cove. Rocks poked and tore at his bare feet. He refused to avoid them, relishing the part of him that could still feel something.

He once thought to invest in a pair of cheap flip-flops, but hadn't made it to a store to buy any. That would require time he couldn't afford to sacrifice. What if she came and he wasn't here?

With his back to the water, James held Emma's beach bag close to his chest, opening it to breathe her in. It had nearly undone him to wash her clothes—wash away her scent—but he had to be prepared, and didn't want them dirty when she came back. But the salty, fresh perfume he so loved remained inside the bag. He inhaled once more and then nestled it on her ledge.

He closed his eyes, listening, wishing, and conjured a picture of her at the water's edge, smiling over her delicate shoulder with full, pink lips, splashing water on her scaly legs, asking him if he wanted to touch her. "I would give anything to touch you," he murmured. A wish. A hope. A plea.

Heart hammering, he turned around. There she was. In the same spot from which she'd left, hair fluttering like fire on top of the water, beckoning him to join her. Pain shot through his chest as he stepped forward, ready to go. Willing to give up everything. Knowing she wasn't really there.

James opened his eyes and watched the memory disperse like smoke as he settled onto the sand to wait.

She'd been gone three weeks.

Most days, he was lucky to make it through school, but only because, in some twisted part of his brain, he believed the future mattered. If she came back, if she found a way to stay, he needed the ability to take care of her, the ability to pack her up and run if necessary, and decent jobs required a diploma. If she didn't come back—he didn't want to think about that.

So he came. Every afternoon. A lot of mornings too. Skipped some classes, and the entire last week of practice. Basketball just didn't feel important anymore. He no longer had the will to fight Mark and Lyle, to smile and pretend he was still alive—because he wasn't. Nothing felt right anymore.

The day Emma left, he missed a tournament game. James didn't care. Coach suggested he see a doctor, get treated for depression—like his father—but James refused. Drugs couldn't bring back Emma, and Emma was the only cure for his heartache. So Coach benched him for playoffs, giving Lyle the starting position James had once usurped. Yesterday, they took third in State. Now the season was over.

"I miss you, baby," he said, knowing she couldn't hear him, but needing to say it anyway. "I miss your voice. And your smile. I miss seeing you in the halls at school and finding your car in the parking lot and fighting with you. You can fight me all you want—just come back, okay? Please."

The sun moved from high above his head and dipped toward the horizon as he talked to the sea, begging it to carry his words to Emma. He told her how her grandmother called to check on him often, to ask if he'd seen her swimming, how Keith was seeing a therapist to help with his stealing habit, and also with losing his sister. He told her how her parents were working harder than ever, and how her dad had stepped up his research, desperate for a way to bring her back, but that they refused to give up hope, the same way he did.

"Heather hates me," he said. "She thinks I'm the reason you left, and that I wrote that letter instead of you. Yesterday she accused me of murdering you and threatened to sic the police on me." Squeezing his eyes closed, he shook his head. "If the situation was reversed, I'd think the same thing."

Eventually, the rhythmic sway of the water lulled him quiet, and he spread Emma's towel on the sand so he could lie there and rest his throbbing head. He never imagined himself capable of being in so deep. His stomach growled, but he didn't move. The sun slipped below the horizon and the stars blinked to life. One. Two. Seven. Twenty. A hundred. He lost count. Darkness rolled over the world and into the cave, and James didn't move. Considered sleeping there. Wondered if she'd come in the night. Thought of school. Decided to drop out. Thought of Emma. Remembered why he had to graduate, and pushed himself up. He should go home, try to sleep, even though he never slept anymore.

He stood, shook out the towel, and folded it into her bag, noticing as he did, the glint of something shiny near the wall of Emma's ledge. His throat constricted as he picked up the tiny pearl, first thinking it had come off her necklace long before, but when he turned it over and around, realized it didn't have a hole through it. Searching his mind to remember how well he'd checked the ledge yesterday, he realized that it hadn't been here. He would have noticed. He paid attention to everything in this cave.

Could it be a sign from Emma? Just in case, he removed his earring and left it where the pearl had been, a sign that he was still here, still waiting, though waiting had never been his style. Maybe he should find a way to go to her, bring her back.

With renewed hope, he hooked his fingers into his shoes and felt his way along the wall, wondering when it had become too dark to see. Feeling the ice in his fingers and toes and wondering how long he'd been freezing and not noticed.

With one last glance at the dark water, James clutched Emma's things to his chest. "Be back tomorrow, baby." Then he turned from the cove and hiked up the hill to his bike.

About Nichole Giles

NICHOLE GILES, the author of DESCENDANT (Jelly Bean Press, May 2013), has lived in Nevada, Arizona, Utah, and Texas. She loves to spend time with her husband and four children, travel to tropical and exotic destinations, drive in the rain with the convertible top down, and play music at full volume so she can sing along.

Acknowledgments

EVERY TIME I DO THIS I have a momentary flash of panic that there is no possible way for me to mention every person who has played a role in the creation of my books. I only have so much space, and there are so many people to thank.

First, and always, all my love and thanks to my husband Gary and our amazing children, Brayden, Brittany, Madison, and Mckay. You are the reason I work so hard and the inspiration behind every character and every happy ending I will ever write. You are rock stars for living with a wife and mother who is a writer, and the unconventional lifestyle that is a result of my career choice. I love you all bigger than the universe.

Enormous thanks to my agent, Sarah Negovetich, for keeping me sane, holding my hand (virtually) and encouraging me to work through the hardest stuff. I am lucky to have you in my corner! Loves, hugs, and more thanks to Tristi Pinkston, Heather Justesen, and Michelle Argyle. You ladies are workers of miracles, and some of the most brilliant people in publishing. I am lucky to have you on my team. More hugs to Elana Johnson for standing over me with an umbrella every time the publishing rainclouds have threatened, and for teaching me all the best ways to think outside the box. I hope you never get tired of hanging out with me.

L.T. Elliot has been a stalwart champion of support since this book was in early draft stage, as have Keith Fisher, Windy Aphyrath, Ali Cross, Sheralyn Pratt, and Jenn Johansson. The multi-talented Erin Summerill took my lovely author photo, and is also a great source of support. Special thanks to Brittany Howard who helped me gain the validation I needed at a time when I was ready to give up hope, and who led me to my agent, Sarah. Of course, I cannot fail to mention my FABs, Jennifer, Tiffany, Raylene, and Lori, who have pretty much been the cushions on which I have landed every time I have fallen.

Unconventional thanks to some high school friends who I haven't seen in years, but the memories of whom I have tapped for character traits, conversations, and scenes from, well, all the stories I have written to date. I've heard it said that we are shaped by the people we spend our time with, and I have found that to be true on so many occasions. I see Tova regularly, because she keeps me sane, but Kerry, Eryke, Andi, Johnny, Amy, James, and Malia—you are all heroes for making my high school experience wonderful, despite my limited time in each place. You made high school fun, and are part of the reason I write for young adults.

I would be remiss if I failed to mention my parents, Joe and Pam Petersen, Deanne and Steve Hechtle, and Kay Giles. Carol Giles cheers me on from Heaven, keeping me strong, with the help of my grandpa, Mel Petersen. My grandparents, Jeneal Petersen, and Mona and Ernie Ketchum are the reason

I'm even here, so I should add them in. And in case I haven't mentioned them before, all my siblings. Ryan, Matt, James, Jodi, Chandi, Zack, Daeton, Justin, Cameron, and Troy. Also my enormous extended Petersen, Ketchum, and Giles families—you all have brought me so much joy, and so many of you have shown support in the most important ways. I have never known anyone to have such an enormous, loving family as mine. I love you all!

I am so fortunate to do what I love, and to have such support from many different and wonderful sources. I am living my dream, and you, dear reader, are part of how that dream has become real. Thanks for reading!

www.ingramcontent.com/pod-product-compliance
Lightning Source LLC
Chambersburg PA
CBHW020254120726
47904CB00001B/196